CONTENTS

SHOW YOU THE STARS

Ally Groh

Brian, this one is for you for encouraging
me to follow my heart.

CHAPTER ONE
-ELLEN

Fall 1943

Time waits for no one so the saying goes. As I race toward the teacher's lounge, I nearly trip over something lying in the middle of the hallway. It's a student composition book. Though I'm in a hurry I stop to pick it up. Checking the time on my watch I quickly calculate how much time I have left of my free period. I should bring this to the front office. In the same instant I know it's the right thing to do, I lament the loss of a few precious minutes to myself. Someone will be looking for it though. I know I would be if I had been the one to lose it.

I bypass by the teacher's lounge heading instead for the front office. The students at this school really should be a little more responsible. They are forever losing pencils, notebooks, what have you. I keep extra pencils and paper on hand for just such an occasion. Already my supply is dwindling and it is not yet Halloween. I'm speed walking now. When the next bell rings I have to be back in my classroom.

There are thirty-two sophomores in my next class. Picking up the pace I mentally run through today's lesson plan on the parts of speech. It occurs to me how almost all of my students are taller than I am. I'm not sure how I feel about that. The front office is fairly quiet when I enter. I hand the composition book to the secretary and give her a quick explanation of where I found it. She thanks me and assures me it will be reunited with its owner.

Pushing open the heavy wooden door I finally enter the teacher's lounge. I am met with the familiar sound of voices vying to be heard over the din of flatware scraping against metal lunch trays. The click-clack of my shoes over the linoleum tiles is barely audible. Pulling out a chair I take a seat and join my colleagues at the long table in the center of the room. Next, I pull a brown bag lunch from the depths of my canvas tote.

Instinctively I reach for one of the newspapers in the center of the table. The public high school where I work gets all the major New York publications delivered each morning. I'm not picky I'll read whichever is available. I glance at the cover. Today's winner is The Post. This is the only chance I have during the school day to catch up on current events, especially news of the war.

Turning the first few pages I scan the headlines until an article about women entering the military stops my hand. I take a bite of my sandwich and as I chew begin silently reading. Almost immediately I become engrossed in the article. The words practically jump off the page. I'll admit I don't know much about what women are doing in the military. It's a novel concept. It's so new. According to what I'm reading the Army, Navy, and U.S. Army Air Force now have reserve branches specifically for women volunteers.

"What's so interesting?" It takes me a second to realize that Mr. Turnbull the math teacher is talking to me. Mr. Turnbull came out of retirement last year when Mr. Thorne was drafted by the War Department. In fact the faculty is made up mostly of females and old, formerly retired male teachers nowadays.

Placing my finger on the page to mark my place I look at Mr. Turnbull sitting across the table from me, "The Women's Reserves," I say.

"Letting women in the military is a terrible idea," Mrs. Byrd the Home Economics teacher says uninvited. Then she goes a step further. "An unmarried woman should live at home with her parents." She's obviously scandalized.

My mother raised us to display good manners at all times. I love my mother dearly however, I am sorely tempted to forget the lessons she taught me just for a moment. I have to bite my tongue.

"A woman's place is in the home. She should aspire to be a dutiful wife," Mrs. Byrd is still talking and I wonder if I'd get in trouble if I threw my apple at her head. "An unmarried young lady is expected to live with her parents until her wedding day."

Help me she is still talking. I roll the apple in my hand knowing I would never really throw it at her. I take a breath and smile at how my generation bucks at those antiquated beliefs Mrs. Byrd is still holding onto. We women have come a long way since the Seneca Falls Convention. For example, we can own property and go to college, we have the vote, we can work and earn our own money and now we can even join the military. "It says here that the Women's Reserves will free up more men, so they'll be able to fight," I say. Surely the woman can't argue with that.

"It's still a bad idea," she shakes her head. "This is going to give women notions and ambitions. You mark my words." She has the audacity to point a chubby finger in my direction.

I've never liked being pointed at. It's rude. As I recall, I was silently reading minding my own business. How did I get dragged into this conversation, I want to know.

Mr. Turnbull clears his throat. He looks like the cat that's caught the canary. "I don't believe so," he says. "The ladies should be able to serve this country in its time of need same as a man."

I can't help noticing how Mrs. Byrd is now openly scowling at Mr. Turnbull. He hardly seems bothered by it. Thankfully she lets the subject drop and opens the Women's magazine at her side.

Grateful for the reprieve, I resume reading the Post and finish my lunch. Conversations go on all around but I stay engrossed in the paper. After I finish the article about the Women's Reserves I soak up as much news about the war as I can. Before long, the bell rings and I hurry to my classroom arriving just in time. I take my place in the front of the room as my students make their way to their assigned seats.

The rest of the day passes in a whir. After the last class I slump into my chair exhausted. There's a stack of papers on my desk. It taunts me. Reaching over I grab it and stuff it into my bag. I'll grade those tonight. After a short rest I stand, stretch my back and turn around. Picking up the eraser I begin to wipe the chalk board clean with wide sweeping motions.

On my way out I see Mr. Turnbull sitting at his desk. I approach the open doorway. Sensing my presence, he looks up from what he is working on. "Miss. Cunningham," he says in greeting, "On your way out I see."

Stepping further into the classroom and patting my bag I say, "Bringing work home with me."

"Never ends does it?" He removes his glasses and sighs. "That actually sounds like a good idea."

"Thanks for running interference with Mrs. Byrd earlier," I say.

"No thanks necessary since I was the cause of all that," he says then pushes his chair out from behind his desk. "That woman is a nuisance." He stands and begins gathering papers and other items into his bag. "I think I'll follow your example and bring the rest of this home with me."

"Be that as it may," I say suppressing a smile because I agree, Mrs. Byrd is a nuisance, and "I appreciated your help."

"Think nothing of it," he waves it off.

"Good night," I tell him.

"See you tomorrow," he says kindly.

There's a Navy recruiter's office between the school and my bus stop. I walk by it every day, twice. This afternoon my steps slow as I approach the building. I turn my head observing the poster in the window. I've seen it a thousand times. But for some reason, today I give it a really good look. Three women dressed in white smile at me. They look confident, happy even like they know something I don't. How would it feel to be one of them?

I hear the bus approaching so I get moving. If I miss it, I'll have to wait for the next bus to get home to Bayside. I give one last backward glance at that poster. The thought of volunteering is outrageous. Isn't it? Picking up the pace I hitch the strap of my bag higher over my shoulder. I make it in time. Taking my place in line I straighten my hat and smooth my hands over my coat. The October sky is grey and the air is turning colder. Summer is definitely over.

"I'm home!" I call out entering the apartment. Closing the door I head down the hall to my room. Dropping my bag onto the bed I kick off my shoes.

"In the kitchen," I hear my mother call.

Shoeless I head there to see what's for dinner. The first thing I notice is the steam rising from the big cast iron pot on top of the stove. I peer inside. It's vegetable soup, something we eat of lot of especially since my brother-in-law Eduardo planted a garden in the small patch of earth in front of our apartment building.

"Give that a stir will you?" my mother says removing a loaf of bread from the oven. The scent of fresh baked bread fills the kitchen. My stomach grumbles loudly. "Dinner's almost ready," she says.

I do as asked plucking a long handled wooden spoon from the drawer by the stove. I give the soup a slow stir and watch as the vegetables and noodles swirl around inside the large pot. The soup looks hearty. "Is Bess home?" I ask after my sister while stirring.

"Bess has class tonight. It'll just be the two of us," my mother reminds me. That's right Bess has class on Tuesday nights and Eduardo waits to drive her home.

Grabbing two bowls, napkins and spoons I duck into the dining room to set the table. After the blessing I take a slice of sourdough bread and dip a corner of it into my soup. It's so good and I'm famished. Before taking a second bite I say, "There was an interesting discussion in the teacher's lounge today."

"Oh," my mother says placing her spoon in

her bowl, "What about?"

"How women are joining the military," I say slicing another piece of bread from the loaf on the cutting board sitting in the center of the table. Then I spread a bit of margarine on top.

My mother looks at me curious. "How did that go?"

"Hmm," I say thinking how best to replay the conversation for her. "The home-economics teacher thinks it's a scandalous idea and the math teacher thinks that the ladies should be able to serve their country." I summarize for her.

"What do you think?" she asks.

"I think it's about time," I say. My mother was a Suffragette who fought for the vote for women. I value her opinion not only because she's my mother but because I look up to her. She is the strongest person I know and I am dying to know what she thinks about this.

She covers my hand with hers. "I think it's a good thing," she says and I am relieved to hear her say this. "It's another step in the right direction for women." She squeezes my hand. "It's a very good thing." Her answer does not surprise me when I think about it. She's always been passionate in her belief that women should have more opportunities available to them.

Most importantly women deserve the ability to support themselves and their families financially.

For the rest of the week the idea of volunteering virtually consumes me. These thoughts are so distracting it's a wonder I've been able to accomplish anything at all. It's all I think about until finally this afternoon I find myself stopped in front of that poster. My feet are rooted to the sidewalk.

The door swings open and a woman steps outside. I take in her smart appearance. Her navy blue uniform looks tailored to fit. "I've watched you slow your step in front of that poster every day this week," she says amiably. "Why don't you come on inside," Patiently she waits for me to make the next move.

Forty minutes later I'm standing at the bus stop waiting for the next bus to take me home. An application packet is tucked inside my canvas tote. Tonight's dinner conversation should be very interesting.

CHAPTER TWO-ELLEN

Ellen

A couple of weeks have passed with no news. Today, when I get home from work my mother is in the living room, looks like she's been waiting for me. She rises from the chair. Her eyes are glassy.

Immediately I go on high alert. "What is it?" I ask. "What's wrong?" A dozen scenarios flash through my mind.

"Everyone is fine," she says allaying my most pressing fears.

I almost sag with relief. "You scared me," I say hand to my heart.

"I'm sorry, honey. That was not my intention," she says then reaches into the pocket of her apron. "This came for you today."

Dropping my bag to the floor I take a seat

in the same chair that my mother was sitting in moments before. My heart is pounding. My hands are shaking. It is from the Department of the Navy.

I look at my mother. She looks as nervous as I feel. "Go on," she says nodding encouragingly. "Open it."

Turning the envelope over, I break the seal and remove the contents. I take a deep breath and begin to read.

"Well, what does it say?"

"I've been accepted," I say. All at once a maelstrom of emotions overtakes me. It is a lot to process.

She begins forward and wraps her arms around me. "I'm proud of you," she says, "So, so proud."

Later when Bess gets home she finds the two of us sitting in the living room laughing and crying. The sight causes her to stop short. "What did I just walk into?" she warily asks, slowly closing the door behind her. We beckon her over to sit with us. I show her the letter.

"Oh El," she says looking up from the letter. "You're leaving us." Her face turns sad.

"I'll be back," I say.

She puts on brave face. "They don't give you much time," she lifts the letter grasped in her hand.

I shrug because she's right. I've been given only two weeks to tie up loose ends before I depart for training. I'll have to let the school know first thing in the morning so they have ample time to find a replacement for me. In fact, there are quite a few things I'll need to do.

Reaching over I turn off the alarm clocking blaring on the table beside the bed. Why does time seem to move faster when we don't want it to and slower when we want it to go faster? These past two weeks went by entirely too fast. I stretch while still under the warm covers and think about how today is going to be bittersweet. When at last I throw back the blankets and get up butterflies fill my belly. Anxiety about what lies ahead has my nerves jumbled.

Yesterday, Bess helped me finish packing. We made sure to include everything on the list that accompanied my acceptance letter. Then the four of us spent a quiet evening together at home. We all agreed to treat it as any other night. After dinner we played cards. Bess won the first hand and I won the second. Eduardo then suggested we play Monopoly. That suggestion was unanimously vetoed by Bess, me and our mother. He usually crushes us in Monopoly.

This morning, as I dress in a forest green wool dress and thick stockings it is with a heavy heart. As I'm slipping my feet into a pair of my sturdiest shoes, Bess calls, "Breakfast is ready."

In the dining room I am pleasantly surprised to see two thick slices of fried bacon on each plate. It smells amazing. "How?" I ask bewildered. War restrictions and shortages have made obtaining certain foods difficult and food shopping has become complicated to say the least.

"We have our ways," my mother says coming into the room carrying a platter of fluffy scrambled eggs. Bess is right behind her with buttermilk biscuits.

Eduardo always waits for us ladies to be seated before he'll sit down to eat. His manners are impeccable. He moved into the apartment with us about a year ago, right after he and Bess were married. They met at university when they were both undergrads. Eduardo likes to tell everyone it was love at first sight at least on his part.

All you have to do is look at him and you can see he is one hundred percent in love with my sister. He's supportive and loving. He speaks kindly to her and he shows her respect. He encourages her to be her best self and to pursue her academic goals. Currently, she is working on an advanced degree in her field of psychology.

Eduardo moved to New York from Chile in order to study anthropology. He knew that by marrying Bess he wouldn't be going back to Chile. He accepted that. He says that his home now is wherever she is.

"Coffee?" Bess asks.

Months ago coffee and sugar were added to the list of rationed items. Raising my cup I allow her to pour. A sly smile crosses her face. I smile back. There's enough here for each of us to have a cup and a lump of sugar to add to it so I savor the aroma and the flavor and make it last throughout the meal taking small sips. I forgot how good coffee tastes.

Inevitably, the clock on the wall chimes signaling it's almost time to leave for the station. Bess looks at it then at me. We've never been away from each other for any length of time. I can tell by her expression that she is as torn up over our impending separation as I am. Our eyes meet. It will be okay I silently convey. She nods and visibly swallows. It will all be okay. I'll be back before anyone can miss me. I sigh willing it to be true.

I excuse myself from the table to collect my bags. I am allowed to bring two suitcases with me to training. Standing in the middle of my room I take one last look around. There's a particular picture in a silver frame on my dresser that catches my eye. Holding it in my hand I study the image of Bess and me with our brother Bill. We were at Jones Beach. The three of us were hamming it up for the camera. Those were the days I think with a measure of nostalgia. Then I remember that George took this picture. I haven't thought of him in years.

Returning the picture to its spot on the dresser I turn and reach for my bags. I'll be in Northampton for the next two months during training and after that I have no idea. My contract with the Navy is ambiguous. I'll serve as long as the war lasts plus six months after that. In all honesty, the uncertainty of the commitment leaves my family and me feeling a little anxious. I make one last sweep of the room making sure I have everything.

I emerge from the bedroom clutching two suitcases one in each hand. My mother and sister are in the living room holding their coats waiting for me. "Do you have everything?" My mother asks.

Nodding I say, "I think so." Then I ask, "Will Bill be at the station?"

"Yes, they'll all be there," she confirms. I'm glad. Now that Bill is married with children he lives in Long Island. Since he moved to the suburbs we don't get to see him as often as we'd like and I want to see him again before I go.

My mother hands me my coat. I take it and put it on. It's the beginning of November and already freezing outside. New York weather can be a fickle friend. Some years summers are long and last through October. In others we see snow before Halloween. This morning frost covers the ground. It crunches beneath our shoes. We see Eduardo standing by the car waiting for us. He takes my bags to place in the trunk. He already has the windshield defrosted. Inside the car is toasty warm. The heat is on full blast.

When we arrive at Grand Central Bill, my sister-in-law Gladys and their three year old twins Jimmy and Johnny are already waiting inside. As soon as Bill spots us he comes right over and wraps me in a great big bear hug. "Hey sis," he says, "You make sure that none of those Navy boys give you any trouble."

"Not a chance," I tell him.

"Chin up you'll be back before you know it." He touches his index finger to my chin. "We'll miss you," he says, "And we're proud of you."

"Thank you." I say. When he tries to get away I tug him back. "You're the best brother a girl could have you know that don't you?" Bill ducks his head when as I say this. He doesn't take compliments well. I hope he knows how much I appreciate him. "Love you."

"Love you, too." Bill works for New York Telephone Company. He started working there straight out of high school in order to help support the rest of us. He's earned several promotions since and now has an office and a secretary. "You look very respectable in a suit and tie, very professional," I say straightening said tie.

"Thank you," he says with an indulgent smile on his handsome face. I tell him this every time I see him in a suit.

He's done well for himself at the Telephone Company and he says he likes what he does for a living but sometimes I wonder if he has any regrets about not going to college. I mostly wonder this because he helped pay my tuition. It would have taken me twice as long to finish my education without his help.

Bess once told me that when I walked across the stage in my cap and gown Bill clapped louder than everybody in attendance. She said he beamed with pride. I can picture him like that. I am the first in our family to have earned a college degree. My siblings and I are first generation Irish-Americans. Despite unjust discrimination toward the Irish, our parents did what they could to give us a better life here in America.

      I was teaching at the public high school by the time Bess was old enough for college so I helped her, the way Bill did for me. I love that about our family. No matter what, we support one another in any way we can. That's why when I told them I wanted to join the Navy the fact that they supported my decision meant so much to me. That's why my throat is tight and the backs of my eyes sting with unshed tears. I am surrounded by the people I love most. They are all here to see me off. It's a demonstration of their unconditional love and support.

      Kneeling on the cold tiles I gather my adorable nephews close and drop kisses on their little pink cheeks. I breathe in the clean scent of Ivory soap and talcum powder wishing they could stay sweet and innocent forever, untouched and unaware of what economic depression and war can do to people; wishful thinking. "You two be good," I tell them even as they wriggle to get free. I'm going to miss these little imps tremendously.

      Standing I hug Gladys then turn to hug Eduardo. Bess is next. She's losing the battle to hold back the tears. Her blue eyes a mirror of my own are watery. "Don't," I say bringing her in for a hug. "If you start crying, then I'll start crying and then I'll ruin my makeup." That did the trick I think when I hear her soft laugh. "I'm going to miss you. Promise you'll write."

"Of course," she says, "Of course I will." She pulls back then taking my hands says, "I wish I could go with you."

"Eduardo would be lost without you," I give her a small smile which she returns.

Stepping away from Bess I turn toward my mother. Her arms are open and I fall into her embrace. At this point I am on the verge of tears. We stand and hug for a long time before she takes my face in her hands, looks me square in the eye and says, "This is your moment."

My family accompanies me to the platform where a sharp whistle pierces the air. There's time for one more hug, one more goodbye, one more word of encouragement. Lifting my chin and squaring my shoulders I say, "Be proud of me and don't miss me too much." My heart is breaking a little but I give them my best smile before climbing up into the nearest passenger car. They will be fine I remind myself. Bill has Gladys and the twins. Bess has Eduardo and my mother has them all.

Hours later, I'm in Springfield waiting to catch a connecting train to take me to my final destination, Northampton, Massachusetts. It's the home of the all girl's Smith College which is where I'll be for the next eight weeks training to become a United States Naval Officer. I still can't believe it. Looking around the Springfield station I can see there are a lot of women who like me are waiting for the connecting train to Northampton eager for this next step. There are women here who look to be in their early twenties all the way to middle forties. At twenty-seven I'm not the youngest volunteer here but I'm not the oldest one either.

It's thrilling and exciting. I'm a little intimidated about the unknown, truth be told. I'm still young and I have ambition. I revel in the idea of being a part of something important. I mean, think about it. It's the first time in the history of this country that a woman can join the military. Just thinking about it makes my insides swell with pride.

As I sit here waiting I temper that pride with a healthy dose of reality. I'm old enough and wise enough to appreciate the magnitude of what I'm doing. I've just left home, said good bye to everyone I know and walked away from a good job and the security that came with it. Ponder that.

As the train approaches, slowing to a stop I stand and gather my belongings. As I move to join the others in line adrenaline courses through me. My entire life is about to change. I ask myself, am ready for this? Yes, I am confident that I am.

CHAPTER
THREE-BEN

Ben
Spring 1944

I'll never forget that day. It was about a year and a half ago and I can still recall certain details like how it had been unusually warm for September in Illinois. It was the day I learned that my life was about to change in ways I could only imagine. Little did I know as I'd walked into work that morning that life as I knew it was about to end. I threw my suit jacket over the back of the chair and settled in. By the end of that day everything would be different.

I remember thinking how fortunate I was to have such an amazing assistant. Ann entered my office carrying a steaming cup of black tea and placed it on top of my desk in front of me. "It's not coffee, but it will have to do," she'd said. She was constantly doing little things like that without being asked. Note pad and pencil at the ready she detailed my schedule for the day. I hope that whoever she works with now appreciates her as much as I did.

Ann rattled off my schedule with proficiency. I had a meeting in the conference room that morning and after lunch I was scheduled to go out on one of the work sites for an inspection. There were phone calls from the day before that needed to be returned and in between all of that I would find time to work on designs for a new project.

As I navigated my way through morning meetings and afternoon work sight inspections I could not have guessed what I was going to find when I got home. I remember telling Ann that I didn't know what I would do without her. She replied with her usual, "Let's never find out then."

As I was headed toward the elevator at the end of the day I saw she was still at her desk. She was still working. "Don't stay too long," I'd said.

"I won't," she'd said. I didn't believe her.

"I mean it, go home to your family," I called back over my shoulder.

"I will," she laughed.

"I mean it," I called one last time.

"I'm going, I'm going," she called back.

I remember having the windows rolled down as I was driving home. The sun was shining, the sky was blue for as far as the eye could see. I loosened my tie and rolled up the sleeves of my dress shirt. It was a picture perfect day. I couldn't wait to get home.

When I pulled up to the front of the house I could see Winston through the front window. The minute he spotted me his tail was wagging and he started barking. Quickly, I went to the curb to collect the mail. As soon as I got inside, Winston was at my side, excited to see me. I rubbed his back. "Did you miss me boy?"

He followed me to the kitchen where I opened the back door to let him out. Standing on the patio I began to sort through the mail as Winston ran around the backyard like a lunatic. The latest edition of Standard Catalog of American Cars had come. I remember thinking that it had finally arrived. I'd been waiting for it and was looking forward to reading it.

Placing the catalog onto the round iron table behind me, I flipped through the rest of the mail. There was the electric bill and the phone bill. What came next made my step falter. The unmistakable seal of the Selective Service System glared at me. My heart raced.

With a pit in my stomach the size of

the Grand Canyon I dropped into the closest patio chair then with jerky, almost sluggish movements tore open the envelope. The piece of paper in my hand felt heavy as I read the large, bold, black type at the top of the page, 'ORDER TO REPORT FOR INDUCTION."

My mind raced a thousand miles a minute. The Army, I'd been drafted into the Army. At the bottom of the standard form letter read the time, date and place where I was being ordered to report. I had two weeks to get my affairs in order. I sat there numb almost disbelieving.

In the back of my mind I knew there was always the possibility of being drafted. After all when the Selective Training and Service Act passed all men between the ages of twenty-one and sixty-five were required to register for the draft. That was three and a half years before so when that letter arrived, honestly I was caught off guard.

I lived alone at the time. It was just me and Winston. I sat there in a daze trying to process the news. Thoughts tumbled and jarred in my mind. The knot in my stomach tightened. Winston came to me and laid his head on my knee. I rubbed the top of his head between his ears the way he liked. "Looks like my number's been called, Win," I said. He raised his eyes. "I guess I shouldn't be surprised, but I am." He whimpered like he understood what I was saying.

He stayed by my side as I sat there, stoic. It took some time but after a while I grew resigned to my fate. Once I'd accepted it there was a feeling of calm that washed over me. It was what it was and there was nothing I could do to change it. I knew that.

I called my parent's house. My mom answered. When I gave her the news she started to cry. By cry, I mean she cried like I had never seen her cry before or since. "Please don't cry, Mom," I'd said.

She told me she didn't want me to go. I told her that it wasn't my choice and I didn't want me to go either but that I had to. I would do my duty. My resolve only made her cry that much harder. Softly, I said, "Mom, give the phone to Dad."

"Why is your mother crying?" he'd demanded to know.

"I've been drafted. I have to report in two weeks."

"Oh, son," he'd said. "I hoped this day would never come."

Two weeks after that I left Winston with my parents and my younger sister. Gabby promised to take good care of him. Then I reported for basic training. At thirty-two I was older than most of the men in my platoon. That only motivated me to work harder than anyone else there.

Upon arrival my head was shaved, I was assigned a serial number and given a set of dog tags. I held them in my hand. The two rectangular notched pieces of aluminum were no bigger than the size of a half dollar. Their purpose was to identify my remains should I die in service. Debossed on them were my name, serial number, years I had a Tetanus Toxoid shot, my blood type (O positive), the name of my next of kin (my dad) and the address where he could be located. I pulled the chain over my head and tucked the tags beneath my undershirt. They were required to be worn as part of the uniform.

I was also issued several pairs of the Army's standard olive drab green fatigues, a pair of heavy black boots along with several other items I would be required to wear. The Army also supplied toiletries as well as items used for camouflaging.

During those seventeen weeks of boot camp I became part of a unit. We ate, slept, worked and studied as a unit. We did hours of physical training as a unit. We learned how to load, unload and clean our weapons. We marched for miles in full gear. We were forced by our instructors to learn the Army's protocol. Even the smallest mistake could result in having to partake in challenging physical punishments or extra kitchen duty. Did I mention I hate kitchen duty?

I pulled my weight, followed orders and made it through boot camp. The rigorous weeks of mental and physical training had transformed me. By the end of basic I was stronger mentally and physically than I had ever been. I felt ready to fight anything.

Most recruits are sent elsewhere for further training after basic depending on the assignment. Me? I'd been tagged for the Army's new specialized training program, ASTP for short. It was created as a means to train highly qualified soldiers in the fields of engineering, science, medicine, dentistry, psychology and roughly thirty foreign languages. The government earmarked over two hundred and twenty seven land grant universities throughout the country to house these programs.

Next thing I knew I was on my way to Blacksburg home of the Virginia Polytechnic Institute where I am currently stationed. It quickly became apparent that the locals call it Virginia Tech for short. I like the moniker. It's much easier to say than Virginia Polytechnic Institute. To be frank it's not the assignment I expected. I assumed I'd be assigned to the Army's general infantry and sent over to Europe or somewhere in the Pacific. Instead I spend my days in a classroom teaching structural engineering to soldiers.

A knock on the door pulls me back to the present. Looking up I see Sergeant Joe Cavanaugh standing in the open doorway. He's a fellow Army instructor here at Virginia Tech. Unlike me, who had zero teaching experience before being shipped to Blacksburg, he's a former college language professor. This assignment isn't too much of a stretch from what he's used to. That is if you don't count the uniform, haircut or any of the many regulations we're under strict orders to follow at all times.

"I got a letter from Dan yesterday," he says stepping inside the empty classroom. Dan is Joe's cousin. "He just got a new assignment," he tells me and I can see the worry on my friend's face.

"Where?" I ask

"Italy," he says.

"That sucks," I say. It really does. There's been a lot of action in Italy recently. "Does the letter say when he leaves?"

"Three weeks and he wants to see us before he goes. He said to tell you 'that's an order'."

Typical Dan I think, "I see he's still lording his superior rank over our heads," I say and start to pack up. "Of course we're going to see him," I add. I can use the time I have saved up. "I've got some leave, what about you?" I ask.

"Yeah," Joe says.

"Good, let him know we'll be there soon." Dan, a lieutenant in the Navy, is stationed in Washington D.C. which is only a few hours from here.

"I definitely will," Joe says.

I finish stuffing papers and books into my messenger bag to bring home to work on tonight. When I'm done I hit the lights on the way out. Outside in the parking lot someone calls my name. "Sergeant Rosenberg!" Turning, I see a familiar face. It's a soldier from one of my engineering courses. "What can I do for you, Private?" I ask as he draws near.

"Need your help, sir," he says producing a notebook. He flips it open. "I'm having trouble with one of the calculations you gave us."

Joe says he'll catch up with me tomorrow. I give him a nod then turning back to the soldier asking for help I surreptitiously glance at the name patch on the front of his coat. As I listen to Private Dawes explain his question I quickly ascertain where his confusion lies. It's a technical concept regarding strength to weight ratio. Glancing at his notebook I see he's missing a step in the equation.

I pose a question then wait giving him time to think. I don't automatically point to the missing piece of the equation. Spoon feeding him the answer would not be doing him any favors. There won't be anyone to feed him answers in a few months' time when he's in the middle of a hostile situation and it's up to him to figure out how much weight a hastily constructed bridge can hold. He'll have to figure it out on his own and he'll have to do it quickly and accurately. His life and those of the men in his unit may depend upon it.

So I wait for him to recall that the strength to weight ratio of any given material is the strength of that material divided the mass of the material. In reality it takes him about two minutes to recall the answer and I watch his eyes light up when he answers with, "The mass of the material, sir."

"That's correct," I say. Two minutes might not seem like a lot of time, but when you've got to get a platoon of men across a river and the enemy is closing the distance between them and you, two minutes is a long time. I hold out my hand and he places a pencil in my grasp.

Turning the notebook so that he can see

the calculation he's struggling with I say, "Look," and pointing with the tip of the pencil I say, "You skipped a step."

He looks closer. "I did."

"Here," I make a few corrections then review the problem with him making sure to detail every step. "Do you see it now?"

He nods, "Yes, thanks Sergeant."

I look him square in the eye and serious as a heart attack I say, "Study this problem and all the others. You need to be able to do them in your sleep."

"Yes sir," Dawes says somberly.

"You're dismissed Private," I say and he turns to go.

As I make my way through the teacher's lot I wonder what will happen to Dawes and others like him after they leave this place. Chances are high they'll be sent to the front. Classes here are condensed versions of what would take months to teach under normal circumstances. It's my job to impart as much practical knowledge as I can in the shortest amount of time possible. What these soldiers learn here will mean the difference between life and death in combat.

Spring 1944

CHAPTER FOUR
– ELLEN

I can arguably say that the two months I spent in Northampton were the longest two months of my life. Officer training was nothing short of grueling. I thought winters in New York were cold. Cross my heart and hope to die, Massachusetts is colder. Long days were filled with physical fitness sessions, classes, war drills, marching, watch duty, lessons, lectures and exams only to be followed by more of the same.

For the first few weeks of training we wore the clothes we brought with us. We looked ridiculous marching in civilian clothes and shoes with a Navy issued hat. Just the thought of it makes me want to laugh a little even now. It was in early December when our uniforms finally arrived. A dark blue wool uniform is for the winter months. It consists of a white button down shirt, dark blue tie, single-breasted jacket and a six-gored skirt.

It comes accessorized with two pairs of shoes, a pair of black Oxfords and a pair of black pumps, as well as a brimmed hat, black gloves, black leather purse, rain coat and winter coat. There's also a spring and summer uniform. It's similar to the dark blue but that one is made from a white light-weight material and is worn with white shoes. Plus if we want we can wear a gray and white striped seersucker option but only in the summer months.

It is Josephine Forrestal, the wife of the Under Secretary of the Navy that we have to thank. At one time she had been a fashion editor at Vogue. When the Navy formed the Women's Reserves Mrs. Forrestal used her connections at the magazine to convince Mainbocher (pronounced 'Maine-Bow-Shay') to design the uniforms.

Being from New York I've heard of the fashion house, but I admit knew little about it. Originally from Paris, apparently Mainbocher is the epitome of haute couture. His fashion is famous for its sophisticated elegance. The designer is credited with creating the strapless dress and jeweled cashmere sweaters. He's dressed royalty, members of the aristocracy, dignitaries' wives, Hollywood stars and now, us.

When war first broke out in Europe Mainbocher was forced to leave France. He relocated to New York City, specifically on 57th Street right next to Tiffany's jewelers. As we were being fitted for our uniforms someone said that the New York location is a replica of the former Paris salon. It is something I'd like to see with my own eyes. Perhaps I'll take Bess and mother there next time I am home.

You may consider what I'm wearing couture, if you please. In all seriousness though, the Navy's uniforms are functional as well as feminine and beautiful. The design is a classic, flattering fit and the best part is Mainbocher did the design for free. He did not bill the Navy.

At the beginning of January my mother, Bess and Eduardo travelled by train to Northampton to watch me receive my commission. I was over the moon that they could be there. Bill and Gladys weren't able to come, but they sent their regards and it meant a lot knowing they were thinking of me. It was then that I got my official orders letting me know where I would be stationed. I could barely contain my excitement the last week of training. I really wanted to know where I would be next.

And here I am living in Washington, D.C. working in the Navy's intelligence department. It was the assignment I had wanted so badly to get. I had to control my excitement when heard I'd earned this position. It was an honor to receive such an assignment one that I felt ready and prepared for.

And look at me now, sitting at my desk in my designer Navy whites. Mine is one in a sea of desks jammed into a large open office space. I'm surrounded to the front, back and sides by rows and rows of other desks occupied by Navy personnel and civilians employed by the Department of the Navy. Currently, I'm working on a file that requires my full attention and I'm trying my best to concentrate.

The problem is the type writers, more specifically, the noise emanating from them. There's a lot of them in here and the acoustics of this big open space only makes the noise that much more distracting. I'm trying to block out the tap, tap of the keys. The sound is all around me. It's inescapable.

The loud ding of the carriages as they reach the end of the page then swoosh of the carriage return levers being pushed back into position are what I find most difficult to ignore. All of the taps, dings and swooshes are a jumble of chaotic noise. Thus concentration is an elusive concept for me at the moment.

The good news is I've made new friends. I live in a small apartment on Florida Avenue with Jane Darby and Phyllis Reid. It's strange yet edifying my new found independence. The three of us work together here in the classification department. Jane is a no-nonsense kind of girl. My first impression of her was that she's a little too serious for her own good but it turns out there's a fun side to her. Jane is tall and slender and there's something classic about her style. She exudes confidence and I would say she's got natural leadership qualities. We work a lot but we also find time to go out, mostly on the weekends. There is so much to do in this city. She is the responsible one. She keeps us out of trouble. Most of the time.

Then there's Phyllis. She's taller than me and shorter than Jane. Her curly hair and warm brown eyes reflect her personality. She's an open book. People can't help themselves, they like her immediately. I did. She makes you feel like you've known her for forever. Her laugh is infectious and she's a hugger. But the thing that I like best about Phyllis is that she says what's on her mind. I don't have to wonder if she's trying not to hurt my feelings. On the flip side I never know what's going to come out of her mouth. She keeps things interesting that's for sure.

Vera King, Jean Gray, and Lorraine Farmer also work in Classification. They live on the first floor in our same building. Vera is a debutante from Connecticut. If I had to describe her in one word it would be classy, with a capital C. That girl could write a book on deportment. She went to finishing school so she is the expert on what is and what is not considered proper behavior. Sometimes we follow her advice and other times we simply drag her along into whatever antics we're getting ourselves into.

Jean is shy and quiet most of the time. However, I've seen her be chatty and she's got a quirky sense of humor. Hers is the face of an angel but more importantly she has a big heart and is kind to everyone she meets. She also happens to be the most patient person I know.

Lorraine is a mid-western girl through and through. She keeps her thick chestnut brown hair long. Her big brown eyes are expressive. Whatever she's feeling is usually written all over her face. She's approachable, fun to be around and she loves to dance. She and I usually eat lunch together. More often than not she fills me in on Hollywood articles she reads in magazines. Because of her I know what movies are coming out and when and who is starring in them. If she wasn't in the Navy she would make a great reporter, I think.

Tonight the six of us are going to the first in a series of classes being offered to anyone here who wants to learn how to speak Chinese. The class is being offered by a Lieutenant Commander who once lived and studied in China. We thought it might be helpful to learn the language. Being able to speak Chinese could possibly aid us to advance our positions within the Bureau.

A quick check of the clock on the wall tells me that we're out of here in a few minutes. I close the file in front of me and set it on the corner of my desk. Jane will be by to collect it any moment now. I open the bottom drawer of my desk, pull out my purse and set it on my lap. I still can't believe it came with the uniform. I reach inside and my hand finds what I'm searching for. Using the little round compact mirror I reapply my lipstick and check my reflection. I dart a quick glance to my left then right. Through my peripheral vision I see the other girls doing the same thing. At precisely four o'clock we stand, grab our hats and make our way to the door. We're going to grab an early dinner before class.

It's not a surprise when we get to the restaurant to find the place is packed like a can of sardines. To say this city is overpopulated is the understatement of the year. Most of the people who live here are either in the military or civilian employees working for the government. We watch as Vera approaches the hostess stand. A few seconds later she's waving us over so that must mean that thankfully, we're in luck. We're shown to a booth and we proceed to cram into it three on each side of the table.

Conversation begins before we even get settled. There is never a lack of things to talk about when we're together. We place our orders, sip our drinks and all the while trip over ourselves in order to be heard. When the food arrives the conversation slows for a short time while we dig in. At some point during the meal someone mentions work and before we know it we're talking about Lieutenant Cavanaugh and how he's being deployed to Italy in a few weeks.

"He's one of the good ones," Jane says.

"He is," Jean agrees.

"He'll be missed that's for sure," Phyllis says before taking a sip from her Coke glass. "On a lighter note," she adds," I hear his party is going to be quite the to-do." She means his going away party.

"No offense to the Lieutenant but it'll probably be like all the other boring cocktail parties we have to go to," Jane says this right before popping a fry into her mouth. It's not fair how she can eat anything and never gains a pound.

"No, Phyllis is right," Vera says leaving me convinced she knows something we don't. "His party will be different."

"How will it be different?" Lorraine asks. Vera has our rapt attention.

"Because his is being held at the Army Navy Club in Arlington," she says.

"Are you sure about that?" Lorraine fires at her. "That club is members only."

"I'm sure. Phyllis and I overheard Captain Knight speaking with Lieutenant Cavanaugh last week. The Captain is a member," Vera says.

"And you're just telling us this now?" Jean demands planting a hand palm down on top of the Formica table for emphasis.

"Sorry," Vera has the grace to blush.

Phyllis who also looks a little sheepish says, "We meant to tell you but that was the day we had that emergency meeting. It slipped our minds."

Vera nods, "I just remembered actually. I think there's a memo going out tomorrow. It should have all of the details then we'll know for sure if it'll be at the club or somewhere else."

Idly twirling the paper straw in my root beer I devour this tidbit. The clubhouse in Arlington is exclusive. Suddenly, I can't wait for Friday night. Now it's unusually quiet around the table. I assume we're all wondering what the inside of the Club looks like and thinking of how we're going to miss the Lieutenant when he's gone.

"Did you know," I say interrupting the silence, "that the first paper straw was invented by someone from D.C? It was in the 1880s I believe, I can't recall the exact year."

Lorraine nudges a bony elbow in my side. "Why do I get the feeling you're about to tell us about it?"

I grin at her, she knows me so well. Pulling the straw from my glass I begin, "The story goes like this. One day a man by the name of Marvin Stone was drinking a mint julep." Jane interrupts me with a comment about mint juleps being one of her favorite cocktails. She never can pick just one drink and stay with it. I shoot her a look. "As I was starting to say, he was sipping a mint julep through a stalk of rye grass and it was leaving a gritty residue in his drink."

"That sounds gross," Jean pulls a face. She's hilarious.

"You know what they say? Necessity is the

mother of all invention," Phyllis adds her two cents.

"You're saying a straw is a necessity?" Jean asks trying to keep a straight face.

"No one wants grit in their drink," Jane says definitively.

When the six of us are in the same room it becomes difficult to tell a story without interruption. I forge ahead rushing to get the rest of it told before I can be interrupted again. "An idea came to him so he wrapped strips of paper around a pencil. After carefully removing the pencil he glued the paper strips together and voila the first paper straw was invented," I say triumphantly finishing my thought.

"Where did you learn that?" Phyllis asks skeptically.

"At the Smithsonian, I balance fun outings with intellectual ones. What?" I shrug my shoulders at the incredulous looks my friends are throwing my way. "I'm a former teacher; I can't help it."

"Oh El," Phyllis wraps an arm around my shoulder and squeezes. "Don't ever change."

CHAPTER FIVE- ELLEN

Back at the Navy Bureau we locate the room on the Third floor of the building where the language class is being held. We are not the first ones to arrive. Two young men in tan officer uniforms are already inside. They stop talking as we enter the room. From the looks of them I'd say they're in their mid to late twenties. By the insignia on their shoulders, I see they are lieutenants.

Even though they out rank us Ensigns, we don't salute since we're indoors. There's a lot of protocol to remember. We find seats around the conference table. Phyllis is on my right, Lorraine to my left. About five minutes later the instructor enters the room. His hands are full. Once he unloads his burden he straightens to his full height then looks around the room. There are only eight people in here. He was probably hoping for a better turnout.

After brief introductions our instructor, Lieutenant Commander Howard dives right into the lesson he planned for the first class. He tells us that over the next several months we'll be cultivating a basic understanding of the Chinese language. "By the end of this course you should be able to engage in conversational Chinese with one another," he says. The girls and I exchange looks. Chinese is not an easy language to learn.

Monday through Friday my days consist of coding and classifying military files. This morning, as Vera predicted a memo circulated containing the details for Lieutenant Cavanaugh's going away party. Sure enough, she and Phyllis were correct. It is being held this Friday night at the Army Navy Club in Arlington.

Last night before we left class, our instructor handed out vinyl records. He told us to listen to them for thirty minutes every day, if possible. On them are voices speaking in Chinese. We are to sound out the words by repeating what we hear. The idea is that by listening to the record we'll be able to practice proper pronunciation. There's a record player at the office so Lorraine and I decide to take the first thirty minutes of the lunch hour to start learning Chinese. The others were not interested in staying back with us.

"You two sure know how to clear a room," Lieutenant Cavanaugh says coming out of his office. "What are you listening to?" he asks looking flummoxed.

"We're learning to speak Chinese, sir" I say grinning widely. "Would you care to practice with us?" I ask innocently. He's our superior officer. We report directly to him with any issues or concerns we may have. We have found him to be fair, especially to us women.

Shaking his head, he gives a little laugh and says, "No thank you. I'll pass. You two carry on, though."

Thirty minutes later we turn off the record player and head downstairs to the cafeteria for something to eat. Descending the stairs Lorraine asks, "What are you wearing Friday night to the Lieutenant's party?"

I sigh because I've been so busy lately I really haven't given it much thought and because I hate to see our Lieutenant go, especially to somewhere dangerous. We hit the bottom of the stairs and round the corner. There we find the line for the cafeteria is long. Everywhere we go there are long lines for service. It's frustrating. Every day is hurry up and wait. From our vantage point we can just see the glass refrigerated case with pre-made sandwiches. "What do they have today?" I think aloud.

"Hold on," Lorraine says stepping out of the line to get a better look. When she's back she says, "Egg salad on white or Turkey on wheat."

"Does the turkey have cheese?"

"Looks like it might be cheddar," she says nodding.

"Mustard or mayo?"

"I couldn't tell," she says.

"Thanks," I say contemplating the options and leaning toward turkey and cheese.

"Don't mention it, now about the party?"

She's like a dog with a bone sometimes. "I have no idea what to wear," I admit with a shrug.

"Your black cocktail dress looks pretty on you," she suggests.

"Thank you," I say. Lorraine is thoughtful to say so. I love my little black dress. I picked it up at Bloomingdales the last time I was home. I had three days in between training and having to report for duty here. While I was home my mother, sister and I did some shopping. Bess insisted I buy it. She said I would need a few formal dresses for special occasions. She was right as usual.

Inching closer to the counter Lorraine

says, "I'm still trying to decide what I should wear. I have a new dress. I was thinking about wearing that one."

"What does it look like?" I ask interested.

"It's red, A-line skirt with rhinestones at the shoulders." Her face lights up as she describes it. "But, I'm not sure it would be appropriate for the party," she finishes.

"Why not?" I ask genuinely confused. The dress sounds beautiful to me.

"It's red," she says like I'm supposed to know what that means.

"So?" I prompt.

Turning her attention back to the refrigerated case, she mumbles, "Maybe I'll wear the blue chiffon."

"Lorraine," I say placing my hand on her arm. I wait for her to turn my way. When she looks at me I say, "Wear the red dress." I'm emphatic because though I haven't seen it I know she is going to look beautiful in it.

"You think I should?" There is doubt in her voice.

"I do," I insist.

"I'll think about it," she concedes. She's been working on gaining more confidence. I really hope she chooses to wear the new dress. What could possibly be a bigger boost to a woman's confidence than a gorgeous red dress?

Finally we've made it to the front of the line. I end up going with the turkey on wheat. Lorraine asks me to get one for her, too. I grab a bottle of Hires root beer for me and a bottle of Coca Cola for her from the refrigerated case. I hand her one of the sandwiches and the Cola.

"Thanks," she says taking them.

We pay the cashier then head outside. It's such a nice day today it would be a shame not to get some fresh air. There's a bench in the small park across the street and we head over to it. Sitting down I pull back the paper wrapper and pick up one half of the turkey sandwich. It's mayo. The sun is warm and feels good on my face. It's a bright blue cloudless sky overhead and a gentle spring breeze rustles through the leaves. Popping the top off the bottle of soda I take a sip. The cold bubbles tickle my tongue.

"How are you wearing your hair for the party?" Lorraine revives our earlier conversation.

I almost choke on a laugh. "I've got a few ideas," she says ignoring the fact that I'm coughing.

"Ellen be serious," she says eyeing me.

"Let's put pin curls in our hair before bed Thursday night," she says.

"Ugh, I detest sleeping in pin curls." I say on a groan. The pins always poke my scalp when I sleep with them in. It's so uncomfortable and I have a hard time sleeping.

"Don't complain," she says patting one of my knees. She amuses me sometimes. Sometimes I want to strangle her. "You know your hair always looks amazing when you do the pin curls."

Hanging my head in defeat I agree to do what she wants. I don't argue with her. I can't because I know she's right. I hate it when that happens.

CHAPTER
SIX - BEN

Dan is not exactly known for writing letters so Joe and I were unfazed to find a mere paragraph from him tucked inside of an envelope with a travel brochure. In summary he told us that he was looking forward to our visit, that we won't believe how crowded it is in Washington and not to bother looking for a hotel room because according to him it's impossible to find one. Seems we'll be staying at his place. I made sure to pack a sleeping bag.

I didn't mind when Joe asked if I'd drive us to D.C. instead of taking the train. It's about a four hour drive. He said he'd pitch in for gas and I have enough ration cards saved up. When we stop for fuel about midway between Blacksburg and D.C. the attendant asks, "Where're you boys headed?"

"D.C," I tell the old guy. Then ask him to put four gallons in the tank.

"I'll need to see your ration card," he says holding out his hand.

Reaching into my back pocket I retrieve my wallet, flip it open and remove the card. He takes it eyeing the information on the front of it. My name and address, the car's make and body style and registration number are all there. Only after he's satisfied the car matches the information on the card he punches a hole in one of the unit tabs at the bottom and hands it back to me.

Then he turns toward the pump. He gets the pump going then comes back to ask us more questions. He's a chatty fellow this one. Only now he's standing near the passenger's side. "What's in D.C?"

Joe rolls down the window. He tells the guy that we're going to see his cousin. As the gas is pumping Joe says, "He's a Navy man. He's about to ship out."

"Where are they sending him?"

"To Italy," Joe says.

I've been looking at the road map as the pair talk. When I look up from the map I'm in time to see a frown appear on the old man's face. "Been lots of action over there of late," he says wearily.

We nod. We know.

Moving from the pump to the front of the

car he swipes a squeegee across the windshield, "You boys in the service, too? You've the look of it."

"Yes, sir," I answer amused to be referred to as a boy. The regulation haircuts are a dead giveaway.

"We're Army," Joe says to be specific. Joe's quite the conversationalist today.

"Thank you for your service," he says. He returns the pump to the tank and comes back around to my side of the car. "That'll be one dollar, seventeen,"

Putting the car in gear Joe and I wave goodbye. As we start to pull away he says, "You boys take care and good luck to that cousin of yours."

The drive is smooth until we reach the outskirts of D.C. where traffic becomes a nightmare. Dan's warning about gridlock did not prepare me for this. I've never seen so much traffic in my life. Tapping the breaks we're reduced to a crawl. "Keep an eye out for a place to park," I say to Joe when we finally pull onto Dan's street.

Pointing to an open space up ahead, Joe says, "There." Parking takes some effort. I haven't had to parallel park in a long time. "Good job," he says when I put the car in park and shut off the engine.

"Not bad," I have to admit. Carefully I open the door and climb out. It's a busy street. Grabbing our duffle bags from the trunk we start walking. Dan has the front door open by the time our feet hit the bottom step. "How was the drive?" he says opening the door wider.

"It was fine until we reached D.C.," I say happy to be out of the car.

Next thing we know Dan's shaking our hands and ushering us inside. He leads us up a flight of stairs to a second floor apartment. "Drop your bags anywhere," he says. The place is compact but surprisingly clean and organized for a couple of bachelors. I like the tall windows in here, too.

Mindful, I place my bag in an out of the way corner of the room. Joe does the same. "I'll give you the five cent tour," he says mostly to me since Joe's been here before and I haven't. "This is obviously the living room," he says.

"The kitchen," he indicates with a wave of his arm to a small kitchen area off the living room. We follow him down a narrow hallway. He points to the right, "Tim's room," he points to the left, "my room and straight ahead at the end of the hall is the bathroom."

The tour takes all of 5 minutes. "At one time this was all one big house. It was chopped up and made into apartments. There are not enough places to live to be able to accommodate all the people moving here." Dan explains heading back the way we came. "Since we entered the war D.C. has seen a population explosion."

"How many apartments are in here?" I ask.

"The building is four stories, two apartments on each floor," he answers.

We're in the kitchen now, "It's small but its home," he says then pauses, "Well, its home for a little while longer anyway." Joe and I exchange a look unsure what to say to that. "Anyway," he continues, "I'm glad you two are here." Pushing away from the counter and subsequently changing the subject he asks, "Do either of you want anything, something to drink?"

Before we get a chance to answer the question the front door swings open and Dan tells us, "Tim's back. Before you got here he ran down to the store."

Tim is Dan's roommate. He finds us all in the kitchen. "Hey," he says coming into the room. He's carrying two brown paper sacks. Dropping the bags onto the counter, he says, "I didn't think I'd be gone that long." Extending his right hand to me he says, "I'm Tim, good to finally meet you."

"Ben," I say gripping his outstretched hand. "Good to finally meet you too."

"Good to see you again," Tim shakes hands with Joe.

"Good to see you, too," Joe says then asks, "What's in the bags?"

Reaching both hands inside one of the sacks Tim pulls out two bottles. Holding them up, he says, "Provisions."

"Think that should be enough?" Joe says joking.

Laughing, Tim proceeds to line up several more bottles on top of the counter. "Maybe," he says tipping his head from side to side. "We'll see."

I can only imagine what the next few days are going to be like. These guys have energy to burn. I'll do my best to keep up with them.

Pulling his keys out of his pocket, Dan says, "Okay then, ready to go?"

Looking to my left I see Joe is grinning, "We just got here," he tells his cousin.

"Yup," Dan says tossing the keys up into the air and catches them, "And now it's time to go out."

I can't help it. I have to laugh. "Where are we going?" I'm almost afraid to ask.

"Just around the corner," Tim says leading the way, "To an Irish Pub."

Cold glass of lager in hand I scan the room as I lean against the bar. There are so many people in here. It's almost claustrophobic. "You get used to it, eventually," Tim tells me. He has to raise his voice to be heard. I'm not so sure I'd want to get used to being this crowded all of the time.

We see Dan and Joe waving us over. Carrying the drinks we head their way. The table is tucked into a corner of the dimly lit pub. Handing Joe one of the glasses I take my seat. Tim hands the other glass to Dan. Over plates of traditional Irish food like Shepherd's pie, bangers and mash, corned beef, and beef stew we finally have a chance to catch up. It's quieter here in the dining room than in the bar area. I break off a piece of Irish soda bread and dip it into the stew.

"Dan's in classification," Tim is saying, "I work in another department."

"Which one?" Joe asks.

"Translation," he answers. "We could use someone with your background," he tells Joe. Joe's fluent in several languages, including Japanese.

"Sorry, property of the U.S. Army," Joe brushes a hand through the short crop of blonde hair on the top of his head. "Is there something you want me to take a look at?" he asks quietly. "I'd be happy to while I'm here."

Tim shakes his head, "Nah, but thanks for the offer."

We talk some more about work. Joe and I take turns explaining how the ASTP works. Sometimes we feel like glorified teachers. "That's what you get for not volunteering," Tim chides us. I know he means nothing by it but he's right. He and Dan volunteered for the Navy after the attack on Pearl Harbor.

They're officers and have important roles in the Navy's intelligence department. Joe and I on the other hand by not volunteering early on were subject to the possibility of conscription. Hence, we are currently at the mercy of the Army, are of the rank and file and had no say in what assignments we were given.

Changing the topic Joe asks, "What are the women like around here?"

Placing his glass back on the table Dan looks at Joe, "Plentiful, beautiful, independent, intelligent, in short, way too good for you."

Joe smirks at his cousin then bursts out laughing. Dan laughs too.

"Did he tell you about the party?" Tim asks me ignoring the cousins' immature behavior.

Nodding I say, "He mentioned something about it."

"I told them," Dan says them pops a forkful of potatoes into his mouth. "This is so good," he says around a mouthful of food.

"Heathen," Joe utters under his breath.

Shooting his cousin the side eye Dan finishes the bite, swallows then washes it down with a swallow of beer. Wiping his mouth on a napkin he says, "It's a going away party in my honor. It's tomorrow night, civilian dress, no uniforms. It's a formal thing. I did mention that part, right?"

"You did," I say. "We're good."

"I expect half the Bureau to be there," Dan says. Seeing the look on Tim's face he huffs out a sigh, "Yes, they'll be there, Tim."

"That's good," Tim says nonchalantly though he can't stop the grin that spreads across his face.

"What are we missing here?" I ask curious now.

"Go ahead," Dan says to Tim scooping more potatoes onto his fork, "Tell them why you have that stupid look on your face."

"I don't have a stupid look on my face," Tim

says.

"Yes you do," Dan says.

Tim looks at me, "Do I have a stupid look on my face?"

I don't know how to answer that because, yes he does. I shrug and he looks at Joe expectantly. Joe nods his head slowly.

"Come on," Tim throws up his hands in defeat and because we're guys we find humor in his discomfort.

"He's in love with the women in the classification department," Dan enlightens us.

"All of them?" I ask.

"Pretty much," Dan nods.

"Just wait until tomorrow night," Tim wraps his hand around his glass of beer and lifts it, "You'll see for yourself." He then proceeds to take a long satisfying drink.

Sitting back in his seat crossing his arms over his chest Joe says, "I can't wait for tomorrow night then."

CHAPTER SEVEN
- ELLEN

I'm standing with Jane and Lorraine when Phyllis approaches champagne glass in hand announcing, "Lieutenant Cavanaugh is late to his own party."

"I'm sure he'll be here soon," Jane says. "I hear he's bringing out of town guests."

Lorraine lifts her glass in a toast. "The more the merrier," she says and I lift mine in agreement.

"Okay, ladies I'm ready for something a little stronger than champagne. I'm off to the bar. Coming?" Phyllis asks and before we have a chance to answer the question she turns on her black patent leather pumps and makes her way across the room toward the bar. At her departure Jane, Lorraine and I look at each other and start to laugh.

"I'll go with her," I volunteer, "anyone else

want to come?"

"Me," Lorraine says.

As we cross the room I pay her a compliment. "By the way, you look fabulous in that dress. Red is absolutely your color." She really does look stunning tonight.

"I'm so glad you talked me into it. I wasn't sure about wearing it tonight," she admits.

"I knew you could pull it off."

A big, bright, confident smile crosses her scarlet lips. I like seeing her this way, confident and happy. "I was right about the pin curls," she gloats. "Your hair looks terrific."

I thank her for saying so even as I wrinkle my nose recalling how difficult sleep was with the pins digging into my scalp all night. I tossed and turned trying to find a comfortable position. I consider voicing my complaints but restrain myself. She's not wrong my hair does look good.

We reach Phyllis who is mid-sentence telling the man behind the bar that she likes her gin martini with three olives. She turns to see what we're having.

"French Seventy-Five for me," I say.

"I'll have a Bees Knees," Lorraine says.

Phyllis turns back to the bartender to

make sure he's heard our orders. He's already two steps ahead of her so she turns her attention back to us. "Look, there's Captain Knight's wife." Phyllis rolls her eyes dramatically. "Don't look," she hisses just as Lorraine and I start to turn around. We turn back to shoot her questioning glances.

"Didn't you just tell us to look?" Lorraine eyes Phyllis.

"I didn't mean turn around."

"Then how are we supposed to look?" protests Lorraine.

Phyllis begins to launch into an explanation of what she meant but stops. Groaning she says, "Don't look now but she's headed our way."

We do not turn around this time. There are rumors around the office that the Captain's wife is stuffy and a bit old-fashioned. I'm the type of person that doesn't put much stock in gossip. I feel it's important to give people the benefit of the doubt. I do my best not to judge others and I believe in forming my own opinions. Mrs. Knight sidles up to the three of us while we wait for our drinks to be made.

"Good evening, ma'am," Phyllis addresses her politely. "Have you met Ensign Cunningham? She works with us at the Bureau."

"It's a pleasure to meet you and please call me Ellen," I stretch out my hand in greeting. Phyllis used my rank in the introduction. Something registers that it bothers Mrs. Knight to hear it said.

"Likewise," she says eyeing me critically up and down making me feel like a toxic specimen on a glass plate under a microscope. Under her breath she grumbles, "Another female officer." I'm what you'd call a people pleaser so I am ready to provide any information she may want to know about me but when I begin to speak she interrupts me, making the conversation about her. "I was a Red Cross volunteer when I was about your age. That was during the Great War," she begins, "That is what proper young ladies do in wartime."

Out of my peripheral vision I can see Phyllis' eyes scanning the room most likely she's looking for a reason to excuse ourselves from this prickly woman's company. Now I understand her earlier reaction when she saw Mrs. Knight coming our way. I feel like I've just been blindsided.

"Red Cross volunteers are invaluable especially in times of war," Mrs. Knight continues.

"Of course they are," I agree because it's true. Out of the corner of my eye I see Lorraine and Phyllis both wince. Too late I've walked right into a trap. My friends should have given me fair warning of what to expect before meeting the Captain's wife. I will hold this against them for the rest of their natural lives.

"Then can you please explain to me why today's young ladies are joining the military when they can volunteer for the Red Cross?" I realize she's seriously asking this of me like it baffles her that women would choose to join the armed services.

With a slight tilt of my head, I think about how to best answer the question. Actually, I'm not quite sure what she's really asking and does she really want an answer? I know why I joined but I don't particularly think my reason would satisfy in this case. I look to my friends for support because they're responsible for the quagmire I'm standing in right now.

"Times change, Mrs. Knight," Phyllis speaks plainly. "We can only tell you what you already know. Congress passed a bill allowing women in the military, the President signed it into law and here we all are." She raises her arms gesturing to the people around the room, many of which are women.

"I'm aware," the Captain's wife says through clenched teeth. Distaste is evident in those three syllables. "This country is going to hell in a hand basket," she huffs, "Women in uniform." We are not wearing our uniforms tonight. In fact we are all looking rather pretty and feminine in our cocktail dresses. Nonetheless, the Captain's wife lets out a long suffering sigh.

Bless her heart, Lorraine attempts flattery, "That's a lovely hat you're wearing, Mrs. Knight."

Mrs. Knight softens a smidge. Bringing her hand to her head she touches the dainty hat that sits there at an angle. It's a simple half hat made of dark blue velvet which matches her dress perfectly. It's embellished with little blue and white beads. It really is a pretty hat I have to admit. She says, "Thank you," to Lorraine. "I see your drinks are ready. I'll leave you ladies to enjoy them," and with that last remark, she is gone.

I blow out a breath before reaching for my drink. "What just happened?" I say before taking a long sip of my French Seventy-Five. It's sublime.

"You just met Captain Knight's lovely wife," Phyllis barely manages to keep a straight face.

"Indeed," I say. "A little warning would have been appreciated."

"I tried," Phyllis reminds me.

What Phyllis said before is true. Thousands of women are serving all over the country. Despite what Mrs. Knight said I truly believe that by being in the military women can do more good than not.

"Let's go find the others," Lorraine suggests. We readily spot Jane. Her sunny yellow gown stands out. We walk over to find her with Vera and Jean. Sidling up to them we slip easily into the conversation already in progress. Jean is wearing a powder blue confection which makes her look more angelic than usual and Vera looks very pretty in plum. So far, tonight is all we hoped. The ball room is stunning with crystal chandeliers and tall windows. The royal blue carpet is so plush my foot sinks into the fibers every time I take a step. Plus, there is a five piece band playing all the popular songs and I am itching to dance.

I take another sip of my cocktail. Relaxing my shoulders I take a moment to take it all in, the room, the music, the people, the food, it's all so wonderful. Best of all, it's Friday night. That means I am free for the weekend which leads me to wonder what to do with the next two days. I look at the faces of my friends. We're nearly inseparable, in and out of work.

"What's the plan for later on?" I hear Jane ask.

"You bored already Janey? The guest of

honor hasn't even made an appearance yet," Phyllis teases.

"Very funny, Phyllis, that's not what I meant and you know it," Jane says indignantly.

Phyllis says, "I know Janey, I'm just teasing you." Then, "I can't wait to see who's with the Lieutenant. That man is a mystery."

"He's professional," Jane amends.

"Same thing," Phyllis counters.

"Actually, we were just discussing ideas of what to do later, after the party wraps up," Vera says interjecting.

I love these girls. I grin knowing that we're going to have a great time no matter what plans they concoct.

CHAPTER
EIGHT - BEN

Dan got held up at the office which means he got home later than expected. "I'm going to be late to my own party," he says now from the passenger seat. I offered to drive tonight and I could tell he appreciated it. The guy should be able to drink at his own party without worrying about driving.

"You're allowed," Joe says from the backseat.

We're almost there now. The gently rolling hills of the Virginia countryside draw my eye. As we round a curve in the road I can see the clubhouse up ahead. The gray stone façade and wide white columns strike an impressive pose. The three-story building is something to behold. The civil engineer in me admires the way the long driveway was expertly planned. I can fully appreciate the verdant green golf course as well as the symmetry of the clubhouse's windows, columns and upper balcony. It is, in my opinion a masterpiece of design.

I follow the line of cars up the main drive to the portico. We file out of the car and I hand my keys to a valet sporting tan pants and a blue blazer, the Club's crest emblazoned on the chest pocket. He hands me a ticket which I stuff into the inside pocket of my dinner jacket. We all follow Dan inside.

At the top of the staircase a staff member directs us to the party. Big band music spills from a set of double doors beckoning us forward. "I hope no one notices our late arrival," Dan mutters. "The plan is to nonchalantly walk in there and act like we've been here the whole time."

"Good luck with that," Tim says slapping Dan on the back. Taking the lead he is first to enter the room. "Great turnout," he comments when we're all inside.

"Wow." Dan is visibly touched to see so many people come to say goodbye to him. Suddenly and without warning, the room erupts into a rousing rendition of 'For He's a Jolly Good Fellow.' Obviously, the idea of blending in did not go according to plan.

"That was hands down the best welcome I ever got," Dan graciously addresses the room when the song is finished and someone in the crowd yells, "Speech!" He steps further inside. "It was only slightly off key." Laughter fills the air over his remark.

"Get that man a drink!" someone else yells.

A waiter approaches carrying a serving tray laden with champagne filled glasses and we help ourselves. Tim raises his glass, "To Lieutenant Cavanaugh may the wind be always at your back my friend."

"Here, here!" the crowd choruses.

A few minutes later the music resumes. "Come on, we'll introduce you two to some of the people we work with," Tim suggests.

"Oh yeah?" Joe's eyes light up at the suggestion.

"Hold your horses," Dan says, "I don't see them just yet."

Joe and I are made to feel welcome. Throughout the introductions no one seems to mind that Dan brought a pair of soldiers with him to a sailor's party. That's good since when it comes right down to it we're all on the same side plus it helps that everyone is dressed in civilian clothes tonight. Now Joe and I don't stand out like a couple of sore thumbs.

"This way," Dan says after a while and we

follow him weaving in and out of people until we come to a circle of women. "Good evening ladies," he says to them.

The circle opens. "Good evening Lieutenant, we're glad you could make it to your party," a woman in a green dress says smiling.

"Long day at the office, Phyllis," Dan replies ruefully. "There was something that needed my attention which unfortunately couldn't wait. But I'm here now and look I've brought friends with me. Ladies, may I present to you to my cousin Joe Cavanaugh," he gestures with his drink hand toward Joe. There's a resemblance between the cousins. They both have the same build and light hair color. Then he gestures to me, "and this is our friend, Ben Rosenberg. Joe, Ben, I'd like you to meet the best of the classification department, this is Vera, Jean, Jane, Phyllis, Lorraine and Ellen."

I'm gob smacked by the sight of them. Now I understand the stupid look on Tim's face last night. The look on Joe's face right now tells me he's thinking the same thing. I just hope I don't have a stupid look on my face.

"It's a pleasure to meet you," the one in red says to us.

"These two fellas here are in the Army," Dan throws that piece of intelligence at their feet like he's the paper boy delivering the morning edition of the Times. "Please don't hold it against them." I watch him try to hide a smile behind the rim of his glass. I eye him skeptically. Dan has introduced us like that to every person we've stopped to talk to so far.

"Would you believe me if I told you these ladies are learning how to speak Chinese?" Dan then says to us.

Immediately I think it's impressive and although Chinese is not one of the languages Joe knows this flash of information about the women is something that he can grab onto and use as an ice breaker. Also, I notice the ladies are starting to exchange worried looks probably wondering what Dan might say next. Join the club, I'm thinking.

"I tell you it's true. In fact they're so dedicated to learning the language they've been driving everyone in the office crazy this week." As Dan begins to elaborate I swear half of them look like they're in shock hearing my buddy joke this way. It makes me wonder how stiff he acts when he's on the job. I get it. I'm that way with the soldiers in my classes.

"They play these recordings of voices conversing in Chinese. Then they repeat the phrases. Over and over and over," Dan is now exaggerating his pronunciation of the word 'over'.

It's fascinating, watching their facial expressions run from worry to shock to finally humor. Dan points to two ladies in particular, the brunette in red and a petite blonde in a black dress. "You know who I mean," he says outing them. He says it with a smile so they'll know he's just teasing them. "In all honesty though I'm impressed you're learning the language and I'm glad to have this opportunity to say that I respect your intelligence and dedication to your work and I'll miss working with each and every one of you."

"Thank you, sir," the one in yellow says. "We're going to miss working with you, as well." The others agree and voice their regret over his leaving.

"Thank you, Jane, all of you. It means a lot to hear you say so." Dan graciously accepts their goodwill and kind words and though they've only just been introduced I can tell that their words are genuine. I'm roused from that thought when I feel a hand come down on my shoulder. I look over to see Dan's got one hand on my shoulder and the other on Joe's. "Is it okay if Tim and I leave you two for a bit? I see someone we need to speak with, officially. We'll catch back up with you a little later." I look over at Joe. He's looking at me like are they serious?

"Sure thing," I manage to say.

"Great," Dan and Tim leave us in the company of some of the most beautiful women I've ever met. Tim is more reluctant to leave than Dan, poor guy. I'm not going to lie. I can't tear my gaze away from one woman in particular. I'm drawn to her.

My eyes dip to where she's holding a glass aloft in her left hand. She's not wearing gloves and my body almost sags with relief when it registers that there is no ring on her third finger. She was the last to be introduced. Ellen was the name Dan had said. She was one of the ones he pointed out about the Chinese records. A million questions flood my mind. Who is she? Where is she from? How did she end up here in D.C., in the Navy? What did she do before the war? What does she want to do when it's over? I have to tell myself to slow down. Be cool.

Apparently, Joe seems to have his act together better than I do. He's talking to these women as if he's already acquainted with them. I just stare at him and marvel at his skill with the ladies. He has them laughing at a story I've heard him tell a hundred times before. I have to shake my head. The guy is good.

The next thing I know he's asking the pretty brunette, the one in the red dress, to dance.

She's nodding and handing her purse to one of her friends. Good for him, I think. As they head toward the dance floor I notice Ellen wink at her friend. They exchange a look I can't quite interpret, a secret female code I assume.

CHAPTER NINE
– ELLEN

Lieutenant Cavanaugh's cousin just asked Lorraine to dance. Inside I silently squeal with delight that I was right about her wearing the red dress. She looks stunning. Judging by the look she just threw me, I can unequivocally state that yes, Lorraine is glad she wore that dress and she agrees, I was right this time.

Watching them walk away I'm struck by how good they look together. The friend, Ben is standing just a few feet away from me, a stone's throw really. He's watching them go, too. He's handsome. I'd have to be blind not to notice. To be more accurate, he's not just handsome he's movie star handsome.

Of course, I'm curious about him. I mean, what's his story? When he turns my way I say the first thing that comes to mind, "So you're in the Army." He nods. I wonder if he's not much of a talker. I press on, "Where are you stationed soldier?" Through my peripheral vision I can see the side of his mouth tip up. I've amused him, good.

"I'm afraid I can't say."

"Oh, why's that?"

"It is classified information, ma'am." He's trying, and failing, to hide a smile. I'm happy to see he's possessed of a sense of humor.

I motion for him to come a little closer and he does. When he's close enough for me to whisper I lower my voice conspiratorially and say, "It is okay you can tell me. I have security clearance. Plus, I'd prefer it if you didn't call me ma'am. Every time someone calls me that I look around expecting to see my mother." Extending my right hand I say, "Hi, I'm Ellen."

He cracks under my masterful interrogation skills and the full force of his smile dazzles me. Laughing, he says, "I'm stationed at Blacksburg, Virginia and I promise never to call you ma'am again." His movie star dimples make my knees go weak. "It's nice to meet you Ellen. I'm Ben," he says taking my hand.

I do my best to remain calm, cool and collected. You see, I can't take my eyes off him. I say, "I wasn't aware there's an Army base in Blacksburg."

"There isn't one. Joe and I are instructors at the University."

"Virginia Tech," I say, "You're professors there?" I ask.

"Not exactly, we're part of the Army's new Specialized Training Program. We work for the Army not the University and we teach soldiers not enrolled students," he explains. He has a nice voice. His words lack the distinct edge of a Northeast accent, instead it's smooth.

"I understand," I say nodding because I do. "My training was at Smith College." The government has been taking over college campuses throughout the country since America entered the war and the military needed space to educate and train men and women. "I'd like to hear more if you wouldn't mind," I say.

Coming closer he says, "I don't mind. But I wouldn't want to bore you."

"You won't," I say.

He's quiet for a moment and I wish I could read his mind. "It's new," he says, "It was created to teach qualified soldiers and junior officers certain skills."

"What kinds of skills?" I want to know.

"Foreign languages, medical, dental and engineering skills," he lists. "Joe's a foreign language instructor." My eyes light up when I hear him say this. "He teaches Japanese. Actually, he was a professor at Ohio State before being drafted," he finishes.

"Were you drafted?" I ask.

Nodding he says, "Yes."

"What did you do before you were drafted? What do you teach now?" The questions trip over one another trying to get out.

"I'm a civil engineer. Before, I worked for the Illinois Division of Highways. Now, I teach how to hastily build infrastructure like roads and bridges or how to dig drainage ditches that sort of thing."

"Is that where you're from, Illinois?" I ask, thirsting for more information about him.

"Yes, Peoria to be exact," he answers my questions easily. I wonder what Peoria is like. Is it a big city like New York? I've never been far from the east coast.

There's a momentary silence where I witness the light in his coffee eyes fade slightly. I think he might be missing home. I can understand. Intending to keep things light I say, "So you're an engineer. I can see that about you."

He looks adorably bewildered by my statement, "Is that so?" he asks.

Finishing what's left of my drink I nod, "It is."

I can tell he wants to ask me what on Earth I mean by that. Instead, pointing to the empty glass in my hand he says, "Would you like another?"

"That would be nice," I say letting him escort me to the bar. While waiting in line he asks, "What are you drinking?"

"It's a French seventy-five," I say depositing the empty glass onto a nearby tray. "It's my favorite."

"Let's see," he pretends to think, "That's made with a little gin, a little champagne, some lemon juice and sugar. Did I get that right?"

Just then Phyllis inserts herself into our private conversation. I didn't even realize she was behind us. That's how engrossed I am by Ben's company like everyone in the room has disappeared and it's just us. "It's Ellen's signature drink and we all think it suits her," she proceeds to explain.

Silently I implore her to stop talking. I try in vain to silence her with just my eyes. It doesn't work. Wrapping an arm around my shoulders she says to Ben, "Both the drink and the girl are equal parts sass and class."

Stunned I wonder how much she has had to drink. I want the ground to open up and swallow me whole right this second. I can hardly believe that Phyllis just said that about me. I'm mortified. I can't even look at him anymore instead I stare at a spot on the carpet below.

A low rumble of laughter shakes the fog of my mortification. "Now that you mention it, I'm pretty sure I detected a hint of both of those qualities in our girl here." Ben is talking to Phyllis like I'm not standing right here. Oh, he's getting me back for the engineering comment I made earlier but that's okay because he just said, 'our girl.'

Phyllis chances a look at me and mouths an *'I'm sorry.'*

The situation is kind of funny. All I can do is shrug my shoulders and say, "I guess the cat's out of the bag. Now you know my deepest, darkest secret, Ben."

Phyllis says that someone behind us is calling to her. It's not true but I let her off the hook and she dashes off.

Moving closer to my side Ben leans down and says, "I like how you handled that."

"Phyllis, she's great," I say waving it off because I have the best girl friends and I know

Phyllis was only trying to be funny.

"I like that you have a sense of humor," Ben goes on, "And who doesn't appreciate some sass now and again?"

Thankfully, it's our turn at the bar because I have no witty come back at present. Instead I suppress a smile. He's nice. We're pressed in on all sides. There is a crush of people around us. Ben's behind me, so close. "I'll take a bourbon old fashioned," he tells the bar tender. Looking at me he says, "What will you have, same as before or something different this time?"

"The same as before," I say. "She'll have a French Seventy-Five," he tells the man. As our drinks are being prepared I can feel Ben's presence. He's trying not to bump into me but it's almost impossible not to given all of the people vying for a drink.

"Sorry," he says after colliding into my back. His hands grip the edge of the bar on either side of me for purchase. He gives me a wry smile. The way his hands are positioned on the edge of the bar makes him look like my own personal body guard.

I smile up at him and say, "No harm done." His smile goes from wry to natural and I am struck not only by his dimples but by how thoughtful he is being. Quickly turning away I watch as the bartender puts the finishing touches on our drinks.

"This is us," I say. Looking over my shoulder I catch Ben watching me and my face grows hot.

When I pass the old fashioned to Ben his long fingers brush over mine. "Cheers," he says and his dark brown eyes lock with mine.

"Cheers," I return.

After wrestling away from the bar we find that the others have scattered and are no longer where we left them. Scanning the crowd for my friends I see some of them are dancing and some are engaged in conversation with co-workers. I'm not sure what to do, excuse myself to join Jane and Phyllis on the other side of the room?

Lorraine and Jean are dancing and I don't see Vera anywhere. Seeing my hesitation Ben gestures toward an empty table and we head over to it. Resting his glass on top of the tall table he says, "Tell me something."

"What do you want to know?" I say, "I'm an open book."

Pausing he studies me. I think he is trying to decide what to ask first. "Where are you from?" I realize that I like that he's easing us into the getting to know you game.

"Born and raised in New York City," I tell

him.

He does the cutest thing. He nods his head and says, "So, you're a city girl. I can see that about you."

It's difficult keeping a straight face as I repeat his words from earlier, "Is that so?"

"It is." He's trying to keep a straight face too. He fires off another question. "What did you do before the Navy?"

"I was a teacher."

"No kidding," he cracks first. "What did you teach?"

"High school English."

"Did you like it?"

"Teaching? Yes, for the most part," I say.

"Does 'for the most part' have anything to do with grading papers?" he asks even though somehow I know that he knows that's what I mean.

"You guessed it," I nod and say, "Not a fan of grading papers either?"

"Not in the slightest," he says.

The beginning notes of Glenn Miller's *Moonlight Cocktail* float around us. "I love this song," I say because I say it every time I hear it.

"Ellen would you like to dance with me?" he asks. When I nod he rounds the table. "I should warn you, I'm not a very good dancer but I promise to do my best to keep up."

Smiling up at him I shake my head. "Why don't I believe you?"

"You've been sufficiently warned," he says holding out his hand.

As I place my hand in his he says, "Lead the way."

So that is exactly what I do.

CHAPTER
TEN – BEN

I'm letting Ellen lead me across the room to where the dancing is. I'm pretty sure at this moment I'd let her lead me pretty much anywhere she wanted to. This girl is smart and beautiful and she's got a great sense of humor. She's not like some of the other women I've met before. She's easy going and easy to be around. She caught me looking at her earlier while we were at the bar. I didn't think she'd notice but when she turned she caught me checking her out. We were so close and her hair smelled so good, sweet like strawberries. I just couldn't help myself.

Even now my eyes follow the seams of her stockings up the back of her calves as they duck beneath the hem of her little black dress. Everything about her draws me in. Turning, she faces me. Did she catch me looking this time? Taking her hand, I draw her near. She places her free hand on my shoulder. I place my hand on the small of her back we begin to move, swaying keeping time with the music.

After a few minutes have passed she says, "I think you lied to me."

"What?" I say a little taken a back.

"You're a great dancer," she says. "You told me you weren't any good."

Ducking my head to hide a grin I say, "I'm okay." Then without warning I dip her. A laugh escapes her pretty red mouth. It's a great sound, her laugh. I'd bottle it if it were possible.

Too quickly the Glenn Miller song ends and the band changes gears. That popular Andrews Sisters song starts. It's fast paced and since it's a song about a bugle boy more people are spilling onto the dance floor. I'm wondering how to extricate ourselves from the crowd when I see Ellen's face light up. Apparently she likes this song too, looks like we're staying right where we are.

Allowing myself to feel the music I match my moves to Ellen's. She's light on her feet. She's graceful and the look on her face lets me know she's enjoying this. I spin her out and back into me. The full skirt of her dress twirls around us. As she comes back to me her hand lands on my chest as she steadies herself. She smiles and it lights up her entire face. I'll dance all night long if that's what she wants to do.

We dance to one more song before she says, "I need to catch my breath."

Her arm entwined with mine I say, "We could go out on the balcony for some air."

"That sounds nice but just for a minute," she says nodding her agreement.

The cool night air washes over us the moment we step outside. Standing near the balustrade Ellen tips her head back and looks up at the endless inky sky. The stars are bright this evening. Pointing she says with wonder wrapped around every word, "Look, there's a shooting star. I've never seen one before." She chances a look at me, "We have to make a wish."

The light streaking across the sky reminds me of summer nights back home. "Have you ever seen one before?" she asks. Moving my gaze from the stars to Ellen I nod, "A few times when I was a kid."

"How lucky you are," she says. I've never thought of myself as lucky.

"On warm summer nights my sister Gabby and I would lie on our backs in the grass and look up at the sky. She liked it when I'd show her where the Big Dipper was high above us. When I was about twelve or so I borrowed a book from the library on constellations. I found it interesting so I memorized the patterns the stars made up. To this day on nights like this, when the stars are this visible I look for them in the sky," I confess searching the sky for familiar star patterns. I don't know why I've just told Ellen all that.

"I don't know what I should be looking for," she says her eyes on the sky.

"There are many constellations and shapes to look for," I say.

"Like what?" she asks moving a little bit closer to where I'm standing. I'm not sure if it's so she can see what I'm seeing or for another reason altogether.

I search the sky for something I can show her. Maybe I can spot Orion or Cassiopeia. There's Leo the lion. I look at Ellen to get her attention. I want to show her where Leo is in the sky. Before I can speak a breeze sweeps in and a lock of hair escapes from the clip she's wearing. The faint scent of strawberries wafts around us. Brushing the hair away from her face I tuck it behind her ear. "What did you wish for?" I ask.

Her voice is soft on the breeze. "I can't tell you," she says, "Or it might not come true."

There is something about her. "Whatever it is," I say, "I hope,"

Suddenly the door behind us flies open. "There they are," I hear Joe say. "See, I told you I saw them come out here." Joe, Tim and Dan come walking over to where we are, Ellen's friends not far behind.

They surround us and it's no longer just Ellen and me. Whereas I'm happy to see the others I can't help feeling a little disappointed that we've been interrupted. "It's a beautiful night," says Phyllis. "Look at all those stars."

"They don't seem as bright where I live," Ellen says turning to Phyllis, "I think all the lights in the city take away from them." Hearing her say this makes me want to know more about Ellen.

Dan is to my left, "You having a good time?" I ask him.

"Yeah," he says with a nod. "I am."

"There's quite a crowd in there," Ellen says with a nod toward the balcony doors. "It's really nice to see so many people come out for you tonight, Lieutenant."

My buddy nods again and says, "It's touching. It means a lot to me that they all came."

"You deserve nothing less," I say touching

SHOW YOU THE STARS

his shoulder. "There are a lot of people inside that room who are going to be sorry to see you go. I know I will."

He's silent for a moment. Only after he takes a drink from the glass in his hand he says, "Thanks."

Phyllis moves to Dan's other side and says, "Lieutenant, you seem different outside of work."

"How so?" Joe and I say at the same time.

Ellen's friend Vera answers before Phyllis can. "He's less straight laced."

Upon hearing Vera's pronouncement Tim begins to cough.

"That's it," Phyllis agrees snapping her fingers. She turns to Dan and says, "You're a lot more fun outside work."

Dan clinks the tumbler in his hand to the one Phyllis is holding. "Have to be professional at work. Would you take me seriously if I wasn't?"

"No," Jane answers pointedly.

"Probably not," Phyllis says conceding.

Leaning on the railing Joe says, "I've never seen him serious. What's that like?"

Dan elbows him in the side.

Jane begins to extrapolate. "First of all our Lieutenant here is always professional around the office. He respects those he works with including the females." Turning Jane addresses Dan directly, "Thank you for that," she says to him.

Dan clinks his glass to hers. "You've earned the respect Ensign Darby," he says. Then looking around at the faces before him he says, "You all have."

Putting an arm around Dan Joe says, "How about we drop the military stuff for tonight, yeah?"

Looking around for some sort of indication that it's okay with the others Dan turns back to Joe. "I have no problem with that."

"Would that be okay with everyone?" Joe puts the question out there.

It seems like no one has a problem with it or at least, no one voices a problem with it.

Somehow the guys and I end up spending the majority of the evening at the Army Navy Club in the company of Ellen and her friends. It's no hardship I promise you. Phyllis it turns out is hilarious. We're all having a great time. Every once in a while Dan or Tim or both of them get pulled away by someone who wants to talk to them but they always manage to wind their way back to our little group.

As the party is wrapping up Dan says he wants to hit the Mayfair. "The Mayfair?" I ask.

"A nightclub," Dan says in explanation.

"A very popular nightclub," Tim adds.

I read between the lines and know that means it will be standing room only. I don't love crowds but since this is Dan's night and he wants to continue this party at The Mayfair, I'm all in.

"You're coming, too?" Dan wants to know of Ellen and her friends.

"Is that an order?" Phyllis jokes making Dan laugh out loud.

"You're funny," he says pointing at her. Then to everyone, "When we get back to the city we'll drop off the cars then meet at the club." It's a plan.

An hour later inside the Mayfair Dan leaves us at the table then heads over to the Juke Box. There he drops a handful of coins into the coin slot on the machine. He's there for several minutes. From my vantage point I can see he's making several song selections. I'm curious to know what he's picking.

When he returns to the table Tim asks him, "What songs did you pick?"

"You'll have to wait and see," is all Dan says.

"Huh." Tim says and takes a swallow from the bottle of beer he's holding. "Suit yourself."

"Hand me my beer," Dan says ignoring the look on his friend's face.

Shaking his head, Tim slides the beer across the table to Dan. "You're really not going to tell us?" Tim asks incredulous.

"Nope," Dan says lifting the bottle to his mouth.

About ten minutes later Dan says, "This is one of mine." It grabs us. Joining Dan in raising our glasses we start to sing along. Woodie Guthrie's folk song is playing on the jukebox and it seems like the entire nightclub is singing with us. Joe slings an arm over my shoulder. Practically everyone in here is singing '*This Land is Your Land, This land is my land*' at the tops of their lungs by now. You can barely here the recording itself. It's raucous and it's awesome.

The lyrics remind us of what we're fighting for. Seeing everyone in here tonight singing along is a spectacular display of patriotism and pride in our country. It's an impromptu tribute to everyone who's fighting and for those who've fought and sacrificed all. Looking over at Ellen I am heartened to see she's singing too. Her pretty face is flushed. She and her friends look like they're having a great time. I'm glad they came to the Mayfair tonight.

The song ends and we lower our drinks to the table. "That was something," Tim says, "Good choice my friend," he pats Dan on the back. "You always seem to play the best music."

"Thanks," is all Dan says taking a pull on his beer.

By now we're all feeling loose and comfortable in each other's company but still I'm surprised when Phyllis grabs Dan by the arm and says, "Let's dance."

Unfazed Dan stands and says, "Let's do it."

Not to be outdone Lorraine grabs Joe's arm and demands he dance, too. "I'm all yours," he says standing.

Marveling at what I've just witnessed it takes me a second to realize that Ellen is calling to me, "Hey Ben!" she says from across the table.

Here I go grinning again. I want to play it cool, act nonchalant. "Hey what, City Girl?" I say like no big deal. Her big blue eyes go wide and then slightly narrow. I kid you not she reaches across the table, grabs my tie and tugs on it then she says, "Come dance with me." This girl is slowly killing me. For the second time tonight I follow her like a puppy on a string.

It's approaching one in the morning with no sign of the guys slowing down. After a few dances with Ellen I'm back at the table. She and the others are still out there, cutting up a rug. I begged off saying I needed a minute but that I'd be back. Joe finds me and joins me at the table. Laughing he says, "I can't keep up with them."

"Me neither," I confess ruefully. "I just needed a second."

"Yeah," he agrees. We sit for minute and I sip from a glass of cold water. "How does Dan seem to you?" Joe asks me.

Rolling my head to look at my buddy I say honestly, "I can't really tell. He seems okay to me but I really can't tell for sure."

"I can't tell either," Joe says.

Lowering the now empty glass I say, "Let's keep an eye out for any red flags while we're here."

"Agreed," Joe says absently fiddling with a paper coaster.

When Joe and I finally make our way through the crowded club to where our friends are I catch sight of Ellen dancing the Lindy Hop with some guy I've never seen before. Standing off to the side watching, I take a pull from my beer. When she sees me she throws me a little wave. I lift the bottle and give her a nod in return. She turns her attention back to the dance. She's good.

A few minutes later the song ends and the Lindy Hop is over. That's when I see another guy approach her. I watch her shake her head and say something to him. When the guy gives up and walks away Ellen turns my way and when she sees I'm still here, crooks her finger at me. I pretend like I don't know it's me she's just beckoned. I point to my chest and mouth "Me?"

She points to me and mouths, "Yes you." Her smile is incandescent. It does not escape me that I am the cause of it. Still I shake my head because I don't want to dance anymore. Instead I crook my finger at her. She plays the same silly game with me that I just played with her. My heart skips a beat when I see her start to walk this way.

Stopping in front of me she tips up her chin, "Are you not going to dance anymore?" Her hands are fisted on her hips. She looks not at all intimidating. A curl has escaped from the clip in her hair and I am reminded of when it happened earlier in the evening when it was just the two of us. I want to tuck it behind her ear like I did earlier. Instead I watch as she reaches up to brush it off her face and secure it back inside the clip.

"Is that okay with you?" I ask.

"I suppose," she says.

This girl does have sass. Phyllis was not wrong about that. Together we make our way to the table. Pulling a chair out for her I say, "Looks like everyone's having a good time."

"It does," she agrees taking a seat.

"What about you? Are you having a good time, Ellen?" I take the seat beside her.

"The best," she says turning toward me.

I miss the opportunity to explore her comment further because over her head I see the others heading our way.

CHAPTER ELEVEN - ELLEN

I can't remember the last time I had this much fun. Lieutenant Cavanaugh - Dan is great and so are his friends. Who knew? Speaking of, here he comes leading the pack. They all look as worn out as I feel. My feet are sore from dancing in these shoes all night. I wasn't upset in the least when Ben said he didn't feel like dancing anymore. I was actually a little relieved.

It's been a long day. I've been up since six and I'm completely worn out. A glance at my watch has me doing a double take. I can't believe it's after two a.m. already. My friends collapse onto chairs in a heap of tired limbs. "I can't dance anymore," Phyllis says on a moan. "Why did you make me stay out so late?"

Chuckling Vera says to her, "Since when do you do what anyone tells you to? Also, I'm pretty sure it was you who made us stay out late."

Dropping her head to the table Phyllis must be delirious as she mumbles, "I never do what I'm told, except at work," she corrects herself.

A laugh escapes from Dan, "That's true enough."

Rubbing her back convivially I tell Phyllis we'll be going soon.

"We'll walk you home," Tim says.

"Absolutely," Dan confirms. "It's late," he adds in a way that will brook no argument from us.

"Thank you," Jane says, "We'd like that." She speaks for all of us on this point.

As we make ready to leave Ben grabs his jacket off the back of the chair. He took it off earlier when I pulled on his tie and demanded he dance with me. I have no idea what came over me then but when I saw Phyllis grab for Dan and then Lorraine grab his cousin, I felt a little bold and went for it. Ben tried not to smile, but I could see he wanted to. I liked surprising him. I also liked dancing with him. Covertly, I watch him slip his arms through the sleeves of his jacket then go off with Joe, Tim and Dan to settle the tab.

"I'm exhausted," says Vera slowly getting

up from the chair.

"Me, too," Jean says giving her a hand up. "It was fun though."

"I think Joe has eyes for Lorraine," Phyllis says rifling through her purse looking for something.

Lorraine's head pops up. She gives Phyllis an incredulous look. "Why would you say that?" she wants to know.

"It's the way he's been looking at you all night," Phyllis says pulling a key from her purse and slipping it into the pocket of her dress.

"How has he been looking at me all night?" Lorraine asks.

"Like that," Phyllis says angling her head in the direction of the bar where the guys are standing.

Turning, I see that Joe does indeed have his eyes on Lorraine. Huh, what do you know about that, Phyllis was right. Then I look at Ben. He's looking at me. My insides do this funny little flip thing.

"We're all set," Tim says several minutes later. "We can leave now."

Pushing open the door, Ben holds it while we file out into the night. I'm the last one out and as I brush past him he quietly asks me, "Can I walk with you?"

"Sure," I say looking up at him making eye contact. "That would be nice."

Despite the hour there are still plenty of people milling about outside the club. Stepping around them we head in the direction of home. The city's blackout rules mean the streets are pitch dark and it makes me feel better knowing we're not walking home alone. I appreciate that the guys are with us. Call me old fashioned, but I feel a little safer with them around.

The temperature dropped considerably while we were inside the Mayfair. Wrapping my arms around myself does nothing to ward off the chill. A few seconds later I feel an unexpected weight fall over me. Ben has just draped his jacket over my shoulders. It's warm and it smells like his cologne. I pull it tighter around me. "Thank you," I say looking over at him. I can't get over how striking his looks are.

He matched his stride to mine and there's that dimple again. "You looked cold and I was taught to be a gentleman."

"Your parents would be proud," I say somewhat joking but also serious. From what I've seen of this soldier his parents should be proud of him.

I think back to earlier tonight at the Army Navy Club. I would have liked to ask him more about himself. I like how when he talks he measures his words. He's thoughtful, case in point his jacket is around my shoulders as we speak. I didn't even have to ask to borrow its warmth. I like the feel of it, like it's an extension of him. As we all walk on Ben stays close by my side. He seems like such a decent guy.

The others are all talking, telling stories, being loud. Phyllis is walking beside Dan. They're a few paces ahead of the rest of us. From what I gather she is keeping him entertained. They're talking animatedly. All of the sudden Dan turns around and begins walking backward. He begins to say something about last New Year's Eve. "Hey Ben, remember what happened that night? Let's tell them about how you, me and Joe went up on the roof of the hotel."

"I don't think they want to hear about that," Ben says quickly interrupting what Dan was about to say.

When I raise a brow expectantly Ben looks sheepish. "I want to cover your ears," he says to me.

Dan then says, "Sure they do Ben. It's a good story."

ALLY GROH

"You can tell it later, to Tim," Ben insists and Joe just shakes his head laughing.

Dan looks to Tim with a big goofy grin on his face, "Tim, you're going to love this one."

I'm still trying to reconcile the Lieutenant Cavanaugh from the office with what I'm learning about him tonight when I hear Tim say, "Can't wait to hear it, wish I could have been there."

From out of the corner of my eye I see Ben shake his head. He shrugs when I throw him a questioning glance. "Dan's a bad influence."

"I heard that, Buddy," Dan says on a laugh.

"It was meant to be heard," Ben returns also on a laugh.

We see no cars out on the road and make our way across the street. We continue on toward Florida Avenue. Because I'm curious I ask, "Have you had a chance to see any of the city since you've been here?"

"Not yet," Ben shakes his head.

"Tomorrow," Joe says, "We're doing some sight-seeing. Dan and Tim are going to show us around."

"That's right," says Dan and it's now that I notice the little slur to his words. "We can all go together," he insists.

"Sure thing," Phyllis says to him. Then she looks to us and shrugs her shoulders.

I know I'm not about to argue with the boss especially when he's had a few drinks. Besides, we've just reached our building.

"This is us," says Lorraine.

"All of you," Joe asks. "You all live here?"

Jean answers, "Yes we do."

I remove Ben's jacket from around my shoulders and immediately miss its warmth. Extending it to Ben I say, "Thanks again."

"My pleasure," he reaches for the jacket. He holds it in his hands.

"It was really nice to meet you," I say.

"Likewise," he says.

Feeling Lorraine's touch on my arm I realize that the girls are already heading up the steps. "Well, this is good night," I say.

"Goodnight, City Girl," he says to me. His eyes search my face. He smiles warmly and those dimples appear. He is so handsome.

I catch up with the others. Ascending the stairs we hear Dan's voice. He is certainly chipper this evening. He calls up to the lot of us, "We'll call you ladies tomorrow. Remember, you're coming with us."

Standing at the top of the steps I turn to see Dan has one arm around Tim and the other around Joe. I think he's leaning on them. I look to Ben who's standing a few feet away from them putting on his jacket. When he's got it on, he looks up. Locking eyes with me, he says, "See you ladies tomorrow."

Jane gets the front door unlocked. Inside in the entry way she, Phyllis and I head toward the stair case. Our apartment is on the second floor. Vera slips her key into the lock of their first floor apartment but before she gets the door open Lorraine sounding puzzled asks, "They'll call us tomorrow?"

Phyllis halts on the third step. "Oh, I forgot to mention Dan asked for our phone number earlier," she explains, "So I wrote it on a cocktail napkin at the Mayfair and gave it to him."

"Do you think they'll actually call?" Jean wonders aloud.

We all turn to look at the wall phone.

CHAPTER
TWELVE – BEN

I want to sit by Ellen but by the time I board the bus the seat beside her is already taken. Her friend Lorraine is sitting there. Doing the next best thing I take the empty seat behind her. A few seconds later Joe plops down beside me. It turned out that last night at the Mayfair Dan got their number from Phyllis who wrote it down on a cocktail napkin after he asked her for it. Thank you, Dan and Phyllis.

They met us at the bus stop. Earlier, Dan called over to their place to let them know when and where to meet us. As we stood around waiting for the bus, everyone except Joe and I debated about where we should go first. After some deliberation it was decided that the National Mall would be our first destination. The plan is to check out the monuments and museums down there.

As the bus chugs forward I pull from my pocket the trifold brochure Dan mailed to us a few weeks ago. I thought it could be useful so I brought it with me to reference. As Joe looks out the window I quietly scan the information available about the monuments along the National Mall. When I look up I see Ellen's reflection in a small round mirror. Our eyes meet and hold for a few seconds before she snaps the mirror closed.

Turning around in her seat she asks me, "What are you looking at?"

Holding up the brochure in my hand, I turn it showing her the cover.

"May I see it?" she asks

I slip it to her through the opening between our seats. Dipping her head Ellen examines it with what looks to me like genuine curiosity. I'm sure she notices the pencil marks and notations that I've made in the margins. Idly, I wonder what she might think about me writing in there. With her attention still focused on the paper in her hands she says, "You've put a lot of thought into what you want to see while you're here."

I nod, "A little." I'm pleased she didn't think

it was foolish to mark up the paper with my ideas.

"Do you like to see new places?" she asks.

"As much as the next person I guess; how about you City Girl?" I shoot back.

"Very much so," she says. "I haven't been many places though. I haven't had the opportunity. I'd love to travel and maybe I will someday, when the war is over," she says wistfully.

"I hope you get the chance," I say for her ears only.

She rewards me with the most beautiful smile, "thank you," she says. She's a sweet person. If I had more time to spend with her I think I could fall for this girl. But, I don't. Joe and I are leaving in a few days.

At the bottom of the stairs leading up to the Lincoln Memorial I offer my arm to Ellen. Together we climb the long column of steps. I have to slow my steps to accommodate her shorter stride. I don't mind in the least. We take our time and when we reach the top to my utter disappointment she lets go of me.

There are ten in our group and altogether we gather at the foot of the statue of the sixteenth president. Ten heads tip back in unison taking in tons of alabaster marble. The statue is enormous. We stand in silent awe.

"You see the hands?" Tim being the first to speak breaks the silence. Pointing upward he continues, "There's symbolism in the hands. Look at Lincoln's left hand. You see how it's clenched?"

Moving a little closer to President Lincoln's massive likeness Vera asks, "What does that symbolize?"

"I read that the sculptor made Lincoln's left hand clenched to represent his unwavering determination to see the Civil War through to the end," Tim answers Vera's question then points to the statue's right hand. "Now look at how the right hand is not clenched."

"It's open," Jean says.

"Yes," Tim takes a couple of steps forward. "The open hand shows Lincoln's willingness to peacefully welcome the Confederacy back into the Union."

Ellen says, "It's strange to think that less than a hundred years ago our country was at war with itself."

"Now we're at war with multiple countries," Lorraine adds somberly.

"Again," Vera adds just as somber.

"As long as evil exists in the world war will always be possible," Dan says. His is a chilling thought but he's accurate in his assessment.

"Evil will always exist it's naïve to think

otherwise," Tim adds gravely. "That's why it's important to do the right thing and to help those who are weaker than us."

"America couldn't keep ignoring what was happening in Europe," I say thinking of the atrocities being done to Jews especially but also to all the other innocent people who've been oppressed and abused and murdered.

"No, we absolutely could not," Jane agrees. "That's why I volunteered for the Navy."

"It's not always possible to avoid conflict," Joe says. "Not when there are those like Hitler and Mussolini in positions of power."

"America did the right thing by getting into this war," Dan says. "We're doing the right thing."

Looking at his cousin Joe agrees, "We are."

We're quiet for a moment and I don't know about the others, but right now I'm thinking about how Dan is leaving soon and he's going to see this war first hand.

As the others wander off in different directions to view the rest of the monument I stay put. The engineer in me marvels at how much work must have gone into creating a project of this magnitude. The amount of people, effort, time, money and skill that was needed to build this monument was not insignificant. I did a little reading up on the history of it. It is impressive.

"What's going through your mind?" Ellen's question interrupts my thoughts. I like that she's made her way to me and I like that she wants to know what I'm thinking.

"I was just thinking about what it takes to make a structure like this one."

"Ah, engineering stuff," she says in that way she has.

"Yes," I confirm, "Engineering stuff."

She nudges me with her shoulder. "I'm just teasing."

I nudge her back, "I know. I like it." I've made her blush.

"Can I bore you with some of the engineering stuff?" I ask not sure of the answer I'll get.

"Please do," she says.

I mentally prepare what I've read about this place. "Okay, stop me when you've heard enough," I say looking into her fathomless blue eyes, eyes that draw me in. She's so pretty. I remind myself to just enjoy her company and have a good time. That's all this can be.

Now that she's been given an out I begin to extoll the features of this place. "The foundation is up to sixty-five feet deep in some places," I begin, "And the undercroft is three stories tall."

"The undercroft?" she asks interrupting.

"The undercroft is the basement. It's three stories tall down there," I say looking down. Then she looks down. We stare at the pink marble floor beneath our feet.

"That's one enormous basement," she says.

"That's for sure," I agree.

"What else can you tell me?" she wants to know.

I gesture to the concrete columns around us. "These are part of the support system, too," I tell her.

Ellen turns slowly making a complete circle. "It's amazing," she says meaning it.

"It definitely is amazing," I agree with her.

Regretfully, Ellen's attention is snatched away. Her friends call her over, "Ellen, come here." For a second she looks like she doesn't know what to do. "It's okay," I say.

She goes to them where they're gathered at the entrance to the monument. Several minutes later I hear Joe say, "Look over here, this way!" Looking over my shoulder I catch him holding his camera aloft. "Let me get your picture," he says to the girls. They're at the front of the monument with the reflecting pool and the Washington Monument both in the background. At the sound of my buddy's voice, they turn around facing him.

"Get closer," he says. At his request they move closer together and link their arms. "Smile," he tells them. I hear a click and see the pop of the flash bulb. I am convinced Joe's just captured a great picture. I'll want to see it when he develops the film. I can't take my eyes off of Ellen. She was beautiful last night all dressed up but today with the sun shining in her hair, she is radiant.

After leaving the Lincoln Memorial we traverse the National Mall stopping to explore points of interest as they arise. Along the way Tim inadvertently sparks a competition of sorts. We end up trying to outdo each other with our knowledge of random historical facts and trivial information about American History. Ellen is exuberant when she learns something new. Her love of learning is infectious. I think she must have been an incredible teacher.

When we reach the National Museum of Natural History Tim stops us before we go inside. "Why don't we all split up for a bit in there? This way we can see whatever exhibits and areas we want. We can't possibly see everything in a few hours," he suggests.

"That's not a bad idea," I comment. His

suggestion has merit.

"We can meet back here in say two hours. Will that give everyone enough time to explore?" Dan suggests.

As soon as we get inside I lean into Ellen and ask, "What do you want to see first?"

"The cultural artifacts," she says with zero hesitation. Honestly, I don't care what I see in here today. I just want to tag along with her. I do a quick scan of the lobby looking for the directional sign that tells us which way to go. "This way," I say and Ellen and I take off toward the section of the museum that houses the cultural artifacts.

Abraham Lincoln's hat is the first artifact Ellen and I stop to look at. It is a tall hat. At six foot four Lincoln was taller than most people of his time period. I once read that even though he was taller than most he chose to wear a tall top hat so that he would stand out in a crowd, even more so than he normally would with his height. I notice how the black silk is faded. The museum has placed placards detailing specifics about the artifacts on display. I am reading that this hat is the one Lincoln was wearing the night he was shot. It was at Ford's Theatre on April 14, 1865. The date strikes me. We're in April now.

CHAPTER THIRTEEN- ELLEN

Covertly I look at Ben who's checking out Lincoln's top hat. I like how he takes the time to read the placard accompanying the exhibit. I've noticed that Ben is pensive and I like that he isn't rushing. He's taking his time to observe all that we've seen today at the monuments. With every hour that passes today, I find more and more about him to like.

Moving on from Lincoln's hat, we stop at various other exhibits. Currently we're looking at a writing box that according to the museum placard once belonged to Thomas Jefferson. It's a portable wooden desk with a hinged writing surface and a locking drawer to store paper, pen and ink. The placard reads that a young Jefferson wrote the Declaration of Independence upon the wooden box and in fact this box was his constant companion throughout his life.

There's so much history surrounding us here. I could spend forever in this museum and never get bored, never get enough. I love learning new things. To me, life would be boring if I ever stopped learning. There is so much that history can teach us. The good and the bad, I want to know all of it.

Some people might think I'm a bit of a bookworm. It's true, I am. I love reading. I believe that by learning from the past like what people did and said as well as the results of those actions and words we can do better in the future. They say that history repeats itself. I don't think that's entirely true, its people's actions that repeat themselves. I only want to know why more people don't learn from the mistakes of others instead of having to find out for themselves the hard way.

I'm inspecting the writing box perched on its stand behind a protective glass case when I feel Ben edge closer to me. His close proximity is a welcome distraction. He smells good. His soft whisper caresses the side of my jaw as he asks, "Do you happen to have a writing desk like this one?"

Holding back a smile at the ridiculous question I say, "I'm afraid not. Plus, I don't think they make them anymore."

"That's a shame," he says shaking his head.

"Why?" I ask.

"Because if you don't have a writing desk then how will you be able to write to me after I leave?" he quietly asks.

Doing my best to keep my composure I say, "Would you like it if I write to you?"

"I'd like that very much," he says.

"I want to," I say.

Walking away from the writing desk we're careful not to bump into other museum goers. Someone squeezes between us and as more people do the same Ben and I get separated. I can see him several feet away but there are too many people now between us. I can't get to him. I want them to move. I don't think he can see me. "Ben," I call and his head swivels at the sound of my voice. As soon as he catches sight of me he begins to make his way through the people to get to me. I don't like this feeling. I like it better when he's near.

When he reaches me he puts out his hand, palm up. I look at it then up at him. When my palm slides over his I am flooded with emotions that I have to work to tamp down. His fingers interlace with mine. Ben is only here for a few days to see Dan before he deploys. It would be unwise of me to let myself think beyond today.

Except, a little voice in my head reminds me that Ben did say he'd like for me to write to him after he leaves.

Gradually I find myself paying less attention to the cultural artifacts I was so keen to see and more attention to my companion who is using every opportunity he can find to ask me questions about myself. What do I like to do for fun? Are there museums like this in New York? Where did I go to college? I answer them all. I tell him that I like to read books, write poetry, go to the beach, go dancing, spend time with my family and my friends and go to the theater. Yes, there are museums in New York, lots of them and I visit them as often as possible. When I tell him that I attended Columbia he abruptly stops walking. Since I wasn't expecting him to stop short, I nearly trip over my own two feet.

"You went to Columbia? he says.

"Yes, why do you say it like that?" I ask.

"Columbia is ivy league." Stopped in the middle of the gallery he's practically making a spectacle of us now. People are starting to stare and more than a few glares are flung our way as people have to walk around us. Nevertheless, Ben holds his ground.

"Keep your voice down," I say laughing

while simultaneously tugging on his hand. Slowly we resume walking. Placing a hand over his heart he lowers his voice and says, "City Girl, I think you might be out of my league."

"Don't make fun," I say.

"Never," he says shaking his head from side to side. "I might tease but I will never make fun of you, Ellen. I think way too highly of you to ever be anything other than respectful."

Now it's my turn to stop walking. No man, other than my brother, has ever said anything like that to me and it touches me deeply. "What would you like to see next?" I ask. I'm not willing to explore how his words just now made me feel. Temporary, I remind myself. Ben is here temporarily.

"Honestly," he says looking into my eyes, "It doesn't matter to me as long as I'm spending time with you. I'll go wherever you want." Gently he squeezes my hand. "Come on, we still have time to see a few more exhibits before we have to meet up with the others. Where to next?"

We view a few more of the artifacts on display. We hold hands as we point out this or that to each other. The whole while I enjoy being with Ben. He's attentive and respectful.

I'm reminded of the qualities I appreciated for my sister in Eduardo. Looking at Ben, I think that Bess would probably like him for me. For a second I try to picture bringing Ben home to meet my family. What I wouldn't give for that to be possible.

At the designated hour Ben and I meet up with the others by the museum's exit. The last to arrive are Dan, Phyllis, Joe and Lorraine. When we're all together Vera wants to know what is next on the agenda.

"The Tidal Basin?" suggests Jean, "The cherry blossoms are in bloom."

On the way across town Ben sits beside me on the bus. As we pass through the city I tell him how much I admire the blend of historic and modern architecture that there is here. "It reminds me a little of myself," I say.

Sometimes I feel like I have one foot in the past and one foot in the present. That may sound odd. What I mean is that I love things and stories from the past. Also, I appreciate my life and the people in it but at the same time I keep focused on my future. I like the way Ben looks at me when I say this like he understands what I mean, like he gets me.

As we descend the bus Ben offers his hand to help me down the steps. He's thoughtful and gentlemanly and I like that he is. There is a walking trail around the Basin and we head toward it. Everywhere we look there is an explosion of pale pink blossoms. It's like nothing else I've ever seen. As I had hoped he would Ben makes sure to walk beside me.

"They bloom like this every year," I hear Lorraine telling Joe a few paces ahead of us.

"People come from all over to see them," Tim says somewhere behind us.

"They're breath taking," Jane says. "I could never tire of seeing the trees like this. It's a shame they don't stay this way for long."

"I expected there would be a strong scent," Ben says after a while.

"I did too," I say. Instead there is only a faint pleasant scent.

Further along the walking trail Ben withdraws the worn brochure from his back pocket. I like how he's made notations in there. I like that he's curious and researches things.

"What is it?" I ask after noticing his expression has changed. He's frowning. It seems out of character for him.

He looks up from the brochure in his hands. His gaze swings from the trees, to me, to the others.

"Ben, what's up?" Dan says when he notices how Ben and I have dropped back several paces. They all stop now, turning to look at us wondering what is wrong.

Ben hands the tri-folded paper to Dan. He looks at it. A minute or so later Dan's expression also changes. He grows solemn.

"Tell us," Phyllis demands.

Dan begins reading aloud from the brochure. We listen quietly as he reads, "The cherry blossom trees were brought to Washington, D.C. in 1912. They were a gift of friendship to the people of the United States from the people of Japan." He stops reading. Shocked we stand here looking at the gorgeous trees that line the Tidal Basin. They were a gift of friendship from Japan. I slip my hand into Ben's seeking the comfort of his touch.

"Then what do you call Pearl Harbor?" Joe says to no one in particular.

I pivot from side to side searching the faces of my friends. It's because of Japan's attack on Pearl that our lives are now different from what they might have been. Had there been no attack we might have avoided active participation in the war. We'll never know. I might still be teaching high school English. If so I'd never have met these amazing women whom I now call my best friends. I look at Ben and feel him squeeze my hand. Most likely he never would have been drafted. He'd be in Peoria building things and I'd never have met him.

I don't think I'll ever understand how countries can go from friend to foe in a short span of time. I look over at Dan. He's leaving soon. I hate that he is going to war. I hate that so many people are forced to suffer. Even as I wish that we could have avoided war, I believe we are doing the right thing because I believe it's wrong to sit by and watch others suffer when you can do something about it.

CHAPTER FOURTEEN - BEN

Not long after the revelation over the trees we left the Tidal Basin. Tim suggested we see if we could get into a steak house he's wanted to try. After about a thirty minute wait we were shown to a table. It was fortunate they could accommodate all of us. Because of the size of our party the chairs are pushed close together. Right now there are about four different conversations going on between everyone but at this particular moment all I can focus on is the fact that Ellen is sitting next to me and her leg is touching mine under the table.

I top off her glass, careful not to spill any red wine onto the white linen cloth. "Can I ask you something?" she says when I set the bottle back down onto the table.

"You can ask me anything," I say and of all

the things she could ask me, she wants to know about my family. I tell her I have a sister. "Her name is Gabriella but everyone calls her Gabby. She's twenty, a bit younger than me. She lives with our parents," I tell Ellen this and add, "And I owe her one because she's taking care of my dog, Winston while I'm away."

"Winston, as in Churchill?" she asks.

"Mm hmm," I nod.

"That's a good name. What kind of dog is he?" she asks.

"Winston is an English Springer Spaniel. That's sort of why I gave him a proper English name. He's a great dog. I got him when he was a puppy. I hope he remembers me," I say.

"I'm sure he will. What about your parents?" she says.

"They'll remember me," I say with a grin.

She bumps me with her shoulder and raises an eyebrow. She doesn't dignify my comment with a comment of her own however. I think she's too sophisticated for that.

"Okay," I say. "They live in Peoria. My father is retired."

"What did he do?" she asks.

"He was an engineer," I tell her.

"Like father, like son," she says.

"Something like that," I concede.

"And your mother?" she asks.

"She keeps busy. She volunteers at the local Red Cross. I couldn't say exactly what she does there but she's dedicated to doing what she can to support the war effort. I imagine a lot of mothers and wives and sisters are doing all they can to help," I say this while thinking about how Ellen and her friends went above and beyond by volunteering for the Navy despite not knowing how long they would be away from home.

Changing the subject Ellen asks me, "How long have you been in the Army?"

Leaning back in my chair I turn my head to get a better look at her. "About a year and a half; I have another year and a half to go," I say. Then I ask her, "How long have you been in the Navy?"

"Not that long," she says.

It sounds like she might be evading my question so I say, "Not that long?"

"Five months," she says clarifying.

"How much longer do you have?" I notice she left that part out.

"Until the end of the war, plus six more months," she says.

My jaw drops. I couldn't possibly have

heard her correctly, could I have? "Did you say till the end of the war plus six more months?" I ask in disbelief.

Slowly she nods. "Yes, it's the same for all of us," she says indicating with a flick of her hand the other women at the table.

I nearly choke on my wine. Ellen will be in the Navy until the end of the war and then some.

"We all knew the terms and conditions when we volunteered," she says. The more I learn about her the more impressed by her I become. I was joking earlier at the museum when I told her that she might be out of my league. But, honestly she just might be. She's amazing.

I'm of the opinion that you can learn a lot about others by asking questions and hearing what they have to say, especially about the people they are close to. From the way Ellen answers my questions about her family I can tell they are important to her. When she tells me that she lost her father when she was just six, I literally don't know what to say. She's actually attempting to make me feel less uncomfortable, to put me at ease. I can't imagine losing a parent that young or at any age for that matter. "It must have been devastating," I think aloud.

"It was a long time ago," she says. She takes

a sip of wine then places the glass back down on the table. Her fingers linger on the stem of the glass. "You want to know something," she says her eyes remain fixed on the dark liquid in her glass. She doesn't look at me as she says, "My mother never remarried after my father died. She told us that he was her soul mate and that love like theirs is irreplaceable." Finally she looks at me.

In that moment I know that I want love like that. I want to know what it feels like to love someone so completely there is no room left for anyone else. I reach my hand to cover hers under the table. Again, I am at a loss for what to say.

"What's it like, living in a college town?" Ellen changes the subject yet again. I shoot her a grateful smile glad to move on from heavier topics.

"It's different from when I was in college," I say.

She interrupts with, "Where did you go?"

I don't mind her interruptions. I like that she's inquisitive and wants to know about me. "In Chicago, at the Illinois Institute of Technology," I say, "It's where my father went." Clearing my throat I return to what I was saying about what it's like living in Blacksburg. "Nowadays, most of the students on campus are military or they will be upon graduation. The mood around campus is serious most of the time," I explain.

She nods in understanding. She's seen this for herself I imagine when she was in training at Smith. "What do you do for fun there?"

I like how she tries to see the silver lining in things. She's optimistic. "Well," I say shifting in my seat to fully face her now. I like how she shifts too so we're face to face. "There's a movie theater." She nods. I know she likes the picture shows, which is why I start with that. "There's always some kind of pickup game of basketball or baseball or football going on at the campus I can join in on." She rests her chin in her hand. Have I mentioned that her eyes are so big and blue I want to swim in them? "Also, I like to read." Her eyes sparkle when I mention that I like to read. "And, I like to go for runs. Running keeps me in shape and it's a way to burn off extra energy and stress when I need to."

I'm jolted by an elbow in my side. I turn to see Dan looking at me with an odd expression. Apparently I didn't hear him the first time he tried to tell me to move so that our waiter can put my plate down in front of me. I move to sit back. I completely lost track of where we are and what we're doing. I hear Dan's low chuckle beside me. Ignoring it I tuck into my dinner and spend the next hour paying attention to what's going on all around the table. All the while I am hyper aware of Ellen beside me and the light scent of strawberries in her hair.

The restaurant is not far from home so we decide to walk. On the way we come upon an ice cream shop. Ellen's friend Jean wants to stop there. "Their ice cream is the best I've ever tasted," she says. "I'm serious, we need to stop here. You will thank me for it."

I'm not at all surprised when I hear Tim say, "I could go for ice cream." I look over in time to see him shrug his shoulders as Dan smirks at him. Tim is loving being around the ladies.

It's only when I hear Ellen say that she loves the ice cream there that I echo Tim and say, "I could go for ice cream, too." I want to wipe the smirk off of Joe's face when I say this. But, it works and in we go.

I order two scoops of rum raisin. I know exactly what I want. Ellen however is finding it harder to make up her mind. "There're too many choices," she says sounding bewildered. Finally she settles on a dish of toffee ice cream. I pay for her ice cream and mine before we step aside to let the rest of them order. As we wait for the others, Ellen and I push a few tables together then sit down. We're joined a little while later.

"This is like heaven in my mouth," Ellen says as if she's never had anything this good before. "Want to taste?" She holds a spoonful of her toffee ice cream up for me. Before she even has a chance to register what I'm about to do, deftly I swoop in, close my mouth around the spoon in her hand and devour the ice cream in one fluid motion. This draws a laugh out of her. I love the sound of her laugh. Have I mentioned she has a great laugh?

When I offer her some of my rum raisin she allows me to feed her like a civilized person. It's all I can do to keep the spoon steady. She takes a taste then gently dabs at her mouth with a paper napkin. After a few seconds she tells me, "I like mine better."

Throwing my head back I laugh out loud. I can't help it. She has me in stitches. I've never met anyone like her. When I stop laughing I say loud enough for everyone to hear, "Phyllis was right about you, Ellen."

"Right about what?" she looks adorably indignant with a hand on her hip eyebrow raised in question. I believe she knows what's coming.

"You've definitely got sass, City Girl," I say.

Phyllis voices her agreement from across the table, "She sure does."

At this Ellen shakes her head. Looking up at the ceiling she says to know one in particular, "Phyllis, she's a peach."

Phyllis shrugs a shoulder and says, "What can I say?"

In an aside to Ellen I quietly say, "Your friends are great."

"So are yours," she says in return. I can tell she means it.

Back outside I stay by Ellen on our walk home. "What made you join the Navy?" I'm constantly asking questions of her. She's like a novel I can't put down. I want to keep reading to see where the story will take me. "I mean I didn't have a choice, I was drafted but why'd you volunteer?" I'm curious especially after she told me about how she's in this for who knows how long?

"It felt like the right thing to do," she says. "I put a lot of thought into my decision."

"It was a brave thing to do," I say sincerely because I think she is brave. It takes a lot of courage to actively decide to leave everyone and everything you know for the unknown.

"Thank you for saying that. There are those who think women don't belong in the military," she says knowingly.

"You shouldn't care what other people think," I say. My heart thuds in my chest when I am rewarded with her smile.

"I agree," she says, "But sometimes it's not that easy not to care, you know?"

"I can understand that," I say. She's right. Sometimes it's hard not to care what others think about you. Growing up Jewish, I've experienced my share of adversity. There are places that Jewish people are not permitted. I have a lot of respect for Ellen and all of the women who ignored the noise and did what they thought important.

"This is the first time I've lived away from home," she offers.

"What about when you were in college?" I ask.

"I still lived at home then."

"Ah, then this must be quite an experience for you," I say.

"It sure is," she says. "Living with Jane and Phyllis is definitely an experience." She makes a funny face and laughs softly.

"What's so funny over there?" Phyllis says to us. She's a few paces behind me and Ellen.

"Nothing," I say and now Ellen and I share a little secret between us.

On the way to the girls' place I point out things to Ellen like street patterns and storm drains. At an intersection we stop to wait for the traffic light to turn red before we can cross. When the light changes color we go. The streets are crowded and I smile to myself when I feel her slip her arm through mine. When we hit the other side of the street I draw her closer shielding her from oncoming foot traffic. I like how she fits me.

Rounding the corner onto Florida Avenue Dan suddenly says, "We need to stop at my place for a second and then we'll be back, if that's okay?"

"You want to come over?" Lorraine says. Confusion tinges her words.

"Yes, we would. Thanks for asking," Dan says innocently enough.

Laughter ensues and there we go; looks like we'll be back. We leave the ladies on their door step with a promise to return a little later. I for one am grateful for Dan's audacity.

"See you soon City Girl," I say to Ellen.

CHAPTER
FIFTEEN- ELLEN

When the guys get here we show them up to the rooftop. It's the best part of the building. We've turned it into an outdoor space where we can entertain. We've placed some outdoor furniture up here. Jane, Jean and Lorraine added potted plants all around. The plants are starting to bloom and the colors and sweet scents add to the charm of this little oasis we've created for ourselves. Tim sets down the bag he carried up here. "This view is awesome," he says whistling his approval.

"We're fond of it," says Vera peering inside the bag. She pulls out a bottle of gin with one hand. Then reaches inside the bag with the other, out comes a bottle of wine.

"We weren't sure what you'd want," Joe says from where he's standing looking out over the city. It's dusk and the setting sun paints a pretty picture across the sky, "So we brought a variety of libations to go around."

"Help your selves," Dan adds setting down a growler of beer and a stack of paper cups.

Ben catches my eye and smiles at me. I'm glad they came over tonight. I wasn't ready to say good bye to him just yet. I'm not sure how long he and Joe will be in town and I'm a little afraid to ask. This weekend has been one of the best I can recall. I don't want the thought of Ben leaving to cast a shadow on it, not yet at least.

Tim withdraws two packs of cards from the side pocket of his jacket and places them on the table as well. "In case anyone wants to play."

"We have dominoes. I'll go get them," Jean offers heading back inside.

After three games of gin rummy I beg off. Joe, Lorraine, Jean and Tim continue to play. Dan, Vera, Phyllis and Ben are playing dominoes. I plan to sit back and watch the others play for a while. Getting up from the table I move my chair over a ways. Grabbing one of the throw blankets we keep up here I open it and cover my legs.

It can't be more than ten minutes that pass before the dominoes game is over. By the look of triumph on Phyllis' face I gather she was the winner. Ben gets up from the table and looks around. He spots me sitting over here. "I'm going to sit out the next game," he says. Then I watch as he moves his chair and sets it down next to mine. "Hey," he says taking a seat beside me.

"Hey," I say. "Had enough?" I ask.

"Phyllis is dangerous to play with," he says. "Had to stop or else she might have cleaned me out," he jokes.

I laugh softly at his comment. "She can be ruthless," I tell him. "Do you think Dan will be alright if you leave him at the table with her?"

His grin is mischievous, "Maybe, maybe not." At my look of shock he says, "Vera's there. I'm sure she'll make sure Phyllis doesn't eat him alive."

At the thought of it I laugh. "You have a great laugh," he says softly.

"Thank you," I say dipping my eyes to my lap. We sit here for a little while not saying anything more, me sipping my gin and juice and Ben working on a beer.

The sun has gone done. The others have tried to continue playing cards and dominoes by flashlight and lantern light but it proved difficult. Tim put away the cards and Jean the dominoes.

Chairs were rearranged and blankets spread. The night sky is black except for the stars in the sky.

Looking up at the sky I say to Ben, "I love it up here at night."

"I can see why," he says looking out over the city and up at the sky.

The city lights are dim because of blackout curtains in windows.

"Would you show me some of the constellations?" I say not taking my eyes off the stars over us.

Reaching over Ben grabs hold of the seat of my chair pulling me closer to him. He flashes a grin at me. Then leaning in bringing our heads closer together he points upward. "Can you see the Big Dipper? It's right up there."

"I see it," I say locating the only constellation I'm familiar with.

"Those two stars on the end of the cup point to Polaris, that's the North Star. Some people think that Polaris is the brightest star in the sky. Even though you can easily spot it, it's actually not the brightest," he explains.

Searching the sky I locate Polaris. "I see it."

"That's the tip of the handle on the Little Dipper. Can you spot that one?" he asks.

Nodding, I say, "Yes, got it."

"The Big Dipper is part of Ursa Major the Greater Bear and the Little Dipper is part of Ursa Minor the Smaller Bear," Ben says pointing out each one in turn.

I'm caught up in the sound of his voice in the way he's explaining how to look at the night sky of how close he is at this very minute. "Unlike other stars, Polaris mostly remains in the same place in the sky. That's why people use it to orient them wherever they are. As long as you're facing Polaris, you know you're facing north," he explains his voice soft as if his words are for my benefit alone.

"Show me more," I say. I am greedy for more of his voice of his attention. I would happily stay up here forever just to listen to him talk.

"See those three stars up there? They are in a line." At my nod he continues, "Those make up Orion's belt. Orion is the Hunter." Moving his arm a little higher he says, "Above those three stars that make up the belt you can see his shoulders. A little higher is his sword. He's also holding a shield, that's that cluster over there. Below his belt are the stars that make up his legs."

I want to keep him talking. I want to keep

him all to myself for a little longer. "Tell me more."

Even in the dark I can see he's smiling at me. "Okay, let's see," he says. A few seconds later, "Over there, that's the Lion, Leo. Look for a backwards question mark," he tells me and I search for the shape.

Searching the sky, it takes me a minute but then I see it. "Got it," I say when I finally spot it.

"The backwards question mark is the head of the Lion." Moving his arm slightly to the left he says, "There's the rest of the body, it looks like a sideways triangle."

I feel rather than see Ben roll his head to look at me, like a moth to a flame I turn my head, too. He is so close now. Only a few inches separate us. His eyes lower to my mouth and my breath catches. I forget how to breathe.

"Ellen," my name is a whisper, "I really want to kiss you."

I can't speak. I can only nod. When his lips touch mine my eyelids flutter closed. I'm lost.

"I've wanted to do that for the last twenty-four hours," Ben says touching his forehead to mine. Our breaths mingle in the cool night air. The back of his hand brushes the side of my face. "I meant what I said earlier today. I want you to

145

write to me."

Nodding I say, "I'd like that too."

Smiling he kisses me again. "Good."

Since he brought it up I have to ask, "When do you and Joe go back to Blacksburg?"

He takes my hand and interlaces our fingers. "Tomorrow afternoon," he says and immediately I think that it's too soon. I want to ask him to stay longer. Seeming to read my mind he says, "We couldn't get any more time away. We were lucky to get this leave approved."

We ended up staying out until well after midnight. Actually it was closer to two A.M. when Jane and Jean had the good sense to suggest we call it a night. Getting up at seven this morning wasn't easy. I woke with a smile though thinking of that kiss on the rooftop last night. That smile however is replaced with a sigh when I remember that Ben is leaving today.

We're meeting the guys for lunch at the Parrot at noon. Dan suggested it last night when we were up on the roof. After lunch Ben and Joe are driving back to Blacksburg. Their short visit is almost over. I'm glad they got to see Dan before he ships out. Under the stars Dan told us he was glad the weekend turned out as it did. He assured us he wouldn't have wanted to spend it any other way.

"I'm just sorry it couldn't have lasted longer," he'd said.

"Us, too," Phyllis was quick to agree with him. She spoke for all of us.

The Parrot is one of my favorite places in all of D.C. to go to eat however even the prospect of having lunch here does little to cheer me up. All I can think about is how this may be the last time I ever see Ben. It seems that after only a short time in his company I've grown very fond of him.

The food was as delicious as it always is here and I've done my best to stay optimistic. We regaled Joe and Ben with tales of the office. There was some nonsense about Chinese recordings being played during lunch time. Lorraine and I shared a look when Dan brought it up. I think she's formed an attachment to Joe. She seems as down as me today. Ben nudges me gently in the side. I turn and give him a real smile. I don't want his memories of this weekend to be clouded by my melancholy.

Eventually, it is time to go. We've stayed as long as possible. As we're getting up from the table Ben places a hand on my arm and says, "Hang back with me?"

Nodding I say, "Okay." I know I'm only prolonging good bye. He and Joe are leaving soon and Dan leaves in a few days.

We let the others go on ahead of us. Standing outside the restaurant watching them walk away, Ben asks, "How are you doing?"

"Okay," I say, "You?"

"Okay," he says.

When we round the corner onto my street I feel the tightening in my chest begin to grow. My feet drag. They are two cinder blocks scraping the sidewalk. I hadn't expected to meet Ben let alone form an attachment. I can say with complete confidence that he is unforgettable. I could live to be a hundred years old and never forget this man.

We stop in front of my building. Unlacing our fingers he runs his hands up my arms. His beautiful face is marred by a sadness he can't hide. I suppose I must look sad to him, too. "I don't want to say good bye," I say into the uneasy silence that hangs between us.

"I don't either," he says emotion getting the best of him.

Wrapping his arms around me he draws me to him. Laying my head on his chest I inhale and let the breath out slowly. I wish we could stay like this. I wish he was stationed in Washington like the rest of us. I wish so many things.

"It's nearing time," he says above my head and I have never hated time more than I do right now.

Reluctantly though, I slip from the embrace. Ducking my head I turn to go. I make it up two steps before Ben catches my hand halting my flight. When I turn he reaches for me, lifting me. We are eye to eye. My heart thuds in my chest. I don't want him to go. Stay with me I want to say though I know he can't. When our lips touch it is soft and heartbreakingly sweet. I cup his face with both hands memorizing him.

Slowly he lowers me to my feet then takes my hands in both of his. "I have to go," he says quietly. "I don't want to, but I have to."

"I know," I say. He has no choice, I know this.

Making my way up the steps I can feel he's watching me. Will I be unforgettable for him the way he will be for me? It takes every ounce of restraint I have not to turn and run back down the steps and throw myself at him. Only when I reach the landing do I turn around. "Good bye, Ben," I say with a little wave. It's all I can muster. I am incapable of anything more.

"Good bye, City Girl." He's looking up at me, hands in his pockets a sad smile on his face.

Holding back the tears that threaten, I get the door open and slip inside. When I am alone in the dimly lit entryway I let myself cry careful to be quiet about it.

"El, is that you?" It's Jane. She's up on the second floor landing the door to our apartment open behind her.

Swiping at the hot tears with the sleeve of my blouse I call, "Be up in a second."

CHAPTER
SIXTEEN – ELLEN

There are two sayings my mother uses with regularity. The first is that things happen for a reason. The second is that all good things must come to an end. Sadly, the one about good things coming to an end is true, at least in this situation. Ten weeks ago Ben and Joe went back to Blacksburg and Dan was sent to Italy. The office is not the same without him.

Every once in a while we run into Tim sometimes in the cafeteria, sometimes in the hallway. When we do he often stops to talk to us. Last week, when Jean ran into him he told her that he'd gotten a letter from Dan. He said that Dan is aboard the USS Plunkett a navy destroyer somewhere off the coast of Sicily.

Life goes on and we keep busy. Every week it seems more and more people arrive here in the capitol city. Everywhere we go there are long lines for service. There are waiting lists for housing, traffic is terrible, the streets are crowed, the busses are usually filled to capacity and the sidewalks overflow with pedestrians. It's hard to get around the city.

Despite the inconveniences associated with the current overpopulation problem Jane, Phyllis and I have a little tradition we like to keep. On Thursday mornings the three of us have breakfast together at the corner drug store before going into work. We have to leave the apartment extra early on those days to ensure we'll get seats at the counter but we think it's worth it. It's a way to take some time for ourselves and have someone else make breakfast for us.

This morning we're the first to arrive. The closed sign is still in the window. Checking my watch I see we have about three minutes before the store opens. As we wait outside I appreciate the summer weather. It's pleasant early in the morning. I'm making an effort to appreciate the little things.

Once the door is unlocked and we're allowed in, the three of us make our way to the luncheonette counter. Hopping up onto one of the red vinyl stools, I carefully smooth the light weight fabric of my white skirt and place my hat on the counter in front of me. Turning to the girls I say, "Don't let me forget to pick up a new lipstick before we leave. The one I have is almost out."

"What color are you thinking?" Phyllis asks me.

"What else is there?" I say teasing, "Red of course."

"Good, because Hitler hates red lipstick and red nail polish," she says reaching for a menu.

"How do you know that?" I ask her reaching for one myself.

Jane looks over at us and confirms what Phyllis just said, "It's true I read it in Vogue. Wearing red lipstick is a form of patriotism."

"And beauty is your duty," Phyllis says to us then to me she says, "Check out Elizabeth Arden's Victory Red. You'll like it."

"I definitely will, thanks," I say and make a mental note to do just that.

We order and while waiting for our food to come out, I add a splash of cream along with a teaspoon of sugar to my tea cup. From the corner of my eye I see two Army officers entering the store. They look young, maybe early twenties. Just inside the door they remove their hats and carry them under their arms. They're headed this way.

"Two of Uncle Sam's boys at nine o'clock," I say under my breath so that Phyllis and Jane can both hear me. There's something about the men that doesn't sit well with me but I can't say what. There's still quite a bit of rivalry between the military branches and though most of it is good natured, we can never be too careful.

Although we girls stick together there is the very real concern that a lot of people don't like it that women are allowed in the military now. I won't go anywhere by myself. You just never know what can happen. As much as women have advanced there are still those who think we belong at home.

Coming to a stop behind us one says to the other, "I see the cooks and bakers are with us." The other one laughs. We've just been insulted. We can't see them but we know they are either referring to the color of our uniforms, white being the same color as an apron or they are referring to the idea that women belong at home in the kitchen cooking and baking. Either way, we are not amused.

Just as I finish telling myself it would be best to ignore these two soldiers Jane very slowly swivels on her stool. Phyllis and I turn around to see. What is Jane doing? She's beginning to stand up. Phyllis and I exchange looks of surprise. Her eyes widen. So do mine. Oh Jane what are you doing, I think.

Jane puts on her haughty face. I don't like it when she makes that face. "Do you boys have nothing better to do this morning? Must you pick on women to make yourselves feel superior?" She narrows her eyes. "If you don't mind you can find somewhere else to stand. Go on, run along." She makes a shooing motion with her hand as if they are no more than two flies who annoy her.

"It was just a joke," one of them says clearly offended by Jane's attitude toward them.

Jane addresses me and Phyllis, "Did you take it as a friendly joke?"

Phyllis crosses her arms and glares at the two men in olive green. "No, I did not," she says.

I cross my arms, too. "Neither did I," I say.

"Lighten up," the taller of the two says.

"Lighten up?" Jane repeats enunciating each syllable. She puts her hands on her hips. Standing straight and tall she stares at them. I swear I have never seen her act like this before. I am glued to my seat. "We are United States Naval officers and we eat little boys like you for breakfast. I suggest you learn some respect."

Phyllis' eyes almost bulge out of her skull.

"Take it easy lady before you have an aneurism," tall guy says to Jane.

Then the other one says something to Jane that I will not repeat. He is foul. When Jane is called a name that I prefer not to repeat Phyllis starts to rise. I place my hand on her arm. She looks at it then at me. I give a little head shake. We're here for Jane, but she has this one.

"Do you kiss your mother with that mouth?" Jane says to the soldiers nonplussed. She does not raise her voice. She maintains an outward calm. I can only guess if it's a ruse. It probably is. I wouldn't be able to stay calm if someone had just spoken to me that way.

Being a woman in a man's world is not an easy thing. I'm in awe seeing Jane stand up to these two bullies. I want to stand up and cheer. Go Jane. I don't however. Leaning forward in my seat I watch with rapt attention. This isn't the first time we've been insulted or had comments made to us but it is the first time any of us has addressed it. It has been our practice to ignore the incidents and pretend they do not bother us.

I mentioned that there are rivalries

between the branches. This morning though it's more than friendly rivalry. When the two soldiers walked in here a few minutes ago, they noticed the three of us sitting at the counter and they deliberately came over. Apparently they don't believe in women having the same rights as men. Either that or they think it is okay to harass women. Neither is acceptable in my book.

"Take a seat if you plan to eat," the cook comes to the counter to break it up. "You two can sit down there," he points to a couple of stools on the other end of the luncheonette counter where the soldiers can be far away from us.

When they're out of earshot Phyllis lowers and voice and says, "Who are you and what have you done with our friend, Jane?"

Blowing out a shaky breath Jane sits down. "I'm tired of being harassed by people like them," she says. Swiveling our stools we face the counter once more. Jane then adds, "I couldn't sit here and let them get away with insulting us. I'm sorry to have embarrassed you."

"Are you kidding me?" I say. "That was amazing."

"Jane, you're my new hero," Phyllis says reaching for her coffee. "Seriously, you were magnificent."

Jane breathes a shaky laugh and reaches for her cup. Hopefully, we'll never see those two ever again.

Our food arrives and we eat quickly. As I pour thick maple syrup over the short stack of pancakes on my plate I wonder what my mother and Bess would think about how Jane handled herself this morning. You can be sure they'll learn about this story in my next letter to them.

After finishing our breakfast in peace Phyllis waits by the door as I buy the Victory Red lipstick and Jane buys the latest issue of Vogue magazine. On the way to work sitting in the back seat of the car I angle my body until I have a clear view of myself in the rear view mirror. Opening the tube of lipstick I just purchased I twist it until the fiery red lipstick pops up. I swipe it over my top lip then over my bottom lip. Then I press my lips together. Blotting with a tissue I ask, "Well, what do you think?"

"Good choice," Jane looks at me through the rear view mirror as she drives. "Hitler would hate it."

"Phyllis turns in the passenger seat to get a good luck. "I like it," she agrees with Jane.

Easing back into the seat I say, "You were right, Phyllis. I feel very patriotic in Victory Red."

Cupping a hand to her ear Phyllis says,

"What did you say? Can you repeat that?"

Laughing I say, "You were right."

"As usual," she adds and Jane groans.

Since the invasion of Normandy last week our department has been exceptionally busy. As soon as we arrive at the office I'm inundated with work. Whenever I feel like I've finally got a handle on the files assigned to me another load gets dumped on my desk. Even so, thoughts of Ben are never far from my mind.

Vera whose desk is next to mine is fanning herself with a manila folder, "It's hotter than hell in this place."

"It is," I agree. This building gets stuffy. There are so many bodies in here and the windows are closed. About five years ago the largest air conditioning system in the world was installed in the Capitol Building. The Senate and House Office Buildings were part of the project so those offices get cooled with forced air. Unfortunately, this building did not get air conditioning.

It is little moments like this I remind myself to not complain. I'm sitting in an office behind a desk while so many of our military personnel are on warships or in tanks or in fields.

I wonder how Dan is and pray he's safe.

Eyeing the papers in front of me I continue with my work of classifying documents. After some time passes I allow thoughts of Ben in. I wonder what he's doing and how he is. Has he or Joe received any recent news from Dan? Does Ben think of me? I have to stop this. I push those thoughts aside. I can't afford to get distracted. It is imperative that I concentrate all of my efforts on what I'm doing.

CHAPTER SEVENTEEN – ELLEN

Lorraine and I started calling class day 'Chinese Day.' The others tease us mercilessly about it, too. But, we don't mind the teasing. We just think it's easier to call it that than 'Chinese Conversation Class Day' so it stuck. In keeping with the routine we established back in April the six of us hang around after work before class. We make it fun. Cocktails are usually involved. Food is always involved. Sometimes I can sneak in an errand or two as well.

We're at the Parrot sharing a charcuterie board when I casually mention that in a little while I have to head to the tailor's. My new seersucker uniform is ready to be picked up. I brought it there a few weeks ago to be taken in. "Does anyone want to come with me?" I ask.

"I'll tag along," Vera says volunteering to come with me.

"Thanks," I say relieved. I don't like to go anywhere alone if I don't have to, especially at night.

Thirty minutes later she and I are pushing open the door of Vesik's Tailoring. Blessedly, the shop is air conditioned and for a moment I am tempted to skip class and stay here till closing time. Vera seems to get her second wind. "I'm so glad I volunteered to come with you," she says smiling in the cool comfortable shop.

Pulling the pink sales slip from my purse I present it to the clerk behind the counter, a thin woman with a friendly face. From among the rows of garments lined behind her she locates mine. Carrying it over her arm she leads us toward the changing room.

Taking a seat on an upholstered chair Vera says, "I'll wait right here." She's perfectly content to sit in the air conditioning and wait for me.

A few minutes later wearing the seersucker and a frown I emerge from behind the curtain and step in front of the mirror. Mr. Vesik, the shop owner and tailor is waiting for me. "The suit fits like a dream don't you think, Miss Cunningham?"

he says evidently unaware of the frown I'm wearing.

"You know Mr. Vesik," I say looking over my shoulder at him, "Some people have nightmares."

The tailor looks dumbfounded, "Miss?"

Motioning with my right hand to my left shoulder I say, "There's a ripple in the seam, right here."

"A ripple? A ripple? Where is there a ripple? Who sees a ripple?" he says looking around the little shop. I look to Vera for help. Then all of the sudden I'm momentarily caught off guard when Mr. Vesik clutches a handful of the jacket at the center of my back and pulls it taut. I almost stumble but catch my balance. "Tell me, where is the ripple?" he's asking now.

"In your hand," I say in frustration. If I had known it would be such an ordeal to have the suit taken in I never would have bought it. The Navy Exchange did not have any summer seersucker uniforms in my size so I bought this one thinking I could have it made smaller. Bad idea I'm realizing too late.

It takes ten exasperating minutes to convince Mr. Vesik that the shoulder seam needs to be taken out and redone. Vera, another patron-

bless her, and I are finally able to convince him. Unfortunately, it will take at least another week possibly three weeks before I can have it. I wouldn't be surprised if Mr. Vesik put my jacket at the bottom of the list of items needing mending.

I change back into my whites then Vera and I leave the air conditioned tailor's shop. Heat and humidity greet us on the other side of the door. Placing our hats on our heads Vera mutters, "It's hotter than hell in this city." This time when she says it, I don't feel like laughing. It is hot.

With a monogrammed handkerchief she pats the back of her neck. Even in this intolerable heat Vera is a classy lady. The air around us is thick. The heat wave that's been hanging over D.C. is oppressive. Even the light-weight material of our whites feels heavy and uncomfortable. "I want to look at shoes," Vera says as we begin walking. "Let's go to the Exchange."

The shoe selection is toward the back of the store. "I'll meet you there in a minute," I tell Vera when we get to the Exchange. "I want to see if they have any officer hats in my size." Because I'm tiny I normally have to have hats special ordered for me. The ones they have in stock are usually too big and don't fit properly.

When I was at Smith for training we were given temporary hats to wear. The one they gave me wobbled on my head. I'm not kidding. As I make my way toward the counter I remember how for the first month of training we had to wear those Navy issued brimmed hats with our civilian clothes.

At the time I was busy trying to remember rules and protocol and a million other things that I didn't pay much attention to how we looked, at least not until our uniforms came in. I just knew that the hat was too big for me. Thinking on it now, we must have looked ridiculous in civilian clothes and brimmed hats marching all over campus. It's funny how training seems so far away even though it was not even a full year ago.

Approaching the WAVE counter I see who's working tonight and slow my pace. She's the one who sold me the seersucker. The one who convinced me to buy it and take it to Vesik's to be fitted. I stop in my tracks. What to do?

She's assisting someone and hasn't noticed me. That's good because the last time I was in here, aside from convincing me to buy something that was too big for me, she had the audacity to say to me, "Well maybe you're just too small for the Navy," when I complained to her that they didn't have my size in stock. Pivoting, I turn and follow Vera. The hat can wait.

The classroom is sweltering. Whose brilliant idea was it to take this class? Looking around I can see we're all miserable even Lieutenant Commander Howard looks like he doesn't want to be here. All I want to do is to go home, take a shower and change into one of my favorite cotton nightgowns.

Lorraine, sitting to my left leans in and says, "Tomorrow after work let's go to Shoreham's."

"Yes, please," Jean says in whispered tones. She would not want the instructor to think she is not paying attention to the lesson.

The Shoreham hotel has a pool where we sometimes go swimming after work. I nod my assent. Swimming is a brilliant idea. For now I put up with the discomfort and set my mind to the new set of words we're given. I practice writing the Chinese characters and before we leave, I accept the next record given to us by our instructor.

On the way to the car Phyllis says, "Every time we play one of these blasted records it makes me think of Dan, excuse me Lieutenant Cavanaugh.

"He's Dan to us," Vera says quietly.

"Yeah," Phyllis nods. "He's Dan to us."

I hop in the back seat of Jane's car. Phyllis takes the front. Vera drives the others home in her car. "I call first dibs on the shower," I say before either of my roommates is able. It's a game of ours to see who can call first dibs. I smile feeling victorious. Rolling down the window I enjoy the wind on my face as Jane takes us home.

"Jane, there's something here for you," Phyllis says going through the mail in the entryway, "Something for me and something for you," she says handing me a small parcel.

Excitedly I take it. I love getting mail. My mother and Bess can be counted on for a parcel at least twice a month. We climb the steps to our second floor apartment. When we get inside and turn on a light I see the return address. It's from Ben. Just like that my discomfort from the heat and humidity are forgotten. "Someone else can use the bathroom first," I say. "I can wait." I thought he'd forgotten about me.

"Is that from Ben?" Phyllis peers over my shoulder.

"Yes," I say. I am inexplicably happy. I open the packaging to find a well-worn book. It is entitled <u>An Easy Guide to the Constellations</u>. Running my palm over the cover I am touched by such a thoughtful gesture.

"Why did he send you an old book?" Phyllis asks perplexed.

Recalling that last night on the roof I say, "We talked about the stars and the constellations when he was here. I guess he thought I might like to have this." I hold the book close. I will cherish it.

"Sounds boring," Phyllis says oblivious. "I'll shower first," she says heading toward the one little bathroom the three of us share.

Jane slips off her jacket and shoes, "She's a peach, that one." We share a laugh. Phyllis is something else alright.

When I'm alone in the living room I open the cover. Tucked inside is a slip of paper. Removing it, I bring it closer to the table lamp. Sitting on the couch I read the words in Ben's own hand.

Ellen,
This is the book I told you about, the one

that started my interest in the stars. I found it in a book shop near campus and I wanted you to have it. Those few days in April with you were the best I've ever known. Never stop looking to the stars.

Ben

Slipping the paper back inside the book I close the cover. Those days were the best I've ever known, too.

CHAPTER EIGHTEEN – ELLEN

I pin a note to the door for Lorraine, Vera and Jean to see when they get home. It's a quick scribble telling them to meet us at Shoreham's pool. Then I dart up the stairs so I can quickly change into my bathing suit. I throw a sundress on over top of my suit and slip my feet into a pair of sandals. Grabbing my bag, sun hat and sunglasses I leave the bedroom and run smack into Phyllis.

"Oof," I grunt catching my balance.

"Have I told you lately how graceful you can be?" Phyllis jokes. "I've got the towels," she tells me holding up the three folded towels she just plucked from the linen closet.

We meet Jane in the kitchen. She is

filling three Thermoses with water from the tap. Rummaging through the cabinets I grab a bag of pretzels and some boxes of Cracker Jack. "This should tide us over until dinner," I say.

We're out the door in no time flat. At the bottom of the stairs we run into Lorraine who when she sees us says, "We got your note. Vera and Jean are almost ready. They want us to wait for them. They said they'll be right out." A few moments later they appear wearing sun dresses, big hats and Hollywood style sunglasses. Locking the door behind them they follow us outside.

When we get to Shoreham's we're met with a sign hanging on the gate by the pool area.

"You've got to be kidding me," Vera says indignant.

"What is it?" I say, unable to see around her.

"Since when is the pool closed on Mondays?" Incredulous Jane moves past Vera approaching the gate. We were just here last Friday after work and I don't remember seeing this sign.

"What are you doing?" Lorraine gasps watching Jane try the handle.

"It's unlocked," she says entering the enclosed space. I marvel at her. She's been acting like a whole new person ever since that incident with the Army officers at breakfast last week. She drops her bag and towel onto a lounge chair near the pool. Edging closer to the water she slips her sandals from her feet and dips one foot into the pool. "What are you all waiting for?" she says looking over her shoulder at the rest of us hovering just outside the gate.

"What if we get caught?" Jean asks. I can tell by the way she says this that she's worried about getting in trouble for being here when the pool is supposed to be closed to the public.

"We won't," Jane pulls the cover up over her head revealing the sunflower yellow two-piece bathing suit she's wearing.

"How do you know that?" Jean wants some reassurances.

"The gate was unlocked," Jane says matter of fact. Sitting at the edge of the pool she hooks her legs over the side. "Come on ladies," she waves us over. "Get in here. The water feels fine." To our surprise she doesn't wait to see if we are willing to be her partners in crime. No she does not. She slides her body into the water as we look on.

Now she's fully immersed, looking refreshed as only a dunk in the pool on a hot summer day can do for a person. That does it.

The rest of us can't get in the water fast enough. Lorraine is the first to follow in Jane's footsteps. Jean still looks nervous. Hooking my arm through hers I say, "Come on." Tugging her through the gate we join the rest of our friends.

Believe me when I say that I'm not the sort of person to ignore signs or deliberately break the rules and neither are the others. However, in this particular instance after an exceptionally long day inside that stuffy government building coupled with the recent record high temperatures we throw caution to the wind. And, if I'm being totally honest, it didn't take all that much cajoling on Jane's part. I was ready to drag Jean in here kicking and screaming if necessary. But, I'm glad it didn't come to that.

Submerged at last I sigh with relief. I don't even mind the chlorine haze clinging to my hair and skin. I'm glad Jane talked us into this. I'm feeling better already. I relax and turn on my back. Clearing my mind, I just float.

I see Vera at the shallow end of the pool. She raises her sunglasses to the top of her head. "Who has anything interesting to share?" Vera loves to know what's going on, who's doing what, who's dating whom.

"I had the day from hell last week," I offer flippantly never guessing that she or the others would actually want to hear about it.

"Oh that's a funny story, El. You have to tell it," Phyllis insists.

My head whips in the direction her voice is coming from. When I sight her she's grinning. "You would think it was funny," I gripe at her.

"Won't you tell us?" Jean pleads her palms together prayer like. "Now my curiosity is roused. I need to know what happened."

I let out an exaggerated sigh, "Okay," I begin, "I will tell you about the day from hell." Pointing an accusing finger in Phyllis' direction I say, "For some strange reason last Wednesday morning the alarm clock didn't go off."

"I've already apologized to you and Jane about a million times," Phyllis says. "Are you two ever going to forgive me for forgetting to set the alarm that one time?"

"Probably not," Jane and I say in unison.

"Jinx," Jane says to me.

"As you can imagine we all woke up late last Wednesday. Picture the three of us trying to get ready for work. There's only one tiny bathroom and we have half the time as we usually would to get ready." Most days it's a challenge to get out the door on time. That day it was nearly impossible. Laughing at the memory I say, "Have you ever applied your makeup without a mirror?" At the horrified looks I'm getting from Lorraine, Jean and Vera I guess that they have not. "Don't do it," I say. Shrugging I say, "My lipstick was a tad crooked. Aside from that, it wasn't too bad."

Phyllis does this little cringing thing with her face which I ignore. It's her fault we ran late and I couldn't get in the bathroom to use the mirror. Continuing I say, "Then, while we were running to the car I dropped my gloves and they landed on the sidewalk in front of our place."

Vera says, "Those white gloves are so hard to keep clean."

"Tell me about it," I say. When I picked them up off the ground dirt smudged the otherwise snowy white cotton. I was not pleased.

"I'm still trying to get the dirt stains out," I tell her.

"Clutching the dirty gloves and my hat in one hand and my bag in the other I bumped my head on the door frame as I practically flung my body into the backseat of Jane's car." I hear snickers from the other end of the pool. Ignoring them I say, "Thankfully, Jane got us to work on time." That morning when we pulled into the parking lot there were precious few minutes to spare before we needed to be inside the building.

"You're welcome," Jane says magnanimously. She weaved in and out of traffic that morning. "After the war you could become a professional driver," I suggest to her.

"After the war," she says, "I'm not sure what I'm going to do," she adds thoughtfully. "We'll have to wait and see, I guess." Her words give me pause. I realize that I haven't given much thought to what will happen to us after the war. Jane's right, we'll have to wait and see.

"We leapt out of the car. I almost knocked my hat off my head in the process. There we were, the three of us hustling across the parking lot. All the while I'm trying to straighten my hat and pull on my dirty gloves."

"At least you were able to fix your lipstick in the car," Phyllis says helpfully.

"At least," I say laughing a little at the memory.

Sweet Jean interjects. She says, "You three did look a little frazzled that morning. No offense," she adds quickly.

"None taken," Phyllis tells her reassuringly.

Continuing with the story I say, "As soon as we got inside I was assigned a bundle of correction sheets that were completely unreadable, unintelligible and un-code-able. It was ugly." Now I'm animated talking with my hands and waving my arms around. Just thinking about last Wednesday has me stressed all over again.

Before I say another word Jane calls to me, "You should have marked them with 'NEC'." NEC stands for Not Elsewhere Classified. That's what we use when we're in doubt about something we're coding.

"If only it were that easy," I say shaking my head at her suggestion. "By lunch time I was starving. There wasn't any time for breakfast and my stomach felt hollow."

"Dramatic aren't we?" Phyllis says looking at me over the top of her sunglasses. I just give her a look. It's her fault I didn't have breakfast that day.

"Lorraine went with me to the cafeteria and on our way down there we ran into a bit of an issue," I say.

"That's right," Lorraine confirms.

"Someone told us that the cafeteria ran out of stuff to make more sandwiches. Oh, and they were short staffed. So, we decided to try somewhere else," she tells everyone. Skimming her fingers over the surface of the water, Lorraine then says, "Wait till you guys hear this next part. "We ditched the cafeteria and walked across the street to the hotdog cart. El and I got frankfurters, chocolate cake and coffees from there."

"That doesn't sound terrible," Jean says.

"Just wait," Lorraine tells her.

Letting out a sigh I press on. "I ordered my hotdog with extra mustard," I explain. "But, to my horror," I say then pause for dramatic effect.

"What?" Jean asks eyes going wide in anticipation of what's coming.

"The hotdog was hard," I say. I couldn't even break it in half with my fingers."

"That's weird," Jean says.

Nodding I say, "I noticed something sticking out of the bun."

"What was it?" Vera's cringing now.

"It was a piece of cellophane wrapper," I tell her.

"You mean it was cooked in the cellophane wrapping?" Jane asks disbelieving.

"Apparently," I manage.

"And the hot dog cart guy didn't notice that when he cooked it?" she asks like I would know the answer.

"Apparently not," I shrug. "I was so hungry I almost didn't care so I just removed the wrapper as neatly as I could which wasn't very neatly at all by the way because it was covered in mustard." I look at Vera who is still cringing.

"You're not going to believe this," Lorraine preempts this next part.

I've got everyone's undivided attention. "I finally get the wrapper off and take a bite. But," I pause.

"What now?" Jean practically demands to know.

"It was still hard," I say.

"Ew, gross," Vera almost gags.

I ended up throwing the hot dog in the trash. "That's the last time I get a frankfurter from that street vendor," I pronounce. I don't for one second swear off all hot dog vendors. Let's face it. I'm from New York and New York is famous for their hot dogs. Contrary to what Phyllis says, I am not that dramatic.

"I don't eat hotdogs," Vera says, "You don't know what's in them."

Ignoring Vera's comment Phyllis asks me, "Did you get to eat anything?" She might actually be feeling bad for me.

"Chocolate cake and coffee," I tell her.

"Poor Ellen," Jean says sympathetically.

"That's not the end of the story," Jane interjects.

"It's not?" Lorraine looks genuinely dismayed on my behalf. She's a kind soul.

"Unfortunately, there's more," I say.

"Really," Jean asks incredulous. "Are you making all this up?"

"I wish I was," I tell her.

"On the way home from work we stopped at Vesik's to pick up our dry cleaning." Out of the corner of my eye I see Jane and Phyllis. They're trying not to laugh. They are also avoiding making any eye contact with me. I remember having a headache and wishing I could just lay down when we got home. "The skirt of my uniform had a wrinkle left in it," I tell them exasperated.

"Vesiks," Vera grumbles. She feels my pain.

"We know how much you love to iron," Phyllis teases. She knows how much I do not love to iron.

"That stinks," Lorraine says sincerely.

"I took some aspirin for the royal headache I ended up with and set up the ironing board. I tried but I couldn't get the wrinkle out with the iron. I had what I thought of as a moment of brilliance. I'd fill the bathtub with hot water for my bath and at the same time use the steam inside the bathroom to get the wrinkle out of my skirt," I say.

"That was a good idea," Lorraine says. "Steam is good for that."

I look at Lorraine with a blank expression on my face. But was it a good idea? "I pinned the skirt to a hanger," I tell them, "then I hung it on the towel bar over the tub. Then I turned on the hot water and watched as the room filled with steam. I was so ready to soak in that tub. By the time it was full and I turned off the water the wrinkle was almost gone."

"Oh thank goodness, El," Jean says, "I was worried something terrible was going to happen to your skirt."

Jean is so sweet I almost don't want her to hear what happened next. "Jean, cover your ears," I say to her. She doesn't.

"I left the bathroom to get a change of clothes and when I returned everything was fine.

When I closed the door though, the skirt fell off the hanger."

There is a collective gasp and Jean says, "Oh, no!"

"Oh, yes," I nod slowly.

"Phyllis and I heard her scream," Jane says picking up the thread of my story. "We thought someone was trying to murder her in there. We banged on the bathroom door until she opened it. She was holding a sopping wet skirt over the tub wringing it out. We felt so bad for her."

Phyllis then says, "Jane grabbed the skirt out of Ellen's hands, ordering her to get in the tub and relax. We told her we would take care of the skirt for her. Sorry El," Phyllis says in an aside to me, "Once Jane and I realized you weren't hurt, we laughed long and hard over that skirt."

"I don't blame you," I tell her. "I would have laughed, too if it wasn't me it happened to."

"So sorry you had such a horrible day," Jean says.

"No wonder you call it the day from hell," Lorraine adds.

"That's still not the end," Phyllis says placing her sunglasses on top of her head.

"There's more?" Vera says disbelieving, "How much can happen to one person in a twenty-four hour period?"

"Unfortunately, Phyllis is right." I too push my sunglasses to the top of my head. The sun is hiding behind a cloud. I am so ready to get this story over with. "After the bath I changed into my pajamas and hung out with Phyllis and Jane in the living room. I still had a headache so I told them I was going go to bed early."

When I see Lorraine I notice she's got her hands hovering near her face. Is she anxious about what I'll say next?

"The moment my head hit the pillow, whack!" I smack the water with my hand sending water droplets everywhere, "The bed fell down."

"Shut up!" Lorraine exclaims.

Vera and Jean have twin stunned expressions on their faces while my roommates are trying hard not to crack up.

"What did you do?" Lorraine wants to know.

"I laid there in shock," I say honestly. I was in shock until I saw Jane and Phyllis run into the room, take one look at me lying on my mattress on the floor and burst out laughing. "Phyllis was laughing so hard she was crying."

"El, even you have to admit it was funny,"

Phyllis is laughing even now. Her laughter is contagious. I can't help it so I start to laugh, too. Soon we're all laughing.

Wiping tears from her eyes Jane says, "The loud noise coming from the bedroom startled us." Then she tells everyone, "We couldn't just leave her like that."

Jean is clutching her side. "The next time I think I'm having a bad day I'll be sure to remember this story."

"I'm glad I amuse you," I deadpan.

"Whatever happened with your skirt?" Lorraine wants to know.

"It dried. It did not shrink but it did take a lot of effort to get the wrinkles out," says Phyllis. I took care of it for El. It was the least I could do."

"What happened with the bed?" Vera asks.

Jane answers this one. "The wood slats that hold up the mattress had slipped out of place. It was an easy fix."

Happy to be done rehashing the unfortunate events of last Wednesday I push off the side of the pool and do a few easy strokes with my arms, kicking my legs behind me. We linger in the pool a while longer. By six we're getting hungry. The snacks aren't enough. Getting out of the pool we dry off and throw on our cover ups. We gather our things and before leaving we make a collective effort to ensure the area looks exactly as it did when we arrived. Jane closes the gate firmly behind her making sure that this time it is locked.

CHAPTER NINETEEN –BEN

Removing my hat, I do a quick visual scan of the book shop I've just entered. It's not far from campus and I often find myself in here perusing the shelves looking for something new to read. I spot Joe by the fiction section. Heading in his direction I can see he's holding a thick, heavy book and is reading its cover. "Looking to do a little light reading?" I say approaching him.

"Oh hey," he says by way of greeting. "Have you read this one?" he asks turning the book so that I can see its cover. He's holding War and Peace.

Shaking my head I say, "Tolstoy is too heavy and depressing for me."

Joe looks back at the book in his hands contemplating my words. After a moment he nods and says, "Yeah, you're right." He re-shelves the book. "What are you looking for?" he asks genuinely curious to know.

"Not sure yet," I say scanning the shelves for anything new that may have come in since the last time I was here. "I'm just looking for something that will take my mind off of things for a time, you know?"

"I do know," he says. He does. This week he got a new set of students. His previous language students have all been deployed. He doesn't know where to, though.

In two more weeks the soldiers I've gotten to know in my classes will deploy to the front. Even though I know it's coming, I still have a hard time with it. "I just finished reading Fitzgerald's Great Gatsby. Ellen suggested it to me. She thought I would like it," I say. "She was right."

"She still writes to you?" Joe asks.
"Yes," I say.
"Huh," he looks at me.
"What does that mean?" I ask wondering.

Joe leans his back against a row of books. "What kinds of things does she write about?"

Okay, I think to myself. I'll play along. "She recommends books to read, The Great Gatsby," I remind him.

"So you're literary pen pals?" he suggests. "What books do you recommend to her?" He's failing miserably at keeping the smirk off his face.

"No we're not literary pen pals and I don't usually make any book recommendations to her. She's the one with an English degree from Columbia. I did send her a book on Constellations, though," I say proudly.

"Ben, Ben, Ben," Joe hangs his head. "You sent her a book on the stars?"

"Yes I did," I say nodding.

"And why would you do that?" he's asks bemused.

"You wouldn't understand," I tell him taking a few steps down the row. I don't need to stand here and take this abuse.

He hurries to catch up. "I'm just kidding," he says afraid to have offended me.

"I know," I tell him, too easily letting him off the hook. "Do you remember the night before we left D.C.? We were outside up on the roof."

"How could I forget?" he says wistfully.

For a second we're both quiet each of us recalling our own memories of that night. Dan was having fun playing Dominoes with Phyllis. I don't think he cared that she won most of the games. I look at Joe and wonder if he's thinking about Lorraine. They spent quite a bit of time around each other.

"Well," I break the silence, "that night I pointed out some of the stars and constellation patterns in the sky to Ellen. When she asked how I knew so much about them I told her about a book I had read on the subject. I saw it in here a few weeks ago and thought she might like to have it," I explain. "So I mailed it to her."

"I wondered what the two of you were talking about that night," Joe says what he's thinking. "She let you kiss her, if I recall."
"Uh huh," I nod.

"Does that nerdy star crap really work with girls?" he asks.
"I kissed Ellen and she's still writing to me," I tell him. "What do you think?"
"Can you show me where you found that book?" he says oh so very nonchalantly.

Stifling a laugh I say, "In a second, let me find something to read over here first."
"Right," he agrees. "I want to find something as well."

We search the shelves, every few minutes pulling one showing the other. "Steinbeck?" Joe suggests. He's got The Grapes of Wrath in one hand.

Shaking my head I say, "Read it. It's depressing."

He puts it back. Then pulls Gone with the Wind. Holding it in front of his chest so I can see the cover he wiggles his bushy blonde brows. "How about this one Ben, I'm sure Ellen would love it if you were reading Gone with the Wind."

Reaching over I snatch the book out of his hand and put it back. "Funny," I deadpan. Actually, I happen to know that it is one of Ellen's favorite books. Also, she told me that she and her sister watched the movie three times when it came out a few years back. "Be serious," I tell him.

"Serious, got it," he says. "How about this one?"

"That's a good one," I say. "I read it a while back. You'd probably like it," I say of the Salinger novel he's just taken off the shelf.

"You think?" he asks.

"Yeah," I say. "It's about a kid who flunks out of prep school. He has a hard time with the disingenuousness of the adult world.

"Are you saying I can relate to the character?" he asks reading the book's jacket cover.

"No," I say, "You're pretty well rounded from what I can tell. It's an interesting read is all I'm saying." I keep searching the selves for something for me. It's difficult since I keep being interrupted. Out of the corner of my eye, I see he hasn't put The Catcher in the Rye back on the shelf.

Reaching up I pluck a novel from the shelf to examine the cover. "Have you read this one?" It's my turn to ask.

Shaking his head Joe says, "No, I haven't, not yet."

I proceed to read the book's jacket. I'm looking for a little escape. I'm not looking for anything heavy or depressing. I think this one might be it. "I think I'll get this one," I say.

"The Maltese Falcon," Joe reads the title aloud.

"Yeah, it's a crime novel," I say.

"Let me know how it is," he says.

We pay for the books and leave the store. Placing our hats on our heads we start off on foot toward campus. I don't drive unless I have to. I walk everywhere or ride my bike. I'm saving my gas rations. It's the middle of the summer and Blacksburg is hot. Right about now I suspect most people are at home getting ready to eat dinner. There are a few people out and about, otherwise it's fairly peaceful.

Clearing his throat Joe begins, "About Ellen's letters."

"What about them?" I ask.

"Does she ever mention any of her friends in those letters?" I know it is costing Joe to ask me this.

I act like I have no idea what he's really asking me. "Sometimes," I say deliberately being vague.

"Oh, like what?" he asks also attempting vagueness.

"Oh you know, normal stuff," I say maintaining a straight face. How I'm doing that is beyond my comprehension. Silently I count down from ten wondering how long it will take him to crack and just ask me if Ellen's said anything about Lorraine. Six, five, four.

"Alright," he huffs. "Has Ellen said anything about Lorraine?"

"All you had to do was come out and ask me, Buddy. I would have told you about thirty minutes ago," I am no longer hiding the grin that is at Joe's expense.

He whacks his arm out to the side catching me in the ribs. "Come on," I say.

"Just tell me what you know about her," he demands.

"Since you asked so nicely," I say. "Though you find it so hard to believe, Ellen does in fact write to me. I usually get a letter from her about once a week."

Joe's jaw drops open. "She writes you once a week? Why?"

Quirking a brow at his blatant show of disbelief I say, "Maybe because I always write her back?" Despite the look he's throwing my way, I tell him what I know. "I just got a letter from her yesterday. I have his attention and his face is not so contorted any longer, thankfully. "Ellen and her friends broke into the pool at Shoreham's last week," I say.

"Be serious," Joe says trying to whack me in the ribs again. This time I'm ready and move out of the way of his arm.

"I am being serious," I say. "According to Ellen, Jane was the instigator."

Joe looks at me sideways trying to determine if I'm making this up or not. I give him my best serious face. "I can show you her letter if you don't believe me," I say then immediately regret the offer because I don't want to share Ellen's letters with anyone, not even him.

"Not necessary," Joe says. "So, Jane is the trouble maker," he summarizes.

"Exactly," I say nodding.

"Those girls were fun to be around," he muses clearly remembering the weekend we spent in their company last April.

Nodding my agreement I say, "That's the only derelict news Ellen reported. They are still taking those Chinese classes."

Joe chuckles when I say this. I wonder if he's thinking about the way Dan had introduced us to the ladies at his going away party. How he ratted out Ellen and Lorraine about playing those records at the office.

"D.C. is even more crowded now than when we were there, if you can imagine that," I say. "She says it's been really hot in the city, which is why they broke into the swimming pool. Ellen swears that none of them would ever do such a thing otherwise."

Joe looks at me funny. "Do you really believe that?"

Shrugging I say, "I have no idea."

"Their department has been swamped with work ever since the Normandy invasion. Also, Tim told them that Dan is on the Plunkett, but we already knew that," I add.

Joe nods. "How is Tim?"

"Ellen doesn't say much about Tim other than the fact that they run into him at the Bureau every now and again," I say.

"And Lorraine?" Joe prods.

"Ellen hasn't said anything specific about her if that's what you're asking. Usually she includes all of them when she tells me stories about what's going on there. From what I can tell those girls are always together."

We've almost reached the campus. "Do you think she's seeing anyone?" Joe asks.

"I hope not," I say thinking of Ellen. "Why do you think I keep writing her back?"

"I meant Lorraine, dummy," Joe says.

"I knew that's who you meant," I say. "Ellen hasn't mentioned anything about anyone dating anyone else. So, probably not," I say. "Do you want me to ask her?"

Joe whips his head to stare at me. "No, don't do that," he says adamantly.

Raising my hands I say, "Okay, I won't."

"Just, if you hear anything," he doesn't finish the sentence.

"You'll be the first to know," I say. I live in an off campus apartment. We're only steps from it. Joe's place is two streets over. "You know, Joe," I start, "You could just write to Lorraine yourself."

He stops, stares at his feet. "I don't think she'd want me to," he says.

"Why not?" I ask.

He blows out a breath, raises his gaze and says, "That last day we were there, at lunch Lorraine told me that she'd like it if we wrote to each other."

"Yeah?" I prod when he remains closed mouthed.

"I sort of told her that I didn't think that was such a good idea," he says sheepishly.

For a really smart guy he can do some really dumb things. "And you said that because?" I am clearly confused.

"I said that because at the time I didn't think it would be a good idea. Ben, those girls will be in the Navy for who knows how long? You and I will in all likelihood get out of the Army way before they get out. There's a war going on. She lives four hours away. We can't get leave. Do you want me to continue?"

I look at my friend with what feels like pity. "What is the harm in writing a few letters to her? If nothing else, you make a friend. Plus you'll have something to look forward to reading when you get home," I suggest. To which Joe holds up the book he's just bought. "Suit yourself," I say. "I'm good with getting weekly letters from the prettiest woman I've ever set eyes upon."

"I have no idea what will come of all this after the war. All I know is that if I get the chance to see Ellen again, I'm going to take it. Until that time comes, I'm going to write her and hope that she keeps writing me back. Everything else is out of our control right now, Joe. Let yourself have a little happiness anyway you can take it. Write Lorraine a damn letter would you?" I finish.

"I'll think about what you said," he tells me. Moving one foot in front of the other, he heads in the direction of his place. "See you tomorrow," he says with a wave over his shoulder.

When I get inside I toss my keys onto the table by the door and remove my hat. On my way to the bedroom I deposit the Maltese Falcon on the arm of the sofa to read later. First, I need to get out of this uniform. When I think about what

Joe just told me, I feel sorry for him. The war has made me look at life differently than I had before.

I'm not sure I would have had the confidence to ask Ellen to write to me before being in the Army. Then again, maybe I might have. What I am sure of is that I'd be kicking myself right now if I hadn't asked. I just wish I had written to her a lot sooner than I did. I guess I thought I could follow Joe's example and not get attached. I'm not wired like he is though.

Sitting on the edge of my bed I unlace my shoes. There is no understanding between Ellen and me. Theoretically, she could wake up one day and decide not to write me anymore. She could also meet someone who lives closer to her and forget all about me. That thought makes me ill.

Standing, I unbutton my suit coat and hang it in the closet. I'll just have to keep writing to her and hope for the best. In the meantime, her letters make me laugh and they give me hope that there can be more for the two of us when the war is over.

CHAPTER
TWENTY - ELLEN

I'm happy to report the heat wave is finally over. It's a warm sunny Sunday afternoon in early September and the girls and I have determined to make it a lazy Sunday. When I got home from church I found a note in the kitchen telling me to go to the roof. When I got up here I found my friends lounging around.

We've been so busy at the Bureau for months now. Between the heavy work load and the Chinese classes we're taking we're usually exhausted by the time we get home. To give you an example of how tired we've all been feeling lately, none of us had the energy to go out this weekend. I know, hard to believe. We ended up staying in on Friday night. Yesterday I caught up on laundry and then Jane, Phyllis and I cleaned our apartment; exciting stuff.

Taking a seat on one of the folding chairs I join my friends. I notice that Jane is lying on her back on a folding chaise lounge. Her eyes are closed and her hands are resting on her stomach. "Is she napping?" I ask in a whisper to Lorraine indicating with my thumb that I'm asking about Jane in particular.

"No," Lorraine shakes her head not bothering to speak in whispers. "She's awake."

"I'm working on my suntan," Jane adds.

There is a cooler on the floor by the table presumably it's full of soft drinks. On top of the table are two bags of potato chips, a box of Cracker Jacks and another bag of Fritos. As I'm checking out the stash that was brought up here I hear Phyllis say, "El, would you grab me a soda, please?" I'm standing by the cooler so I lift the lid and grab a bottle of Coca Cola from within.

"Here you go," I say handing it over.

"You're a doll," she says reaching for the bottle.

While I was in the cooler I grabbed a root beer for myself. Grabbing the Sunday paper from the table I carry both over to a chair and settle in to relax. I still make it a point to read the newspaper. Tucking my feet up under me I start reading about how the British and South African Allied soldiers recently liberated the Italian Renaissance city of Florence.

The article mentions that German soldiers under the command of Albert Kesselring destroyed several historic buildings and bridges before they retreated. I've never been to Florence but that's a place I would love to see someday. Italy is rich in history and I am incensed over the destruction happening there. In fact the senseless destruction throughout Europe bothers me so much I want to scream.

I can't fathom what it must be like to have a war happening where you live. How scary it must be when bombs fall overhead and enemy troops tromp through towns and villages taking whatever they want, terrorizing the residents and occupying towns. A shiver runs down my spine at the thought of it. So many lives have been lost and homes and businesses and schools have been destroyed. Millions of people are displaced and for what?

My thoughts are all over the place and I wonder if Ben has read about Florence or about Rennes, France which was liberated by the Americans the very same day as Florence. I'll admit it does feel good to read about something positive.

Lowering the newspaper and reaching for the bottle of soda on the floor by my chair I notice that Jane is turning pink. Like me her skin is fair which tends to burn easily. I grow a little concerned for her so I say, "Hey Jane, you should probably turn over. You're starting to burn."

Eyes still closed face tilted toward the sun she says, "I will in a few minutes."

Sometimes she can be stubborn so I let it drop. She'll turn over when she's ready. I take a sip of my soda, place the bottle back on the floor by my chair and pick the newspaper back up. It's important to me that I keep up on current events. Through my work in classification at the Bureau I'll get bits and pieces of what will happen or what has happened but I never get the full picture.

I only get the news after the fact like the rest of the population. Several minutes go by when I hear Phyllis say, "Jane, flip over. You look like a lobster."

I hear a huff and see Jane finally flip onto her front. That's good.

I finish with the paper and ask if anyone wants it. "I'll take it," Vera says. Getting up from my chair I walk it over to her then make my way to the table with the snacks and other reading materials. There is a small pile of LIFE magazines. Rifling through the stack I see there are several past issues.

On top is an issue from last April. Pausing, I lose myself in a memory. It's been five months since I met Ben last April. Smiling to myself I think of how he still writes to me. He read The Great Gatsby like I recommended. He also wrote to tell me he read the Maltese Falcon. I don't necessarily enjoy crime novels so I don't think I'll read that one even though he said he enjoyed the story.

"Hey El, what are you doing?" Jean asks pulling a chair up to the table. She's carrying a beauty case in her other hand.

Clearing my head I put aside thoughts of one very handsome soldier who I wish I could see again and answer the question. "I'm trying to decide what to read next," I tell her. The April issue of LIFE has the young British Princess Elizabeth on the cover. That could be interesting.

Jean sets the case on top of the table and opens it. She proceeds to set out the items in her manicure kit. She's got a lovely shade of pink there I notice. I look at my red finger nails. Though the pink will be pretty on her I like the red for me, especially after learning that Hitler hates red on women. I feel a sense of patriotic duty to keep wearing it.

Under the April issue with Princess Elizabeth is one from July. Admiral Nimitz is featured on the cover. After the attack on Pearl Harbor he was appointed Commander-in-Chief of the U.S. Pacific Fleet. He's credited with rebuilding the Pacific Fleet and halting Japan's advance across the Pacific.

Last year he was put in control of the Allied Forces in the central Pacific region. So far he's won strategic victories at the Battle of the Coral Sea and the Battle of Midway. Earlier this year his fleet secured the island of Guadalcanal from Japanese control. As you can tell, I keep up with current events. Plus, Admiral Nimitz is a living legend in the Navy.

I pour a handful of Cracker Jack and pick up the Nimitz issue. Resuming my seat I snack on the caramel popcorn and peanut combination in my hand as I read more about the Admiral. We're all quiet for a while and it's peaceful. After some time passes, Lorraine suggests a game of cards. "I'll play," I say volunteering. She, Jean, Phyllis and I clear the table. Lorraine shuffles and deals the first hand.

Jane is still sunbathing and Vera has gone inside for more sodas to stock the cooler. Picking up my cards I fan them out in my hand. "What should we do for dinner?" I ask matching suits and pairs careful not to show my cards. "Don't say Spam," I say to Phyllis before she can get the words out. I'm tired of Spam sandwiches.

"Meatloaf?" Lorraine suggests. She makes great meatloaf.

"I can make macaroni salad to go with it," I offer.

Jean puts three fives on the table in front of her. "I made a Jell-O salad this morning. We can have that for dessert," she says.

"What flavor?" Phyllis asks, picking up a card from the pile of cards in the center of the table.

"Cherry," Jean says.

"Should we eat up here?" I ask since the weather is fine enough.

"Why not?" Lorraine says when it's her turn. She draws a card then plays an eight, nine, ten, jack.

"Nice," I tell her.

We ended up having an early dinner on the roof top then retreated to our own apartments by seven o'clock. I used the time between then and when I went to sleep, at nine, to write home. I owed Mother and Bess letters and I also wanted to write to Bill and Gladys and the twins. After I finished those letters I wrote one to Ben.

This morning as I'm getting dressed for work Phyllis comes into our room declaring, "Jane looks terrible."

"What do you mean, Jane looks terrible?" I ask buttoning my uniform jacket and straightening it. Turning from the mirror I see her rummaging around in the closet. "What are you looking for?" I say. Phyllis is already dressed and ready for work.

Emerging from the closet holding up a pair of white slip on sandals she says, "I was looking for these."

Confused I ask, "Why?"

"Jane can't get her shoes on," says Phyllis heading for the door.

Now I'm very confused. Following Phyllis out of the room I come to a dead stop when I see Jane. Understanding dawns on me. She has the worst sunburn I have ever seen.

Phyllis and I help Jane dress and brush her hair. Each one of her movements is slow and painful. Her skin is hot to the touch. She is in so much pain. I hurt for her. Finally she slips her swollen feet into Phyllis' sandals. "I'm going to get written up for wearing these, but I can't even care right now," she says pathetically.

I drive us to work since clearly Jane is in no condition to drive. Phyllis and I help her to her desk and then we help ease her into her chair. "If you need anything at all, tell one of us and we'll get it for you," I say before heading to my desk from which I intend keep an eye on Jane throughout the day.

I have to hand it to her, Jane is being a trooper. She's not complaining at all but it is obvious to everyone here that she is struggling to do her job. At the end of the day our supervisor approaches Jane and orders her to stay home tomorrow. The relief on her red puffy face is palpable.

When we get home, Jane changes into a loose cotton night gown and carefully stretches out on the sofa. Phyllis and I make dinner. I veto Spam and instead fix three egg salads on toast while Phyllis whips up a cherry tomato salad.

"How are you feeling?" I ask Jane placing a tray of food onto the coffee table in front of the sofa.

She gives me a pitiful look. Yup, I imagine she feels awful. Phyllis comes into the room then with a copy of the Farmer's Almanac in her hand. Plopping into the arm chair she opens it and starts flipping through the pages.

"What are you looking for?" I ask her.

"Remedies for sunburn," she says and I think that is both genius and thoughtful of her.

Jane asks for some water. "Here you go," I say picking up the cup of water I carried in on the tray with the egg salads and bringing it to her hands. Holding the bottom of the glass I help as she slowly drinks from it.

"Thank you," she says when she's had enough. Taking it away I place it back down on the tray.

"I found something," Phyllis announces.

"What did you find?" I ask.

"First, do we have an aloe plant?"

"No," I say shaking my head.

"Darn. Apparently, the gel is good for burns," she says.

"My mother says it's good for practically everything," I tell her. "We should get one for the apartment," I say and make a mental note to see about getting an aloe plant for in here.

Phyllis nods but keeps looking in the book for more remedies for Jane. "Okay, here," she says pointing to something on the page. "It also suggests applying diluted apple cider vinegar to the affected area." She looks up from the book. "Do we have any of that?"

"We might. I'll go check," I say heading toward the kitchen.

On my way to the kitchen I hear Phyllis saying, "It also says that you can put coconut oil on the affected skin."

I call back to her from within the kitchen, "I'll check to see if we have any of that, too." After searching high and low through every cabinet and drawer I find neither apple cider vinegar nor coconut oil. "We don't have either," I say when I return to the living room empty handed.

"The Almanac gives one more suggestion," Phyllis says looking to me and Jane, "Dissolving either Epsom salts or baking soda in bath water and soaking in it."

"We have Epsom salts," I say triumphantly, "And baking soda." Kneeling next to the sofa I ask Jane, "Do you want me to run a cool bath for you with some Epsom salts after we eat?"

She gives me a small smile. "I would appreciate that," she says.

After dinner I run the bath for Jane. Using the sensitive skin on the inside of my wrist I adjust the temperature being careful not to let it get too warm or too cold. Pouring in a generous amount of Epsom salts I swirl my hand around in the water until the salts are completely dissolved.

After we eat, Phyllis and I clean up the kitchen. She washes and I dry the dishes while Janes hauls herself off to the bathroom to soak in the tub. When the sun goes down I pull on a cardigan sweater and head up to the roof to look at the stars. It's something I like to do now. Being up here on nights like this makes me feel closer to Ben. Does he look at the sky and think of me? A girl can hope can't she?

Armed with a flashlight and the book on the constellations I take a seat in one of the folding chairs wishing he could be here with me. I would ask him to point to the constellations and tell me about the mythological creatures they represent. I would only half pay attention to what it is he would say. I would only be paying half attention because I'd be distracted by how handsome he is.

Opening the book in my lap I remove a photograph from between the pages. I put it in there a few weeks ago. Shining the flashlight over the photo I sigh wistfully. Ben sent it to me in one of his many letters. It's a picture of us. Joe took it with his camera the day we toured the city. Ben thought I would like to have something to remember that day by. I love looking at this picture. He's smiling in it, as am I. Picture or no, I will always remember that day.

CHAPTER TWENTY-ONE – BEN

I've just finished a four mile run. I pushed myself hard today. It was a good run and I was able to keep my speed up. As I slow my pace and work to control my breathing I finally stop to appreciate there's a breeze in the air and that the leaves are starting to turn. As I make my way up to the door of my apartment I also appreciate how quiet Blacksburg is at this hour. I prefer to run in the early morning hours because usually no one else is out and I can be alone with my thoughts. That was especially important to me this morning.

The newspaper is waiting for me on the door step. Picking it up I carry it inside with me. I toss it on the kitchen table and reach for the refrigerator. Pulling a pitcher of cold water from within I pour some into a glass and down it quickly. Through the connecting archway I see into the living room. On the coffee table are the papers I left there last night.

Running my hands through my damp hair I blow out a breath. I was handed orders yesterday by my commanding officer. I immediately requested permission to go to D.C. for a few days. My request was denied. It is too far from here, I was told. I need to be closer in case of an emergency I was told.

Since then all I can think about is how will I be able to see Ellen before I go? I leave at the end of the month. That doesn't give me much time. While on my run I wracked my brain for a solution and I think I may have come up with something. Now all that's left to do is find out if it will work.

Up until now, Ellen and I have only exchanged letters; we haven't spoken over the phone. Long distance is expensive and while I don't mind the cost to speak with her, her schedule is full and the girls have a shared phone in the lobby of their building. It wouldn't be convenient for Ellen if I made a habit of calling her I'd imagine.

Eyeing the phone that's hanging on the kitchen wall I contemplate what I'm about to do. She'll either say yes, or she won't I tell myself. I hope that she'll say yes. I'll never know unless I call her though. Taking a deep breath I dial the number I've long memorized.

"Who is it?" I hear on the other end of the line.

I'm pretty sure it's Lorraine who's answered the phone so I venture to ask her, "Is this Lorraine?"

"Who wants to know?" she asks defensively. I imagine there must be lots of men calling their place.

"It's Ben," I say, "Is Ellen there?"

"Ben, hi hold on a sec while I run upstairs to get her," Lorraine says.

"Thank you," I say and prepare to wait for Ellen to come to the phone. In the background I can hear Lorraine calling Ellen's name and then I hear the sound of footfalls.

She comes on the line and for a moment I can't speak. Finally I choke out, "Hey City Girl." Hearing her voice again is indescribable. I've missed her more than I want to admit even to myself.

I'm not entirely sure how to say what I must. So I decide to just say it however it comes out. I don't plan it so it's not perfect. "I got orders yesterday," I say, "And I'd really like to see you before I deploy." There's silence. "Ellen, are you still there?" I ask afraid she's hung up on me. I wait.

"When are you leaving?" she asks quietly. She could not have expected this. I wasn't expecting this.

"Soon," I say, "Two and a half weeks."

"Where are they sending you?" she wants to know but I can't tell her. It's a classified mission. Even I don't know where they're sending me yet.

"I don't know yet," I say, "I haven't been told."

The days in between learning I'll be leaving Blacksburg, calling Ellen to ask her to meet me and today have been interminable. Finally, finally I am this close to seeing her after months apart. I left Blacksburg right after my last class let out and have been on the road for almost two hours which is within the distance I am permitted to travel without needing to take leave.

The night breeze blows in through the

open windows rustling my short hair. The radio is turned up, a folk song blaring through the speakers. Hanging my left arm out the window, I feel the wind push against my open palm.

I pull into the parking lot of the hotel where I've booked a room for tonight and tomorrow night. When I suggested we meet halfway between our two assignments, to my relief Ellen agreed. Honestly, I had no idea if she would or not. Checking my watch for what seems like the millionth time today I surmise she should be here soon.

Getting out of the car, I stand and put on my hat. I'm still in my uniform. I didn't stop to change before heading out of town. I'm not above admitting that I'm nervous about seeing her again after all this time. Closing the door I lean against the driver's side of the car and take a deep steadying breath. The air is chilly tonight. I let the breath out slowly. My heart is pounding.

A set of headlights alert me that a car is pulling into the parking lot. I stand up straighter. It has to be her. I can feel it in my bones. The head lights swerve as the car pulls into a parking space. My pulse races and my hands begin to shake as I recognize the car. She's borrowed it for the weekend. She has the best friends.

I've pictured this moment in my mind so many times but now that it's here I don't know what to expect from Ellen. What if she doesn't feel the same about me as I do about her? What if I'm not how she remembers me? What if I'm standing here asking myself too many questions instead of going over there? She's just shut off the lights.

She's getting out of the car. The moment our eyes connect I am moving. Pushing away from the side of my car I go to her. Not stopping until I am within arms reach, I sweep her up and crush her against my body. Overcome by emotions hitting me all at once I cannot speak. So I just hold her. I feel her slip her arms around my middle.

She wraps her arms around me so tight I almost can't breathe. Do I care? Not in the least. Emotion clouds her words, "You're here."

"Of course I'm here," I say into her hair. There's nowhere else I would rather be in this entire forsaken world than here with her right now I silently think to myself.

"Let me look at you," I say putting space between us so that I can look at her. I reach for her hands and hold onto them. I am incapable of letting her go now that she's here. I still can't believe she agreed to this. I search her beautiful face. Using the pad of my thumb I wipe away a tear that slips down her cheek. Her skin is soft under my touch. "Hey," I say gently, "What's this about?"

She shakes her head eyes downcast. I cup her beautiful face with both hands and gently angle it upward until I can look into her eyes. She is exactly as I remembered. "I didn't know if I'd ever see you again," I say grateful for this little bit of time we've both made to be here. Wow, she's really here with me. If I'm dreaming I never want to wake up.

She cups one of her hands around one of mine. I love her touch. "Nothing could keep me away," she says and another tear escapes those big blue eyes. The same eyes I see in my dreams at night. She takes a breath and lets it out slowly. I give her the time she needs.

"Ready?" I ask only when I sense that she is ready to go inside.

She nods and we make our way to the hotel's entrance.

At the front desk we check in as Mr. and Mrs. Rosenberg. This is a small town. It's not like

D.C. where anything goes. I wouldn't want to put Ellen in an uncomfortable position. Besides, the less anyone here knows about us the better.

I hand the room key to Ellen. Carrying both of our bags I motion for her to go first. We climb the curved staircase to the second floor where our room is located. She stops outside number one twenty one. She slips the key into the lock and before she turns it, looks at me from over her shoulder. Then, she slowly turns the key and pushes open the door.

Dropping the bags to the floor I close and lock the door behind us. Turning around I see Ellen standing in the middle of the room. Our eyes lock and I can't explain how but the whole world seems to fade. My entire focus is her. "Hi," I say stepping toward her.

"Hi," she says meeting me half way. Wrapping her arms around my middle she lays her head on my chest. She has to feel and hear how hard my heart is pounding. Resting my chin on her head the scent of her strawberry shampoo fills my senses. This is surreal; it's as if time has stood still yet at the same time I feel like it's been forever since I last saw her. "I've missed you," I say into her hair.

"I missed you more," she says and there,

there's that sass I've missed.

Grinning, because she missed me I say, "That is not possible." Placing a finger under her chin guiding her so that I can look into those fathomless baby blues I ask, "How was the drive? Did you have any trouble?"

"No trouble," she says, "I just couldn't wait to get here."

Running my thumb along her jaw I say, "I can't believe this is happening." Then after waiting far too long I begin to lower my head to hers. Respectfully I ask, "Is it okay if I kiss you now?"

Slowly she nods and a small smile curves her pretty red lips. Lowering my head even further I keep my eyes locked with hers. When our lips are no more than a breath apart she sighs and softly she says, "What took you so long?"

The nervousness and the worry dissolve into nothingness. "I don't know," I say on a breathless huff. "I should have kissed you in the parking lot." I close the gap and I'm struck by a simple truth. Kissing Ellen feels like coming home.

I need to catch my breath. I kiss her lips

one more time. I kiss her temple. "Where are they sending you?" she asks the moment I lean my forehead against hers. She says the words so softly I almost don't hear the question.

I close my eyes. She knows I can't say. "I don't know yet." I don't know and I don't want to think about it at least not right now. I just want to concentrate on the time I get to spend with her.

She fists my shirt. "Promise me you will come back," her voice cracks on the last word.

"Ellen," I say rubbing up and down her arms soothingly, "I promise you that I will do everything in my power to make it back home in one piece." Neither of us is naïve enough to think that my being sent on a classified mission will not entail some measure of danger. I won't stand here and lie to her either. "Let's not think about that now though, okay?" I want nothing more than to come back to her.

"I'm sorry," she says. "You're right." She releases the tight grip on my shirt and smooths her hands over the fabric.

"Come here," I say taking her hand and leading her to the arm chair in the corner. Sitting, I draw her down into my lap. She feels soft and warm and I never want to let her go. We sit like this, quietly for a time. I don't want thoughts of my imminent deployment to mar what little time we get to be together.

When her stomach growls I ask her, "Have you eaten anything?" She's not wearing her uniform so I know that she at least took a moment to change her clothes before coming here.

Shaking her head she says, "No, I dropped Jane and Phyllis at the apartment after work, quickly changed into this and grabbed my overnight bag. I didn't want to waste any more time than that," she says.

It looks to me like she took some care with what she's got on even though she just said that she changed quickly before coming here. I like that she wanted to look nice when she saw me. She looks so pretty in that dress. The dark blue color brings out the blue in her eyes. I run the material of the skirt between my thumb and forefinger. It's soft and smooth. The sleeves are long with cuffs that button at the wrists. I finger the pearl button there.

We should probably go eat. "I haven't either," I tell her. Then I suggest that we go downstairs to have dinner in the hotel's restaurant. "Give me a minute to change into something else before we go," I add. Before letting her up I kiss the tip of her nose. Being able to spend this time alone with Ellen is a privilege and I don't want to rush things.

I know the memories we make this weekend will have to sustain me through whatever I'm about to face. I want to remember every second of it. Plus I want Ellen to know how very much I care about her. "Everything is going to be okay," I say and pray that's true.

Rummaging through my duffle I grab a pair of pants and a light blue button down shirt. I packed this one because it reminds me of the color of Ellen's eyes. Striding to the bathroom, clothes in hand, I tell her, "I'll just be a minute." Ducking inside, I close the door. Catching my reflection in the mirror I stare back at myself. After a second I grin like a fool and shake my head. Then I quickly change my clothes and head back into the room where Ellen is waiting for me.

Like a gentleman I hold the chair for her as she is seated. Then I round the table and take the seat opposite. "Order whatever you'd like," I say perusing the menu. Decision made, I look up from my menu and watch as Ellen studies hers. I drink in the sight of her.

"Ben?" she says my name not lifting her eyes from the menu in front of her.

"Hmm?"

"You're staring," she says and I can hear the smile in her voice even if the menu is covering her mouth so that I can't actually she's smiling.

"I can't help myself," I tell her with a little shrug. Because, I can't help myself; I can't take my eyes off of her.

Two hours go by and I want time to slow down. We've eaten and the table has been cleared of all but our water glasses. When the waiter asks if there will be anything else I defer to Ellen. She shakes her head slightly letting me know we need nothing else from him. "No thank you," I tell him. He brings the bill and I charge it to the room.

After adding a tip and signing the room charge receipt I reach my arm across the table opening my hand palm up. As if we've done this move a hundred times before, she slips her hand over mine. I gently rub the pad of my thumb over the back of her hand. Keeping my voice low I ask, "Shall we go upstairs?"

CHAPTER TWENTY-TWO – ELLEN

I had watched the clock all day at work wondering if the darn thing was broken. Time dragged. Finally, four o'clock came. Jane and Phyllis knew how important this trip was for me and I will love them both till the day I die for being ready to sprint out of the building and to the parking lot the moment we were allowed to leave.

When we made it to the apartment all three of us ran up the stairs. I changed out of my uniform and into the royal blue dress I had laid out on my bed this morning. I slipped my feet into a pair of peep toe pumps. I didn't like the idea of wasting any time before I hit the road but I wanted to look nice for Ben. I grabbed the overnight bag I had finished packing last night. It was by the door waiting for me. I gave Phyllis and Jane hugs and thanked Jane for the millionth time for letting me borrow her car. Then I was gone.

When I was pulling into the hotel parking lot earlier tonight I caught sight of Ben leaning against his car. He was in his uniform. I'd never seen him in his uniform before then. The sight of him took my breath away. I almost lost control of Jane's car. She would have killed me if I had gotten it into an accident. There he was leaning against the car door looking like he'd just stepped out of a magazine. I had to do a double take. He looked so handsome, devastatingly so.

My hands were shaking as I pulled into an available parking spot. I wanted to jump out of the car and run over to where he was. I had to remind myself to put the car in park and shut off the engine first. Once I'd done those things and pulled the key from the ignition I opened the door thinking how I wouldn't be able to get to him fast enough.

When I alighted from the car I was able to take approximately three steps before Ben was right there standing in front of me. The moment his arms came around me I knew I'd made the right decision to come here. I'd missed him. I buried my face in his chest and inhaled his clean scent.

It was strange checking into the hotel as Mrs. Rosenberg. Strange but if I'm being honest, it felt pretty wonderful. I got butterflies in my stomach when Ben handed the room key to me. This is the first time he and I have been alone together. I'm embarrassed about the tears that fell earlier. I was just feeling so overwhelmed by so many emotions. I love that I'm here with him yet I hate that he's being deployed. Everything is so uncertain yet I'm certain that being here is the right thing for us.

His thumb is skimming over my hand. "Shall we go upstairs?" he's just suggested. My cheeks I'm sure are pink with embarrassment though I know I shouldn't be embarrassed. This is Ben, good, worthy, gentle Ben.

Moving my gaze upward from our joined hands I admire the man sitting across the table, his strong jaw line, those dimples and his intense dark eyes that hold my gaze. "Yes," I say a little breathless.

Ben pushes away from the table and stands. Coming around he holds out a hand. Taking it I let him help me up. Arm in arm we leave the restaurant and make our way up to the room.

Along the way I am oblivious of my surroundings. I am only aware of the man at my side. I know we pass by at least one other couple. Ben nods in their direction when they say hello in passing.

When we pass by the front desk the clerk wishes us a nice evening. Ben tells him thank you and for him to do the same. I think I waved a thank you. As we climb the staircase Ben is steady as a rock and I hold onto his arm for support. I don't know why I'm so nervous right now. I've dreamed of being with him. He must feel me looking sideways at him because he turns his head. He catches me watching him. At the top of the stairs he stops us on the landing.

"Everything okay?" he asks sweetly searching my face.

Nodding I say, "Everything is more than okay."

Lightly he sweeps the back of his hand over the sensitive skin of my cheek. "Okay," he says.

Coming to a stop outside of our hotel room door he produces the key from inside the front pocket of his dark pants. Silently he slips it into the lock and turns the knob. I go in first. I go to stand in front of the window. It's dark outside so I cannot see much. I hear the click of the lock, the sound of the key hitting the dresser and then I see his reflection in the window behind me. Turning to face him I reach for him.

Walking us backward a few steps never letting go of my hand he lowers himself so that he's sitting on the edge of the bed. Bringing my hand to his mouth he kisses the sensitive flesh there. "Ellen, I've wanted you for so long." My knees almost buckle at his admission.

When I shyly tell him that I want him too he reaches for me. Placing both hands at my waist drawing me closer he says, "This may be all we ever get."

Softly I touch my index finger to his lips, "Don't say that."

"It has to be said," he looks sad but determined. He's kind as he says, "Please understand that I'm being realistic. I don't want to give either one of us false hope." He tightens his grasp at my waist. "If I make it back I will come to you."

"I'll wait for you," I say close to tears. I hold them back however. I don't want to cry anymore until Sunday. Sunday, I know I will cry the whole way home. For now though, I fight to hold the tears at bay.

Lowering his gaze to the floor between our feet he says so quietly, "I can't ask you to do that. I have no idea how long I'll be gone or if I'll even come home."

Running my hand over the close cropped hair of his bent head I say, "You didn't ask and you will come back." I will wait for him for as long as it takes. I'll wait for him for forever.

Lifting his head he stares into my eyes. His eyes are so dark and full of emotion. I sense he wants to protest, perhaps make me swear that I won't wait around for him. I'm glad he doesn't though.

Ben stands and kisses me with such tenderness. "Don't move." I watch him draw the curtains closed and turn down the light. Then he pulls a small packet from his duffle bag and slips it into the back pocket of his dress pants. When he catches me watching he says, "I wouldn't want to leave you in a family way." When I say nothing he asks, "Are you upset that I assumed…?"

Shaking my head I say, "Not at all." I'm actually relieved that he came prepared. Holding out my hand I beckon him to come to me and he does. This time when he kisses me I know there will be no turning back. I want to belong to this man completely body and soul. He is the keeper of my heart. I am totally and irrevocably in love with Benjamin Rosenberg.

I don't want to think about anything beyond this room. I don't want to think about responsibilities or the war. I want to forget about everything for a little while. I especially want to forget that Ben is going somewhere dangerous.

His warm breath heats the sensitive skin just below my ear, "So soft," he murmurs. I want to make time stop for us. "Do you remember the night we met," he asks. His fingers skim down my right arm. I feel the touch through the satin of my sleeve.

"I could never forget that night," I say a little breathless from his touch.

"I couldn't take my eyes off of you. I thought you were the most beautiful woman in the room." He skims his fingers down my other arm. "Now I know that you are beautiful on the inside as well as on the outside."

Doesn't he know that I am already extremely emotional? His words are almost too much for me to bear. I've worn my hair in loose curls tonight. He reaches out and wraps one of those curls around his finger. Giving it a gentle tug he says, "I thought I would forget about you after I went back to Blacksburg. I thought that you would forget about me, or at least get tired of writing to me." His confession makes me a little sad. I don't like that Ben thought he'd forget me or that he thought that I would stop writing. "But I couldn't. In fact the opposite occurred. You are always in my thoughts. I wanted to come see you again. I never got the chance."

"Don't you know," I start to say, "That you are unforgettable?" I place my hand, palm open over his heart. I feel the steady rhythmic beat beneath the fabric of his blue dress shirt. "You are a good man, Ben," I say meaning every word.

"You make me want to be a good man, Ellen," he says running his fingers through my hair. "You make me want so many things." Then he's kissing me. It's not gentle this time. His kiss is a demonstration of longing and desire.

He makes me feel things I have never felt before. Thousands of little jolts of electricity course through my body. His touch, his warm breath on my skin, the scent of his cologne they assault my nerve endings. He is all consuming. I am on fire.

The only sound in the room is the sound of

our breathing, "Turn around baby," he whispers into the silence. I do as he asks turning and presenting him with my back. He takes his time with each pearl button. When the third and final button is released, Ben strokes the exposed skin and I feel his kiss on the back of my neck. He skims his hands down either side of me. When he reaches the hem of my dress he begins to lift it. "Arms up," he says again in a whisper. I lift my arms for him.

Standing in only my slip and stockings I concentrate on the moment. I've dreamed of this night so many times. I watch as he undoes the buttons down the front of his shirt and tosses it aside. I lose capacity for speech when he reaches for the hem of his white undershirt and pulls it up over his head. His body is perfection all sculpted muscles and lean solid mass. He is a trained soldier. He is magnificent.

He leads me to the bed. I welcome his weight, the press of his body over me. His beautiful mouth is curved into a sad little smile. His dark eyes are serious. "Please don't cry, City Girl," he says stroking my hair. I hadn't realized I was crying. "Do you want to stop?"

Looking deeply into his eyes I say, "No, I don't want to stop." His beautiful face hovering just inches above me loses some of its previous sadness. If he's right and this is all we ever get then I don't want to hide anything from him. So I decide to tell him what I'm thinking and what I'm feeling. "I'm so in love with you," I say. Have I made a mistake by telling him? Should I have kept these feelings to myself? I am not sorry I said it.

A tear slips from the corner of his eye. Touching his forehead to mine he sighs. "You shouldn't love me Ellen. My life is not my own right now. I can't make you any promises, not now. What if I don't come back?" Another tear follows the first. "I want you to be happy."

"I am happy here with you," I say.
He gives me an ironic little frown.
"Being with you makes me happy," I say. Placing my hands on either side of his face I look him in the eye. "You don't have to say it back. It's enough for me that you know how I feel about you," I say.

When we are skin to skin and there is nothing between us Ben looks deep into my eyes all the way to my soul. "Ellen," he says my name like a caress, "I love you, too." Then he is inside me, filling me, shattering me completely.

CHAPTER TWENTY-THREE – BEN

I watch her as she sleeps. Her features soft and relaxed now are so different from how she looked earlier. One of the most beautiful things about Ellen is how expressive she is. When she started to cry last night I could read her feelings. They were written all over her face. When she said the words out loud I was at once overjoyed and devastated. She loves me. I hold onto that.

How am I supposed to watch her drive away from here tomorrow and not totally lose it? Running a hand through my short cropped hair I push that unpleasant thought aside. There will be plenty of time to wallow in self-pity on the drive to Blacksburg. Now is not the time to panic.

She looks so peaceful curled on her side

facing me. My eyes track the slope of her shoulder, the curve of her hip. By the time my gaze makes it back to her flawless face I find her watching me. She's smiling, always a good sign. "Did I wake you?" I ask.

She shakes her head. "No, you didn't wake me," she says her voice sleepy. "What time is it?" she asks moving in closer and laying her head on my chest.

I reach out to grab my watch. I took it off last night and placed it on the table by the bed. Bringing it into view I check the time. "It's only five. You can sleep longer if you want to," I tell her.

I feel rather than see her shake her head. "I don't want to sleep," she says, "I want to spend every possible minute with you awake."

I know exactly how she feels because I feel the same way. I return the watch to the table and wrap my arm around her. "I was thinking," I say running my knuckles over her hip.

"About what?" she says burrowing deeper into my chest.

"Well," I kiss her temple, "I was thinking we could go on a picnic today if you'd like."

She looks up at me. I smooth her hair away from her face. I wish I could wake up to Ellen every morning like this for the rest of my life.

"Where would we go?" she asks interested.

Cupping the side of her jaw I brush her bottom lip, devoid of red lipstick with the pad of my thumb. "There's a park not too far from here," I tell her looking into her eyes. "Would you like to do that? Go on a picnic with me?"

Leaning up on an elbow she touches the side of my face. "It doesn't matter to me what we do today Ben, as long as I get to spend it with you." Her words burrow into my skin and bury themselves somewhere deep where they will remain with me after tomorrow.

"Can I tell you something?" I ask tentatively. It's not easy for me to talk about my feelings. When she nods I say, "I've never been in love before. Not sure I even believed it existed. Then I met you," I say tracing the outline of her jaw. "You came into my life and turned it upside down." A little self-deprecating laugh escapes me.

"I'm sorry," she says not at all sorry. Then she says, "I never doubted love exists, Ben." "My mother made sure that my siblings and I knew our father was a good man who loved his wife and his children. She kept his memory alive for us. She would tell us so many stories of our father that he became a familiar figure in our lives, even though he wasn't with us physically."

Smiling softly she says, "He is always with us in our hearts. My mother wanted my brother to know what it means to be a good man to the women in his life and she wanted my sister and me to know what to look for when we were ready to open our hearts to someone."

I am absolutely still. I stay silent listening as Ellen takes me into her confidence. From what she has already told me I know that her parents shared a deep abiding love. The fact that Ellen's mother kept her father's memory vividly alive for Ellen and her brother and sister is more proof of the love they must have shared.

"Ben," Ellen says making sure she has my full attention which she definitely does. "I've never been in love before either." She trails feather light kisses over my shoulder and up my neck. She stops to whisper in my ear, "You should also know that you are the only man that I'll ever be capable of loving."

Her soft proclamation renders me speechless. I question whether or not I am worthy of such a woman as Ellen. I want to protest and beg her to take the words back. However, I'm not going to do that. Instead, I say, "What did I ever do to deserve you?" Inside I ache for what we may never have.

If I die and I don't come home I don't want Ellen to feel like she's obligated to mourn someone who couldn't give her more than this stolen weekend. Sure, I would want her to remember me and how I once loved her. More than that, I want her to have and do all of the things she dreams of. I want her to live and to find love again. I meant what I told her last night that I want her to be happy even if that means it's with someone else.

She is too good a woman not to have the life she deserves, not to have love. I don't say any of this to her because I'm selfish and I don't want to spend this time arguing or trying to convince her I'm right. Don't get me wrong, I want to be the man in her life. I would give my right arm for the privilege of spending every day I have on this Earth with her.

She's stubborn and I know it would be a futile attempt to try to make her see my side of this so I put it to rest in my mind. Turning my head I catch her lips hoping my kiss conveys even half of what I'm feeling for her. "I love you," I tell her. "I'll always love you," I add knowing full well that it is the absolute truth.

My heart slams against my ribs. Her nearness, her touch, the look in her eyes all work together to cast some sort of spell over me. This beautiful, amazing woman has bewitched me. "What have you done to me?" I say in awe. What has she done to me indeed?

She wraps her arms around my neck and tells me she needs me. She says what I'm thinking. "I need you, too" I tell her. I mean those three words in every possible way a person can need another person. Rolling us so that now she's beneath me her breath hitches and she arches her back. "You are perfect," I say placing a kiss to her neck. As I lose myself in loving Ellen one thought remains clear. She is air, she is light. She is my world and I want to come back to her.

While Ellen is in the shower I call the hotel concierge and request a picnic lunch be prepared for two. As soon as we're both dressed and ready to face the day we leave the room. On the way downstairs I slip my hand into hers. I've never been an overly demonstrative person but with Ellen I crave touch and the closeness we share. We swing by the concierge desk to collect the picnic lunch I ordered earlier.

I loop the basket's handle over my arm

keeping it out of reach of one very curious female. "Come on, Ben" she says reaching for the covered hamper. "Let me see what's inside."

Extending my arm away from her grabby little hands I chuckle, "I thought Catholic girls were supposed to practice patience," I tisk, "How does that saying go?" I try to recall. "Oh, right, patience is a virtue."

She's reaching across my person trying to lift the lid to peer inside. This is fun. "I never learned patience," she says pulling on my arm. She's cute like this. Her determination to see what's inside the hamper is impressive. "Please Ben I have to know what is in there."

I eye her suspiciously. "Why do you have to know what's inside?"

"Because, I just do," she says grabbing for it again. I don't know whether it's the adorable face she's making or the impulsivity she's showing but I fall in love with her a little more. Stopping I hold the hamper still so she can look inside.

Shutting the lid post inspection she says, "That will do."

I try and fail to stop a laugh. Her sass is off the charts. I hope I'm able to see for myself that Ellen will be as sassy at the age of eighty as she is today. "Satisfied?" I ask.

"Yes," she bobs her head up and down.

"May we proceed?" I ask.

"We may," she says once again looping her arm through mine.

"Thank you," I say.

We follow the directions to the park provided to us by the hotel's concierge. When we get to the park we find a flat grassy area and stake our claim to it. Together we spread a blanket, also courtesy of the concierge. Then, I set the hamper down in the middle.

I wanted today to be one that Ellen would always remember with fondness. I wanted whatever we did to be fun and easy. That's why when she wanted to take a peek inside the picnic hamper I kept it out of her reach. Life with Ellen would be interesting. If only I had some guarantees. No, I won't think like that today. Today, I want to play pretend.

Lowering myself to the blanket I get comfortable. Ellen joins me there. "What is one thing that you want to do but haven't been able to?" I ask. Today, I'm playing pretend.

"That's easy," she says, "I would travel."

"Where would you go?" I ask intrigued by

her answer.

"Everywhere," she says almost immediately.

Her answer is surprising, yet not surprising in the least. Shaking my head I say, "Okay, but where would you go first?"

She stops to think about that. She scrunches up her nose as she contemplates where to go first. "That's a hard one. There are so many places I want to see." She's still thinking. "Oh, I know, China to see the Great Wall," she finally says.

"I see," I say playfully tapping her nose. "You want to use your new language skills."

She scoffs and says, "I don't know very much Chinese yet. It's a difficult language to learn."

It's like this all day, easy banter back and forth. We share stories and dreams and 'what ifs'. It's a window into what my life would look like in an alternate universe, one where there was no war going on, no draft, no imminent deployment and separation. I pepper her with questions and listen intently to her answers. I intend to learn as much about the woman who owns my heart as I possibly can in the span of a few hours.

I'm hoping this day will be full of memories Ellen will look back on with fondness. I know I will for as long as I live. We share a bottle of wine and throughout the afternoon we nibble on cheeses, a selection of smoked meats and a loaf of fresh baked bread.

Sated, I lie on my side on the blanket covering the soft grass and pat the space next to me. When Ellen reclines beside me I reach for her hand and bring it to my lips. It seems that when she's near I must always be touching her. I send up a silent prayer grateful for this time. "Ellen?" I say after a while.

She turns her head to look at me when she says, "Yes?"

"I'm really glad we met." I notice her eyes get watery and that was not my intention.

"I'm really glad we met, too," she says. "Ben," she adds after several seconds of silence.

"Yeah?" I say.

"We will meet again, I know we will," she says it with so much conviction that I have no other option but to believe it.

CHAPTER TWENTY-FOUR -ELLEN

Early afternoon sunlight streams through the high windows of Grand Central Station's Main Concourse. "There she is!" I hear my mother's voice before I catch sight of her making her way through the crush of people to get to me. Her familiar Chantilly perfume envelops me, calms me.

It's good to be home even if it's only for a few days. I was granted leave to spend Christmas in New York with my family. I can't tell you how relieved I was when my request was approved. Since Ben deployed it's been increasingly difficult keeping my spirits high. Spending the holiday at home should be just the thing I need.

It's going on two months since we said

goodbye. I cried the entire car ride to D.C. Since then I've gotten only one letter from him. By the time it reached me it was battered and torn. Parts of the letter had been redacted so much it resembled a slice of Swiss cheese. What I do know is that he is somewhere in France. The knowledge does not ease my mind, though. As you might imagine I scour the newspapers and listen to radio broadcasts for any and all news from France.

The hustle and bustle inside the station fades as I am surrounded by familiar faces. Bess and Eduardo are here and so are Bill and Gladys and the twins. As much as I like living in Washington, D.C., I needed to be in New York with my family. I've missed them so much. Bess lunges for me, wrapping me in her arms and holding on for dear life. She says she doesn't want to share me but she does just the same. I'm passed around like a rag doll but I don't mind. With each hug and kiss I start to feel a little better. "Let's go home," I say.

Eduardo takes my suit case from me as we head toward the exit. He is ever so thoughtful. Glancing around it's hard to believe I've been gone for more than a year. Grand Central is as ostentatious as I remember. The enormous War Department mural is still there. I have a deeper appreciation for the meaning behind it now.

Thousands of people pass through this terminal every day. I wonder what goes through their minds when they see the mural with its images of the larger than life soldier and sailor up there encouraging them to buy defense bonds and stamps. I hope they are moved to support the war effort.

Stepping out onto East Forty Second Street we're greeted by a blast of icy air. The winter wind swirls around our little party. A mix of sounds greets us, there's the Salvation Army bell, car horns, conversations. Pedestrians walk briskly by us and I am bumped into by one of them. "It is so good to be home," I say squeezing Bess' arm taking it all in.

On my first full day home which happens to be Christmas Eve, my mother, Bess, Gladys and I do a little last minute holiday shopping. Our first stop is Macy's department store. We take our time strolling through the store admiring the holiday decorations and gorgeous window displays.

After Macy's we ride the subway to Rockefeller Center to see the Christmas trees in the plaza. There are three of them this year. One is trimmed in white, the second in red and the third in blue. They are a dedication to the war effort. There are no lights on the trees again this year because of the blackout rules. Still, they look beautiful.

"Even without the lights they're beautiful," I say.

"They are," Bess says beside me. She puts her arms around me. "I've missed you," she says softly.

"I've missed you too," I hug her back.

It's so cold out here. We duck into a nearby café where we can rest and warm up before heading home. We order a pot of tea and pastries. Seated by the window our attention strays to the ice rink outside. There are some wonderfully graceful skaters on the ice gliding around and around. There are also a good number of unskilled skaters who are doing their best to remain upright.

"What's that down there supposed to be?" My mother says pointing out the window.

"What's what down where?" I ask confused by the question.

"That gold statue," she clarifies.

Bess lowers her tea cup. "That's Prometheus'" she answers knowingly. At my mother's curious stare Bess explains, "According to Greek mythology he was a Titan god of fire." Bess has always enjoyed Greek mythology. I've a liking for mythology myself lately, at least where it applies to the constellations.

My mother tilts her head slightly still looking out the window and says, "He looks like he's falling." At her statement I give it a closer look and upon further inspection I must agree with her interpretation of the gold Prometheus statue in the Plaza. He does look like he's falling.

"They say that the sculptor wanted to make it look like he's falling from the heavens to the Earth and sea," Bess adds. Okay, I think. Prometheus is supposed to look like he's falling. The sculptor did a good job then.

"The ring at the bottom represents the heavens," Gladys adds helpfully. Apparently, Gladys is interested in Greek Mythology as well. We all stare out the window to admire the Greek god a little bit longer. I think it complements the Art Deco architecture in this part of the city.

"I learned something new," my mother says pleased as punch. Before taking a bite of cheese Danish she adds, "You girls are so smart." She takes a dainty bite of pastry then dabs a napkin at the corners of her mouth. "This is delicious," she says. She's not wrong. The tea and pastries are some of the best I've ever had.

Bess and I help our mother in the kitchen preparing dinner, a hearty beef stew which tastes and smells amazing. I can't help compare how Phyllis, Jane and I are barely competent in the kitchen. It's strange being back here. Everything is as it was when I left.

After dinner Bess and I get comfortable on the living room rug where we spread out everything we need to wrap the last minute gifts we bought while we were out earlier. The paper is shiny silver. It's pretty paired with either the forest green or navy blue ribbon. I think I want to use the green ribbon but it's too far for me to reach. Pointing to the roll I say, "Bess, will you hand that one to me, please?" It is closest to her. She picks up the roll of green ribbon and tosses it to me. I catch it easily.

Cutting off a length I tie a bow and tape it to the top of the small box I've just finished wrapping in the silver paper. "What do you think?" I ask holding it up for my sister's inspection.

"Gorgeous," she says.

"High praise," I tease.

"Indeed," she says. "Well, what do you think of this one?" Now it's my turn to rate her wrapping ability.

"Stunning," I say of the gift she has wrapped with silver paper and blue bow.

"There may not be much variety in the goods we're able to source these days, but we girls sure know how to make the most of them," Bess says with a touch of mirth. What she doesn't say but implies is that we girls are also good at recycling, reusing and making things last as long as possible.

We clean up the floor before dropping onto the couch. I switch off the lamp so that the only light in here is coming from the electric colored light bulbs on the tree. 'I'll Be Home for Christmas' plays softly on the radio.

My mother and Eduardo join us only when we tell them that it is safe to come in. We didn't want them to see the gifts we got for them. My mother's carrying a tray. I'm sure Eduardo tried to get her to let him carry it for her. From where do you think I get my stubbornness? On the tray are four glasses. They are from my mother's set of wedding crystal. They only come out on the holidays. She carefully sets the tray on the coffee table.

Eduardo pops the cork of a nice Merlot and pours a little in each glass. We toast to being together and to the Christmas holiday. We sip Merlot and enjoy the holiday songs on the radio until eventually my mother can't keep her eyes open any longer. She says good night and goes to bed leaving the three of us alone.

A little while later Eduardo stands from the chair and stretches. "I'm going to turn in now." He leans over the couch and kisses Bess on top of her head. "Stay and spend time with your sister," he says quietly in his accented English.

I love how sweet he is to my sister. Bess touches his arm as he begins to straighten. "I love you," she tells him.

Covering her hand he says, "Y yo tu mi amor." Then to me he says, "See you in the morning Ellen. It's good to have you home with us."

Resting my head on my sister's shoulder when it's just the two of us I tell her, "You married a good man, Bess. Eduardo is a gem."

"He is," she says in complete agreement.

Cautiously I say, "I've met someone."

She shifts beside me on the couch. This is, I suppose, to her monumental news since I haven't mentioned anyone in a long time, not since George and I broke up and that was years ago. "Will you tell me about him?" she asks.

Resting my head back on her shoulder I tell her, "His name is Ben. We met last April when he was in D.C. visiting a friend. He's in the Army," I pause. She's patient and doesn't rush me for details. I appreciate that about her. "He's in France," I say then stop. Silently she places a hand on my knee. "I miss him," I whisper. We stay quiet. I suspect she senses I'm trying not to cry.

After several minutes go by she says, "Can I ask you a serious question?"

Frantically, my brain works to figure out what she wants to ask. "Okay," I say wondering what she wants to know.

"Is he handsome?" I love how she can make me laugh so effortlessly.

Smiling on a sigh I say, "So handsome."

Bess and I stayed up late last night so now I'm covering a yawn in the church pew hoping no one notices. We stand to sing the last hymn and my nephews wiggle through the adults to make their ways to either side of me. Two little hands hold mine and my heart warms at the attention they've been giving me since I've been home.

From the early morning church service we drive across the bridge into New Jersey. My aunt and uncle live in Montclair. Aunt Nan is my mother's older sister. She and Uncle James have hosted Christmas every year since I can remember. As we get closer I can hardly contain my excitement. I'm looking forward to seeing them and my cousin Belle. Sadly, my cousin Carter will not be with us. Carter is in the Army. He is somewhere in Italy.

My Aunt answers the door and it's all animated screeches and hugs and kisses. We're ushered inside out of the cold. Bill and Eduardo join my uncle in the study. The twins go with them to be with the men.

The rest of us join Aunt Nan in the warm cozy kitchen. She has almost everything prepared so we sit around the big butcher block table while we wait for the turkey to finish roasting. "Ellen, tell us what living in Washington, D.C. is like," my cousin Belle says. Belle is twenty-one. I wonder if she's thinking about becoming a volunteer. I suspect my Aunt Nan would have a hard time with that.

"What do you want to know?" I ask

adjusting my chair.

"Everything," she says wide eyed. "What's it like? Where do you live? Where do you work? What do you do for fun? Do you have time for fun?" Her rapid fire questions are giving me whip lash.

"I don't know where to begin," I say honestly.

"Why don't you tell us about your roommates," my mother suggests.

Now that is a topic I can easily expand upon. For nearly forty minutes I regale the women in my family with stories of not only Jane and Phyllis but also of Lorraine, Jean, and Vera. By the time the table is set and the meal is ready Gladys, Belle, Bess, my mother and Aunt Nan are in love with my friends.

"If I were twenty-five years younger I would join you, Ellen" my Aunt says.

"I want to join you," Belle says and Aunt Nan looks like a deer in headlights.

"It's not all fun and games," I say to Belle. "After dinner, I'll tell you about the serious parts of my work and my life in Washington."

One of my absolute favorite parts about Christmas at my aunt and uncle's house is when we gather around the piano to sing carols. After we eat and clean up the kitchen, Belle sits at the piano. As she sets up several sheets of music it hits me how much I missed this tradition last year when I was at Smith.

When she's ready she splays her fingers over the keys. Before she presses them she says to us, "Does anyone know the words to 'White Christmas'?" It's a newer song. "If not, I have the words here," she says meaning the sheet music in front of her.

"I love that song," Gladys says.

"She does," Bill says moving closer to the piano. "Every time Bing comes on the radio, Gladys stops what she's doing to turn up the sound."

"It's a beautiful song," Gladys says emphatically.

Eduardo scoops Jimmy up onto his shoulders saying, "In my opinion it is the best Christmas song ever written."

"I agree," Belle says swiveling on the piano bench. "Plus, I find it fascinating that it was written by a Jewish person. Think about it," she says, "Probably the greatest Christmas song ever written was by someone who doesn't celebrate Christmas."

I know Irving Berlin wrote White Christmas. I know he emigrated from Russia but I didn't know that he's Jewish, not until Belle just told us that. Huh, she makes a good point there I have to admit. Automatically my mind goes to Ben. Ben is Jewish and he doesn't celebrate Christmas.

Belle begins to play the opening notes. Tucking those thoughts of Ben somewhere safe in my heart to unpack later, I join in signing. It's a pretty song. When it ends I see Aunt Nan dabbing a handkerchief at the tears she can't hold back. Uncle James wraps her up in a hug and gently rubs her back. "Sorry," my aunt says, "I was just thinking of Carter."

Turning I walk to the window and look out onto the front lawn. Ben, wherever you are, I hope you're warm and safe and I hope you know how much I miss you, how much I love you. Please come home to me I think. It is more than a thought, it is a silent prayer.

CHAPTER TWENTY-FIVE – ELLEN

"Phyllis, hurry up. We won't get seats if we don't get there before the store opens," I hear Jane call. She's standing impatiently by the front door, keys in hand. It's Thursday. Yes, we still have breakfast, just the three of us on Thursday mornings before heading into the office. "Come on," Jane adds for good measure.

"Hold your horses, Jane," Phyllis says emerging from the bedroom. "We'll get there with time to spare," she says pulling on her white gloves.

Grabbing my purse and hat I follow Jane out the door. Phyllis brings up the rear. As we make our way to Jane's car parked on the street in front of our building the first signs of spring make themselves known to us. The city is still relatively quiet this early in the morning. The sound of birds chirping has me thinking there must be a nest nearby. Raising my gaze I appreciate the new buds on the trees overhead. It's already April.

If feels like just yesterday I was with my family in New York. Although it was what I needed at the time and I was so grateful to be with them I could only stay there for a few short days. I was back in D.C. two days after Christmas. The gals and I rang in nineteen forty-five together at the Mayfield. The absence of Ben, Dan and Joe was acutely felt.

Ben's letters have been sporadic since his deployment last November and some parts are censured. I presume the Army doesn't want me to know where exactly he is. I find myself praying more now than I ever have before. As I fold into the backseat it hits me that it was a year ago when Dan introduced the girls and I to Ben and Joe. Wow, a year since Dan left us. His letters to Tim are also sporadic. We still see Tim at the Bureau. It's good to see him now and again.

There's been a lot of news coming into Classification. Reports indicate that the Allies are very close to victory. I hope those reports are true. I stare out the window as Jane drives. Ben's last letter sits heavy on my heart. Tucking my purse close to my chest I lower my chin and sigh deeply. "You okay back there, El?" Jane says eyeing me through the rear view mirror.

"All good," I say to Jane lifting my chin to meet her gaze in the mirror. I carry his last letter with me everywhere I go, by doing so I have something of him with me. It's the last thing I have of him. It is dated twenty-five January. It has been over two months since I've heard anything from him. Since then I have written to him at least a dozen times. I'm worried that something has happened. I'm terrified that any day now I'll come home to find a telegram telling me that he is missing in action or worse.

I can't think like that though. I just can't let myself. Staying busy with the girls and at work is the only way I maintain my sanity. Jane parks the car and the three of us get out. The closed sign is still in the door. "See, Jane," Phyllis says, placing her hat on her head, "I told you we'd get here in time."

Not a minute later the door is unlocked and we enter the drug store. We head toward the luncheonette counter and hop up onto the red vinyl stools. My appetite has been minimal but I make an effort and order a cup of tea and an

English muffin. I half listen to what Phyllis and Jane are talking about. My mind wanders as it so often does to the letter inside my purse, the last words from Ben. I've read it so many times I have it memorized.

My Dearest Ellen,

I received your letter dated ten December. I can't express to you how much your letters mean to me, especially over here. Letters from home are all we have to look forward to. Some of the guys are crushed when mail finally gets to us and there is nothing for them. Ellen, your letters are a bright spot in an otherwise dismal existence. Please keep them coming.

It's cold here. I've never known cold like this. The only thing that keeps me going is the thought of you my beautiful girl. At my darkest I think about you and your incredible smile. I think about coming home to you. Ellen, I was wrong to tell you that you shouldn't wait for me. If it's not too late I want to take back what I said. I do want you to wait for me.

The fighting here is bad. It snows a lot. Sometimes we have freezing rain. Some mornings we have to chisel the ice off the tanks because they've frozen to the ground overnight. When fog rolls through our air support can't get to us. That's when the Germans like to attack. Enemy fire is heavy. Our side has taken a lot of hits. Ellen, your love keeps me going. The thought of getting home keeps me fighting through the blizzards and snow drifts. All I want is to see you again.

Currently, I am writing to you from a fox hole. There's a lull in the fighting. The forest around us looks like something out of a gothic novel. The trees, more casualties of heavy shelling and tanks coming through are twisted and hacked and broken. I have to close now. I can hear the sounds of artillery in the distance. Until we meet again, know that I love you.

Yours always,
Ben

"El, what do you think about that idea?" I'm pulled from my thoughts by a hand on my arm.

Shaking the cobwebs from my brain I say, "What? I'm sorry; I didn't catch what you just said."

Phyllis pats my arm and says, "I was just telling Jane that we should do something for Jean's birthday. It's in two weeks. What do you think?"

"Oh," I say embarrassed I hadn't been

paying attention. "Yeah, we should do something to celebrate her birthday. What did you have in mind?"

They make suggestions but nothing solid is decided. I think we should include Vera and Lorraine in the planning. Jane and Phyllis both nod agreeing with me. We decide to talk to both of them sometime today. If we can we'll try to surprise Jean with something fun to do on her birthday. Thankfully, we're not interrupted by anyone bent on insulting our uniforms or our persons this morning and we finish our breakfast in peace.

We arrive at the office fifteen minutes early. Jane parks the car and we walk toward the building. We're back in our whites. We put away the blue wool uniforms a few days ago. It was another marker of the passage of time. The skirt was loose when I took it out of the closet and tried it on again. Lorraine insists it's the stress that's caused me to lose weight. She's probably correct. If it wasn't for my friends, I might forget to eat at all. I'd probably live on coffee and tea alone.

Inside we show our badges to the security guard and he allows us through. Upstairs we see Tim at the other end of the hallway. He's walking in our direction. He greets us with a wave and when we stop him to ask if he has any news of Dan it is with great relief when we see him nodding emphatically. "Yeah, I was wondering if you'd heard yet," he tells us excitedly.

"Heard what?" Phyllis practically demands. There's always been a little part of me that wondered if Phyllis didn't have a thing for Dan. Honestly, I think I might have been a little too preoccupied by Ben last year to pay close attention to how Phyllis and Dan got along that weekend before he left for Italy. I do remember they hung out in each other's company quite a bit. Oh yeah, and she did drag him onto the dance floor at the Mayfair.

Tim smiles wider than I have ever seen him smile, ever. "He's on his way back," he says of Dan. "He's coming home," Tim's jubilation is infectious.

All of the sudden, Phyllis covers her mouth and rushes off without a word. I exchange a look with Jane and she gives the slightest shake of her head letting me know that she thinks it best to give Phyllis her privacy. We don't follow after her. Dan was on the USS Plunkett when it was attacked in January. The Navy destroyer was in the vicinity of Cape Anzio. The Plunkett was hit by a bomb and caught fire. Twenty-three men were killed, thirty went missing and many on board were wounded.

Our department was tasked with classifying documents pertaining to that incident. When we learned that it was the Plunkett that had been involved in the attack and that it sustained casualties the atmosphere in the office changed drastically. You could have heard a pin drop. Typewriters stopped, nobody said a word, the silence was deafening. That is until Dan's replacement came out of his office to tell us to buck up and get back to work.

"Thanks for letting us know," Jane says. "That's great news." It's obvious she means every word of it. It is great news.

I for one am relieved to know that Dan is coming home. It wasn't until we didn't see his name on the list of casualties, missing or wounded that we were able to breathe a sigh of relief.

"As soon as I hear anything else I'll be sure to let you all know," Tim says. Then, holding up a folder marked classified he adds, "I have to hurry right now though. I'll catch up with you ladies again soon."

We let him pass. "Dan is coming home,"

Jane says as if she needs to hear the words again out loud to make them real. Then she does something so out of character. She tugs me into a hug and just holds me for minute. "El, Ben will be coming home soon, too," she tells me setting me back to rights. "Be strong."

The mood in the office is lighter knowing that Dan is okay and on his way back to the States. There is five minutes before lunch. I'm working on something when I hear the Chinese record being played. What the heck? Looking up from the file on my desk I see Jane of all people at the record player grinning from ear to ear. Of course, now everyone is looking at her and wondering if she's lost her mind.

"What are you doing?" I ask her.

She crosses the room to my desk and says, "You recall how much Lieutenant Cavanaugh loved it when you and Lorraine played these records during lunch."

This makes Phyllis laugh and it's good to see her laughing again.

"Um, Jane," I lean back in my chair. "You recall that he was just teasing us about that?"

"Of course I do," she says. "I just thought it was fitting to play it in his honor."

Shaking my head I tell her, "You're a

wacko,"

She shrugs, "Maybe, maybe not." Either way she goes back to the record player and lifts the needle from the vinyl record making it stop. Everyone goes back to what they were doing and a few minutes after that people start dispersing for lunch.

The six of us take lunch together this afternoon. There is something in the air. I think they must feel it too. Whatever it is, I feel the need to be surrounded by friends today. We wind our way downstairs to the cafeteria. We wait somewhat patiently in the long line. Finally we make our trays and pay for our meals. Surprisingly we catch a table at precisely the right moment as another group is exiting. As we sit down to eat we're interrupted by a growing commotion.

There is a buzzing that grows louder and louder. What is happening I'm wondering just as someone approaches our table and announces, "Hitler is dead." Looking around the cafeteria the buzz is growing louder and people are standing and cheering. Some are crying great wracking sobs of relief and joy. Some are laughing. Lorraine, who happens to be sitting beside me grabs onto my hand and holds it. What does this mean?

CHAPTER TWENTY-SIX – BEN

My feet hit solid ground and I want to sink to my knees in gratitude. The fighting in Europe ceased in April but it has taken months of coordinated efforts by the government and military to get us back home. It's controlled chaos right now at the port. I've just debarked. Duffel bag slung over my shoulder I follow the throngs of G.I.s getting off the ship.

I've been here for hours waiting in line to use the telephone. When it's finally my turn I slide into the phone booth and close the glass door in an attempt to block out some of the background noise. Crossing my fingers I hope she's home. It is seven-twenty on a Monday night. She should be home I think. I pick up the receiver and feed a coin into the slot. Holding my breath

I dial the number. It rings four times before someone answers.

"Hello?"

Closing my eyes I lean against the wall. It's her. "Hey City Girl," I have to swallow the lump in my throat to get the words out.

"Ben," her voice cracks and I hear her start to cry. I want to cry, too. I don't though. I hold it together. "You're okay," she says relief in her voice.

"I'm okay," I reassure her. "Did you get my last few letters?" I ask. "I wrote to let you know I was alive and that it would be a while before they started bringing us back stateside. Did you get them?"

"I got them," she says. "I got them."

Good, I think. I couldn't write for a while not during the heaviest of the fighting. We were on the move and then so much happened. I wrote as soon as I could though.

"Where are you, Ben?" she asks urgency in her tone. "Where are you calling from? Are you stateside or still overseas?"

"I'm Stateside," I say, "And you're the first person I wanted to call," I tell her.

"When did you land?"

"We just pulled into port today. Ellen, it's

crazy here. There are so many guys like me. We all just want to get out of here. As soon as I can I'll come to D.C. I want to see you the first chance I get," I say longing to see her.

"Where are you now?" she asks.

"The port of New York," I say ironically.

I hear her soft laugh. "You're in my backyard," she teases.

"I wish you were here to show me around this great big city of yours," I tell her through the phone.

"I wish I was there with you, too," she says.

There's a knock on the door of the phone booth and I know my time is up. "Listen El, there's a long line of soldiers behind me here. They're all waiting for their turn to use the phone. I have to go now, but I'll be there as soon as I can," I have to raise my voice over the complaints outside for me to get off the phone already. "I love you," I tell her. When she says she loves me, too I smile for the first time in a long time.

I hang up the phone and slide the door open. Stepping out of the booth I say, "My girl still loves me," to the next guy in line. He looks at me like he could care less. He's anxious probably to call his own girl. I step out of his way. Hitching my duffel higher on my shoulder I head away from the phone booths to see what I have to do next before I'm free to go.

I was at the train depot early this morning and purchased a ticket to take me to D.C. I slept for part of the journey. I hadn't realized how exhausted I was. I could barely sleep last night thinking about today. When I arrived in D.C., I took a cab to the hotel, checked in, took a long hot shower and put on clean clothes.

Now I'm just sitting here waiting for Ellen. From my position on the park bench across the street I have a perfect view of the main entrance of where she works. Leaning my head back to look at the blue sky up above I shield my eyes from the bright September sun. I've only been in the States for two days and the contrast between here and the devastation of where I've come from is something I'm still trying to get used to.

I get to my feet when I see the doors opening. Scanning the faces of the people exiting the building my heart is in my throat waiting for the sight of her. My feet carry me to the curb at the intersection. All the while my eyes remain fixed on that door. Quickly, I cross the street. There she is. The sight of her takes my breath away.

She's not alone. I recognize the faces of her friends. They're talking about something. Frozen to this spot on the sidewalk, I watch her stop and put on her hat. She looks absolutely stunning. Her hair is a little longer than the last time I saw her. She looks a little thinner as well. I clock the moment she notices me.

Next thing I know she's hurrying to get to me, never mind the people in her way. I propel myself forward and catch her up in my arms, spinning her. Holding her tight she throws her arms around my neck. This is what I went on living for. In the darkest hours when I didn't think I could go another mile or fight another battle, this is what I pictured in my head, coming home to Ellen.

Her face is buried in my neck and her whole body begins shaking. "Shh, Ellen, it's alright now. I'm alright," I say softly, soothingly. "Everything is going to be alright now." I don't let her go. I just hold her as she lets it all out. She runs her fingers over my face, over my brow, my cheek bones, across my lips. "I can't believe you're here," she says. Softly she kisses me almost as if she's afraid I'll disappear.

"Wild horses couldn't have kept me away," I whisper for her ears only as I remember we have an audience. Turning our heads at the same time Ellen and I look to where her friends are standing around watching our reunion. I'll be darned, even stoic Jane is wiping her eyes.

Lorraine steps forward to give me a hug and says, "Welcome back Ben. It's so good to see you again."

"Thank you, Lorraine," I say. "I can't tell you how glad I am to be back here." I look at Ellen after I say this.

"How is Joe?" Lorraine asks me.

Shaking my head, I tell her, "I haven't talked to him yet. He's in Blacksburg still. I expect I'll see him soon though."

Phyllis steps in for a hug and says, "You have to see Dan and Tim while you're here."

"I'd like that," I say hugging her back. I receive warm hugs from all of Ellen's friends before they go.

When it is just me and Ellen I reach for her hand linking our fingers. I raise her hand to my mouth and kiss it tenderly. "I've missed you so much," I say. She agrees to accompany me to the Shoreham Hotel. "I'll make us reservations for dinner," I say as we pass through the front doors and enter the lobby. "While I'm doing that, why don't you call your place and ask one of the girls to bring you an overnight bag." Now I realize that I am assuming much here, but I'm shameless and not above begging her to stay with me if I have to.

"Okay," she says nodding. Relieved, I fish in my pocket for some change and hand the coins to her. She heads toward the phone booth.

I finish making dinner reservations for us then turn back to the lobby to wait for Ellen to finish her phone call. As she approaches me I ask, "All set?"

"All set," she tells me. "Lorraine said she'll be here around seven o'clock and to meet her out front," she adds smiling beautifully.

Reaching out I trace the curve of her jaw. I've missed this woman so much. "We could get a drink at the bar before our table is ready," I say lowering my hand.

"I'd like that," she says slipping her arm through mine. "Lead the way."

I can't stop looking at Ellen. Her skin is glowing in the candle light. She is a beautiful woman. "You're staring," she says lowering her glass. She still drinks the French Seventy Five. There's a hint of a smile on her red lips as she accuses me of staring. Some things haven't changed I guess.

"You know I can't help myself," I say leaning my elbow on the bar. "You're even more beautiful than I remembered." She blushes at the compliment. "I love you," I say quietly. I'm glad you're staying with me tonight." I want to kiss her.

We're interrupted by the hostess who comes over to us to let us know that our table is ready. Placing my hand on the small of Ellen's back we follow the hostess to a linen covered table in the main dining room. There are fresh cut flowers in a vase in the center of it. Again I am reminded that I am no longer in a war torn part of the world.

We linger over dinner until a few minutes before seven. I wait by the entrance for Ellen as she meets Lorraine in front of the hotel. I see Lorraine getting out the car. She hands a bag to Ellen. They hug and exchange a few words. I'm too far away to hear what's being said though. As Lorraine gets back inside the car to leave, Ellen turns suitcase by her side. Angling her head she smiles at me. It's the very smile I dreamed about when I was over there. I go weak watching her make her way back to me. "Everything okay?" I ask.

Wrapping her arms around my middle and laying her head on my chest she says, "Everything is more than okay now that you're here." Her words are exactly what I need.

We take the elevator up to the fourth floor. Inside the room, she unbuttons the jacket of her uniform and places her hat and purse on the dresser. "What time do you have to be at work in the morning?" I ask placing her bag on the ottoman by the arm chair in a corner of the room.

"Seven," she says. "Can we get a wakeup call for six?"

Dropping the room key on the dresser I say, "We can get a wakeup call."

Picking up the phone in the room I call down to the front desk to request a six a.m. wakeup call for Ellen. As I'm on the phone she opens her suitcase and takes out a few items then she carries them to the bathroom. I hang up the phone and listen. The shower is running.

I knock on the door to the bathroom then push it open slightly. "I requested the wakeup call for six," I say. The bathroom is filling with steam. There is fog on the mirror. I take a step inside the room. I undo my watch and lay it on the bathroom counter. Next I slip off my shoes. "Ellen, I'm coming in there with you, unless you tell me not to." I wait holding my breath for her to say something. A few seconds go by with only the sound of running water. "El," I say her name again, "Would that be alright?" I ask for confirmation.

"Yes, it would," she says from behind the curtain.

With shaky hands I shed my clothes letting them drop to the floor. Stepping inside the enclosed space I am met with the most beautiful sight. The air is thick with steam. She's just finished washing her hair. "Strawberries," I say under my breath wrapping my arms around her from behind.

She turns in my arms and stretches up on her toes. Wrapping her arms around my neck she kisses me. Night after frozen night thoughts of this woman kept me sane. Thoughts of her kept me going when I didn't think I had anything left inside of me. There were times I didn't know if I would make it home or not. At my lowest I would block everything else out and focus on how much I wanted to come home to Ellen. And now I'm home and I'm with her.

I hoist her up and she wraps her legs around me. I've fought battles, walked miles, slept in the elements, went without food and shelter countless nights, I've seen atrocities that made grown men cry and I kept going, I endured all of it with the sole purpose of coming back to this woman. Shutting off the water I pull back the curtain. Carrying her out to the bedroom I say, "You and I have a lot of lost time to make up for, beautiful girl."

CHAPTER TWENTY-SEVEN – ELLEN

"I can't believe this is it," Lorraine says uncorking a bottle of champagne. She does it expertly. By now we've had enough practice.

"Neither can I," I say holding two glasses steady as she pours, hers and mine. She moves the bottle from glass to glass so we can all have a little bubbly with which to toast. Don't be alarmed, there are two more bottles waiting for us inside.

My eyes travel from face to face. For me, Lorraine, Vera and Jean this is our last night in D.C. The four of us are out of here tomorrow. It's downright cold up here on the roof as one might expect for February but Jean insisted we had to come up here one more time. It was Phyllis who suggested we bring glasses and one of the bottles of champagne with us. So here we stand shivering.

"Please let's do this before my fingers freeze and fall off," Jane says.

"Hold your horses, Janey," Phyllis says. For the record, Jane does not like to be called Janey.

"Ellen," Jane turns to look at me, "Are you sure you want to go back to New York? I'm not sure I can handle Phyllis all by myself." Phyllis merely scoffs at her.

Wrapping an arm around Jane's shoulders I tell her, "I'm sure." Jane tries to conceal her feelings but I know she doesn't like that I'm leaving.

Our contracts with the Navy have been fulfilled. Jane and Phyllis decided they are staying in though. Seems neither was ready to walk away. I'd considered staying in with them. After a lot of thought and reflection however I decided against it. So much has happened since the end of the war and I'm ready for something different now.

We huddle close together to share warmth. "I'm going to miss all of you so much," Jean says and I know precisely how she feels. Pushing the sad thoughts aside for now I focus on how my nose is cold and my fingers are tingling. The stars are bright though and the city looks pretty all lit up.

I've had plenty of time to reflect on my life in D.C., the friends I've made and the experiences I've had here. I'm grateful for all of it. Lorraine finishes pouring the champagne and the melancholy I've been holding at bay begins to break through the barriers I thought I'd erected. Why does saying goodbye have to be so hard? She stands the empty bottle on the floor by our feet and joins the circle of our huddled bodies.

It's funny how life works. Whatever happens after this I know that I will be fine. I'm not the same girl I was when I left for training in forty-three. When I leave here tomorrow it will be with my newfound independence, renewed self-confidence and a wealth of new knowledge. My mother was right about it being my moment and no matter what I have no regrets.

We link arms and huddle a little closer. I start. "Where ever life takes you, whatever path you pursue or dream you follow," I begin searching each face, making eye contact one at a time, "Just know that I'll always be in your corner to cheer you on. I'm only a phone call away. I love every one of you crazy gals and I can't tell you how proud I am to call you friends. Oh, and you better write to me," I finish quickly before I start to cry.

We go around the circle and when we get to the last person Vera says through chattering teeth that she loves us and she's going to miss us, too. Then she says, "Okay, let's go back inside now. I'm turning into a human popsicle."

We make a bee line for the door. Deliberately though, I slow my pace so that I'm the last one off the roof. I take one last long lingering look. We had so many good times up here. We descend the stairs down to the first floor. We head inside Lorraine, Vera and Jean's place where it's warm and remove our coats.

Unwinding the scarf from around my neck I hear Lorraine saying, "Remember when we met Admiral Nimitz?" Tucking the scarf into the sleeve of my coat I smile at the memory. That had been a truly epic day. I hang my coat on the coat tree by the door before squeezing myself between Lorraine and Jean so I can sit with them on the couch.

"His visit to the Bureau that day was such a surprise," Jean says reminiscing.

"Now there is an understatement for you," Jane says coming into the room. She has an unopened bottle of champagne in her hands. She's just plundered the refrigerator. She gets comfortable on the floor joining us in conversation.

I can already tell that stories and memories are going to be shared late into the night. In order to set the story properly for you first recall that it was Nimitz who represented the United States when Japan formally surrendered last August aboard the USS Missouri while it was anchored in Tokyo Bay.

In our Navy circle October fifth was being referred to as 'Nimitz Day' because he was being given an award that evening by President Truman at the White House. What we didn't know was that while the esteemed Admiral was in town he would be making an impromptu visit to the Bureau building during the day. We were startled when someone came running into the office and yelled, "Look lively, Nimitz is in the building!" There was a momentary arc of panic before we jumped up out of our seats and ran into the hallway hoping to catch a glimpse of him.

I kid you not, the silver haired Admiral stopped to shake each hand. Up and down the corridors of the Bureau building he went. Can you imagine how that felt? I'm still having a hard time believing it actually happened. There was this living legend heavily decorated with medals and military awards all over his uniform and he was shaking my hand and thanking me for my service. It was surreal.

Reaching forward for a bowl on the coffee table I scoop a couple of crackers into my hand saying, "We had a lot of great times together."

Lorraine tugs me back into the couch, swipes a cracker from my stash and says, "Yeah, like Chinese Days." That makes me laugh. We took those Chinese conversation classes for a year. "I still don't have a working knowledge of the language," she adds. That, too makes me laugh because neither do I.

"I can tell you this much," Phyllis says while reaching into the bowl of crackers, "Thanksgiving will never have the same meaning for me again." She pops a cracker into her mouth. "Mm, this is good," she says around a mouthful.

"Nor for me," Jean agrees also reaching into the bowl. She stops and asks, "What kind of crackers are these?" She holds the golden round disc up for closer inspection.
"They're called Ritz," Vera says.
"I like them," Jean says then takes a bite. I

like them too actually. They have a buttery taste to them.

Knowing it would be our final Thanksgiving here we pulled together a feast fit for a king. Well, we did our best with what we could get at the stores. It was a potluck. We ate and played games. It was the day we openly acknowledged that we'd be separating soon. I can't remember who brought it up but by the end of that day there was an understanding between the six of us. Once a year we would spend a week together somewhere. We vowed to make it work.

Tucking her feet up underneath her, Vera who is sitting on the only chair in the room says, "How many cocktail parties did we go to between Thanksgiving and New Year's Eve?"

Jane pops the champagne bottle's cork saying, "More than I can count." Nodding I have to agree with Jane on that one. Extending the bottle she tops off Vera's glass.

"Thanks," Vera says bringing the fizzing glass to her lips. "That reminds me, Captain Knight's wife is still a pleasant woman to be around," she says obviously tongue in cheek.

"Mrs. Knight is a witch," Jean says and my eyes go wide. It is not like Jean to say a bad word about anyone. A bubble of laughter escapes

Lorraine and soon we are all laughing. Jean merely shrugs and says, "Sorry, I couldn't hold that back." Jean is so sweet that her chagrin about calling the Captain's wife a witch in front of us has us laughing even harder.

Catching her breath and holding onto her side Phyllis says, "That a girl Jean. Don't hold back. Say what's on your mind." So okay, there are some things and some people that I will not miss from here like Mrs. Knight for instance.

"Oh my gosh you guys, Christmas was fun," I say remembering how Jane, Phyllis and I dragged a tree for three blocks between the tree lot and home then up a flight of stairs. By the time we got to the apartment we were covered in needles and sap. Plus, it took a lot more effort to get it to stay upright in the stand.

Phyllis sits on the floor and extends her empty glass in Jane's direction. Without needing to be asked, Jane refills it for her. "Christmas was great," Phyllis agrees. The six of us stayed in town and celebrated the holidays together. It was as if we were on a mission to make the most of the few months we had left together.

"And New Year's Eve," I add.

Jane raises her glass as a gesture of approval. "Now that was fun," she says wistful making me wonder what she's thinking in that head of hers. There had been a lot to celebrate. The girls and I had gotten all dressed up and we went to a party at the Shoreham hotel. While we were there I kept remembering the days and nights I'd spent with Ben at the Shoreham when he'd first gotten back from overseas. I haven't seen him since but hope to soon.

"We danced all night," Vera says. We did dance all night. My feet were killing me the whole next day but it was worth it because we rang in nineteen forty-six enthusiastically. The war was over. There was so much to celebrate, so much to look forward to.

In the midst of all of our chatter and laughter the doorbell buzzes startling us. "Are we expecting company?" Vera asks getting up from her position on the chair.

"I don't think so," Lorraine says sitting forward.

Vera crosses the room to the front door and peers through the peep hole. Then she unlocks the door and swings it open. In come Dan and Tim. Jean tenses beside me for a brief moment but then relaxes again. If I hadn't been sitting so close to her I might not have noticed, but I did. I'm sure I did.

Taking off his coat Dan says, "I know there was a farewell thing for everybody at the office yesterday but Tim and I wanted to come over to see you ladies one more time before you head out tomorrow." I can't help noticing how Tim's eyes keep coming back to Jean. Dan folds his coat over the back of the couch.

Standing I say, "That was so thoughtful of you both." Rounding the table in front of the couch I make my way over to Dan to give him a good bye hug. The thing at the office was formal and stuffy and I'm glad that they've come over tonight. Dan and Tim are more than colleagues. They are friends, good friends.

"Take good care of yourself, Ellen. Let us know how you're doing from time to time," Dan tells me. "You know where you can find us. And if there's anything we can ever do for you all you have to do is ask."

Touched I tell him, "The same goes for you." Turning to Tim I say, "And for you," I give him an affectionate hug good bye. He gives me a brotherly pat on the back.

Pretty soon we're all hugging, it's a little ridiculous really but that's how it is with this group. Just the thought of not being around them anymore after tomorrow is devastating. I feel like I'm losing a limb that's how close we've all become.

Dan and Tim easily join in the conversations and the re-telling of stories, many of which they are hearing for the first time. We have them laughing for hours. A few times tonight I feel like crying but manage to stop myself in time. I just want to enjoy this moment with my friends. Don't cry, don't cry, I think reminding myself that we're all going to get together next year. This isn't the end of us. It is just a pause.

When we can no longer keep our eyes open, Dan and Tim head out and Phyllis, Jane and I go upstairs to bed. After three bottles of champagne and a few crackers we're a little wobbly on our feet. Climbing the stairs I'm grateful for the railing. The three of us are unusually quiet as we make our way up to the apartment we've shared for the past few years. After tomorrow this will no longer be my home.

"El?" Jane stops mid-flight and turns to

look at me.

"Yeah?" I say.

"Going to miss you a lot," she says. Unflappable Jane is tipsy tonight.

"Going to miss you, too," I say, less tipsy.

For once, Phyllis is quiet, no quips or sarcastic come backs are forthcoming from her. She passes us on her way up the stairs. As she does so she reaches out and squeezes my arm. Good byes can really sting.

CHAPTER TWENTY-EIGHT – BEN

Closing the car door I quickly jog from the driveway toward the house. The sun is behind the clouds and it is raining fairly hard. The wind almost knocks me over. Holding onto the railing I take the steps two at a time. When I'm under the cover of the porch of my parents' two-story brick colonial I remove my jacket and shake it out. After wiping my feet on the mat I turn the knob and let myself in. I hang my jacket on a hook in the entryway.

Bending down I rub Winston behind the ears. "Hey boy," I say happy to see him. "Did you miss me while I was at work?" He wags his tail letting me know that, yes he is happy that I am home from work. It turned out that my dog did remember me when I returned home from the war. He doesn't like to let me out of his sight now that I'm back.

"Ben is that you?" I hear my mother calling from the kitchen. I head there, Winston trailing behind me. The house is warm and I'm glad to be out of the elements. I'm staying with my parents until I get a place of my own. After being honorably discharged from the Army I came back here. It's been three weeks and I'm starting to settle back into life as a civilian.

I've resumed my job with the Illinois Division of Highways. It took a little time to adjust to being back at the Division but I'm starting to feel comfortable with my position and the responsibilities I've been given. Also, my salary as a civil engineer is much better than the pay I received as an Army Sergeant. That helps in the transition from soldier to civilian.

It's been good to see the familiar faces of old friends and colleagues. They welcomed me back like a returning hero, though I'm no such thing. I'm just a guy who served his country, did his best and made it back in one piece. There are thousands of guys like me who didn't. I'm just one of the lucky ones.

On my first day of work I sought out Ann.

I was glad to see she still works there. "Ben," she'd said hopping up out of her seat and rounding the desk to get to me. She grabbed hold of my arms and looked me over as if making sure I really was all in one piece. "Welcome home," she'd said throwing her arms around me.

Ann is close to my mother's age I suspect. She's a formidable woman not prone to letting her emotions get the best of her. Knowing this only made her display of affection that much more meaningful. "Thank you, Ann," I'd said and leaning closer lowered my voice and asked, "Any chance of you working with me again?"

She winked and said, "Let me see what I can do about that." The very next day, Ann was waiting for me outside my office. "Good morning, Mr. Rosenberg," she'd said in greeting, a hint of a smile evidently hovering around her mouth. She couldn't hide the fact that she was as happy as I was to be working together once more. We make a good team.

"Good morning," I'd said not even trying to hide my smile. Then quietly on the way into my office I said, "Thank you." Ever since, she's been instrumental in helping me get up to speed on everything I've forgotten since I've been gone, everything that has changed since I've been gone and a million other things in between. She's especially been helpful navigating new building codes. Being back at the office, doing what I was meant to do feels right. It's like putting on an old sweater that still fits.

Now I'm on the hunt for a place to live. Once that's settled I can go to New York and finally, finally ask Ellen to spend the rest of her life with me. The thought exhilarates me. Once and for all we'll put an end to the long distance between us.

I can't wait to make our relationship legal and permanent. I'll be the most fortunate of men when I can fall asleep beside her every night, holding her, touching her, knowing that her beautiful face will be the first thing I see when I open my eyes in the morning. I dream of giving her everything she could ever want.

I'm determined to be the kind of man she needs, the kind of man she wants beside her. I will love and cherish her with everything I have, everything I am. I already do. I am ready and more than willing to spend my life making her happy. Because, Ellen's happiness is all I want.

I'm anxious to get everything in place. At last, it feels like we can have it all she and I.

Tomorrow afternoon I have an appointment with a realtor to look at houses. I'm looking for a house with at least three bedrooms. For a moment I allow myself to picture the children we'll have, the children who will fill those bedrooms. The thought makes me catch my breath. Ellen will be a wonderful mother.

"Hey Mom," I say entering the kitchen finding my mother at the counter chopping vegetables. It's strange living with my parents again. I've been on my own since I left for college years ago. Even though I'm practically climbing the walls ready to move into my own house, there's no denying it's been great eating my mom's home cooking every night.

Also, I wonder how Winston will react in a new environment. He's been living here with Gabby and my parents these past few years while I've been gone. He's used to them and this house. It might take some time for him to get used to a new house. Plus, by then Ellen will be here. I clock a look at my dog. "You're going to love her," I whisper to him. He tilts his head looking up at me and barks. "Just you wait and see," I tell him.

Reaching for a carrot slice while simultaneously kissing my mother's cheek I ask, "How was your day?" Peeling another carrot my mother smiles up at me and tells me that she had a good day. I then ask, "How is dad feeling?"

My father was diagnosed with a weak heart while I was overseas. Imagine the shock of coming home and finding him weak and frail, not at all how he was before I left. I'd demanded to know why nobody wrote to tell me about his condition, "Because he didn't want you to worry about him while you were over there. You had enough on your plate," my mother had said voice hushed so my father wouldn't over hear us from the other room.

Later that night after our parents had gone to bed, my sister came to my room. She knocked on the door and when I opened it she said, "Can I come in?" Pushing the door further open I stepped back and let her enter. "I wanted to tell you about Dad," she'd said. "I thought you deserved to know, but they made me promise not to tell you." I stood there in my old bedroom arms crossed. "They didn't want you to worry. They were worried enough about you."

I pulled her into a hug when she started to cry. I don't like when women cry. I wanted to cry. "We were so worried about you, Ben. When you were overseas, all we could think about was you and if you were okay. Don't be mad at them or mad at me."

"I'm not mad, Gabby. Don't cry. I'm not mad at you," I said quietly. It's true, I wasn't mad. I was frustrated and I was out of sorts. It was hard to put my feelings into words. I'd been through hell and back and I'd come home to find my father in poor health. I'd felt cheated somehow. I was restless and I felt helpless.

Gabby and I stayed up late into the night talking. She listened while I told her about my time in the Army. I was careful about what and how much I told her. There are things I saw and did in battle that I will never tell anyone. Things I want to forget. There are things that are better left unsaid. War is ugly business.

I told her about Ellen. She was happy for me. "I can't wait to meet her," she said. Because of our age difference Gabby and I hadn't ever really had a heart to heart before. It was nice and I'm glad we're getting to know each other better. My little sister grew up while I was away. I look forward to spending more time with her.

Now, she and I make a point to talk as often as we can. She's a great person, my sister. She wants to become a librarian. I like that she and Ellen will have a lot to talk about when Ellen moves to Peoria. They both love books. I'm sure

they will become fast friends. Or at least, I hope
they will.

"Today was a good day for your father,"
my mother says scraping the chopped vegetables
off the cutting board and into a cast iron frying
pan. She adds some oil and turns up the flame on
the stove. With a flat wooden spatula she moves
the colorful medley around the pan. She sprinkles
some kosher salt over top and stirs again. A
sizzle and hiss accompany the aroma of sautéing
onions, carrots and peppers. "He's in the living
room. Why don't you go visit with him before
dinner?"

"I'd like that," I say watching as Winston
nudges my mother's leg with his nose. I open a
cabinet and pull out a box of dog biscuits. "Come
on boy, let's go in the living room," I say holding
the biscuit in my hand for Winston to see.
He immediately abandons my mother's side and
comes bounding over to me tail wagging, tongue
hanging out of his mouth. He's predictable, this
one.

As I turn to leave my mother stops me.
"Wait a second,"
"Yes?" I ask.
She points the wooden spatula toward
the counter behind me. The pan on the stove

continues to sizzle. "There's a letter for you. It came today in the mail."

Turning, toward the counter I see a letter from Ellen. I pick it up, happy to have word from her. She's in New York and I'm curious to know how she's doing. Is she transitioning back to civilian life well? What is she doing? How is she spending her time? Does she miss me as much as I miss her?

I miss her so much it hurts. I can't wait until I can go to her. I just need to settle a few more things here first. I smile thinking about the next time I'll see her. As much as she's told me about her family I feel like I know them already. I'm looking forward to meeting them in person. I plan to ask her brother for permission to marry his sister. I figure it's the right thing to do. I always want to do the right thing for Ellen.

"Why are you still in touch with that woman?" My mother asks voice low and my smile is gone. I don't like the way she's just referred to Ellen as 'that woman.'

"Her name is Ellen," I say.
"Ben, she's not Jewish," my mother says like it's her duty to remind me that Ellen is not the same religion as we are.

"I know that," I say.

"Stop writing to her," she says pointing the spatula at me. She doesn't raise her voice. My mother never yells. She rarely raises her voice.

"Why would you say that to me?" I ask meeting her eyes and squaring my shoulders ready to defend Ellen. I don't want to argue. But, I can't let my mom think she can tell me what to do especially not about this.

"Because Ben, you can't keep seeing her," she says matter of fact.

I let the silence hang in the air between us for a moment. "I will keep seeing her," I say defiantly. Then shrugging my shoulders I say, "I love her. I don't care what religion she is or isn't. That doesn't matter to me." It is as simple as that.

"Don't be ridiculous," she says sighing wearily like the weight of the world rests on her shoulders. She softens and says, "Ben, I'm sure Ellen is a nice girl and maybe you fell in love with her during the war. That's understandable, but you're home now. I'm sure you can find a nice way to let her know that what you had is over."

Dumbfounded I stand rooted to the floor, it's like she hasn't listened to a word I've said. I need my mother to understand that what Ellen and I have is not some trite wartime romance that can easily be ended with a few nicely written words. "Mom," I begin. It's my turn to sigh. "I have no intention of ending anything with Ellen." Before my mom can interrupt I raise my hand stopping her next words. "Just listen to me, please," I say keeping my calm, "I'm going to ask her to marry me."

Gasping, shocked my mom hisses, "Benjamin Rosenberg, you will not marry that woman."

"I will, if she'll have me," I say adamant about it.

"You will not." She also is adamant. "You will not marry her," she says with finality turning away from me and jabbing the spatula in the pan on the stove. I've been dismissed.

I watch her vigorously move that spatula around the pan. "Mom," I cautiously start to say, "I'm not a little boy anymore. You can't tell me what to do or what not to do."

After a minute of stony silence I decide it's best to let the subject drop for now. I leave the kitchen. I know this isn't over, not by a long shot but with my father's poor health I'm willing to give my mom a pass. I'm sure she'll get over whatever reservations she has about Ellen. I know that when she finally meets her, Ellen will win my mom over.

Leaving the kitchen, I head toward the living room. Rounding the corner I catch sight of my dad. He's where he usually is this time of day. He's sitting in his chair. A blanket covers his lap. He's looking out the window. The rain is still coming down. The wind whips against the side of the house. "It's nasty out there," I say coming into the room. Lowering myself into the arm chair across from my dad's I pat his knee. "Hey Dad," I say.

I notice how pale his skin looks. He needs more sun I think. Being cooped up in the house can't be good for him. "Hello son," he says. He's happy to see me. "Tell me something interesting that happened today." It's something he always says. For as long as I can remember he would ask me the same question.

I settle into the chair. "Let me think," I say. I take a second before I begin to tell my dad about a new project I'm working on. We're trying to come up with a solution for the high volume of traffic downtown. Something I say prompts him to share a few stories from his working years.

I love talking to my dad like this. I love when he shares bits and pieces of his life that

I didn't know before. It makes me feel closer to him. I sit and let him talk, soaking up the stories he chooses to share. In my mind I can picture a younger version of my dad in each scenario. Then he changes topic and says, "Let's take in a game this year, just the two of us like old times."

When I was overseas shivering in the cold snow waiting for the German tanks to come thundering through the forest I would think how if I made it back home one of the things I would do is take my dad to a Cub's game. Taking in a game at Wrigley Field with my dad was the pinnacle of my childhood. I'd bring my glove hoping to catch a fly ball. We'd eat Nathan's hot dogs. He'd order me a root beer and he'd get a real beer. Sometimes, he'd let me have a sip from his cup. I had to promise not to tell my mom. I never told. Those trips were sacred.

My dad was always patient with me. I would get so excited when we got to the stadium. Over the years the field changed and we were a part of it. We went to a game together the summer before I was drafted. It was the last time we'd been. By then the brick outfield wall was covered in ivy and the old wooden bleachers were replaced with concrete ones.

When I was a kid my dad would explain

the rules of the game to me. He pointed out what was happening on the field. He told me that there were people inside the forest green scoreboard who changed out steel plates for every run and score. That fact always fascinated me. It sort of still does. We'd go to at least one game every summer. My dad would take a day off of work to spend the day with me. Then, on the three hour drive home we would discuss the game and the players and any bad calls made by the umpire.

It's because of him I love baseball. I had thought that if I was lucky enough one day to have a son of my own that when he was old enough my dad and I could take him to Wrigley together. My dad would teach my son the rules of the game, just as patiently as he had taught me. The three of us would toss the ball in the yard. We would discuss the plays and terrible calls during the long rides home.

Sadly, according to his doctors my dad won't be doing those kinds of things anymore. His heart isn't strong enough they say. While I'm troubled by his condition, I'm relieved he's still with us. I'm not ready to lose him. I just got back. We can listen to Cubs games on the radio. For now, it's day by day. "Sure," I say, "I'd like that." I don't have the heart to tell him there will be no more treks to Chicago for him. "Spring training is just around the corner," I add.

Over dinner, across the dining room table my mother won't look at me. If my father notices, he chooses not to mention it. Aside from that, the meal is pleasant. Gabby is not eating with us tonight. She is out with some of her friends. Later, when she gets home I will fill her in on the conversation I had with our mother earlier about Ellen. I'm sure Gabby will take my side.

When everyone is finished I get up from the table, bring the plates into the kitchen and place them in the sink. I help my father back to the living room and into his chair. Spreading the blanket over his legs I ask, "Do you need anything?" He shakes his head. "Okay, I'll come back to help you up to bed when you're ready."

I kiss the top of his head and straightening up say, "Love you, Dad." Then I make my way up the stairs. Closing the door I turn and walk into the bedroom. Leaning against the desk I reach into my pocket and pull out the letter from Ellen. I've been dying to read it since I saw it sitting on the counter earlier.

Just as I'm separating the folded pieces of stationary from the envelope I hear my mom yelling, "Ben, come down here quickly!"

For a second I am frozen, unable to move.

My mother never yells. Ellen's letter falls from my hands. I can't stop to pick it up so I leave it where it lands on the floor. Opening the door I run toward the stairs.

At the bottom of the stairs I find my father slumped in his chair. Please no, please no I say over and over in my head. Please. I check for a pulse. I can't find one. "Dad," I say kneeling in front of his chair. No response. "Dad," I say again a little louder, again nothing. I hang my head. There is nothing to be done.

Getting to my feet slowly I go to my mother. "He's gone," I say gently reaching for her. It's barely more than a whisper really. I can't find my voice. Wrapping her in my arms I hold her and she cries. Numbness settles over my body. I'm not ready for this. He was too young to die. There is still so much I have to learn from him.

CHAPTER TWENTY-NINE – ELLEN

Since I've been home I've dragged my mother and sister through countless museums and book stores. In turn, Bess has dragged me through Macy's, Saks Fifth Avenue and Bloomingdales. Now that my sister is a professional working woman she insists on shopping at these fine establishments. I've enjoyed every single minute with her.

I feel as though there are years of missed opportunities to bond with my sister to make up for. Plus, it's there in the back of my mind the notion that I'll be leaving her again. This time, at least I know where I'll be heading. Though I've never been to Peoria Ben has told me much about his city. The mere thought of seeing Ben again makes me swoon. I love that man and I can't wait to be with him.

During our shopping excursions I let my baby sister pull me along from department to department. Bess is fun to shop with. She's helped me craft my own wardrobe. "We need to get you outfitted for civilian life, El," my sister told me on my third day home. I was wearing a dress I'd pulled from my closet one that admittedly, was several years old, a little worn and regrettably out of style.

In my defense, I've been in uniform for the last so many years and hadn't found the need for new clothes. Now however, faced with the prospect of wearing something new, pretty and stylish I am a willing participant in Bess' plans to pad my wardrobe. So whenever she suggests we go shopping, I agree. Plus, I enjoy the quality time I get to spend with her.

The past two Sundays after church service Eduardo drove Bess, my mother and me out to Long Island. Bill, Gladys and the children live in Hicksville. They bought a house there and I was eager to see it. My nephews have grown into little men with big personalities. I couldn't wait to see them. They are much taller than the last time I saw them. They are bright and sweet and funny.

"Let me see her," I'd said that first Sunday about my little niece, Susan. The newest edition to the family is beautiful, so tiny and so perfect. She's three months old. I was sorry I couldn't be here when she was born. It's a reminder of so much that I missed when I was away. Gladys handed the little pink bundle to me and my heart constricted. "She's perfect," I'd said. I am so very happy for my brother.

Today, as I walk toward Bess and Eduardo's apartment a breeze ruffles the hem of my new dress. Six months ago they moved out of our family's apartment and into one of their own. They were able to do so when Bess finished graduate school and started working for a private practice. I'm bursting with pride that my sister is a doctor of psychology.

Due to doctor patient confidentiality which she takes very seriously she can't tell us that much about her work and what she does. But, she could say that the office where she works caters to New York's social elite. I leave it up to my imagination as to who comes to see my sister the psychologist.

Thankfully for me their new apartment is just a stone's throw away, literally. I can see their building from my bedroom. Bess and Eduardo come over for dinner quite a lot. Some nights after we eat they stay to play cards or dominoes or board games. Eduardo is still good at Monopoly. Some things never change.

The heels of my Mary Janes click clack over the concrete sidewalk. With a hand I smooth the skirt of my smart new dress to prevent it from rising whenever a breeze blows. Not wearing a uniform is taking a little getting used to. I'd be wearing the blue wool now and the whites would be brought out in another month.

For a second I am lost in a memory of life in the Navy. A small smile tilts the corners of my red stained lips as I think of my friends. I still wear the Victory Red lipstick Phyllis suggested. It's a connection to them, one that I want to keep. I miss those girls, all of them. We've been good about keeping in touch. I'll write to them again soon.

Today though, Bess and I are going to see a Saturday matinee show, just the two of us. The Pirates of Penzance is playing at the New Century Theatre. We've been talking about seeing a Broadway show for a while in fact it was the subject of several letter exchanges between us last year. We knew that when I came home she and I would make sure to get tickets. We thought this one would be perfect.

I climb the steps to their third floor walkup and knock on the door. "You look so pretty," Bess gushes after opening the door. "That dress is perfect for you." She would say so, she picked it out. Right here in the hallway I do a slow spin so she can see the whole thing. Initially, I was drawn to the pattern, a dark blue and emerald green plaid. I especially like the gathered shoulders, v neck line and large bow at the cut of the v. The dress is belted at the waist and looks quite sophisticated if I do say so myself.

She steps back allowing me to enter the apartment. I step inside and Eduardo comes to greet me saying, "How are you, Ellen?"

"I'm well, Eduardo," I tell him, "Thank you for letting me borrow Bess today," I say lightly.

"She is happy to have her sister home," he says of Bess kissing the top of my head affectionately. "I like when my wife is happy."

Bess smiles saying, "I am glad to have my sister home." Grabbing her purse she turns to me, "Ready to go?"

We hail a cab to take us to the theatre. It drops us off in front. Once inside we find our seats. "I've been looking forward to watching this show with you all week," Bess says.

"Me too," I tell her. Taking her hand I give it a light squeeze, "Me too." When the lights begin to dim over the audience we turn our full attention to the stage. The pit orchestra begins to play and the curtain rises. I love the theater.

After the show Bess and I make our way on foot toward Times Square. As we walk Bess is caught up in her own personal monologue dissecting the costumes, the music, the plot and much more about the Pirates. She has a lot to say it's hard to get a word in edge wise. I finally find an in and interrupt her, "Let's eat at the Horn & Hardart Automat."

"You read my mind," she says excitedly before falling right back into what she'd been saying, something about the set design this time. She finishes her commentary as we draw nearer to the restaurant. The two story façade is impressive with its stained glass windows. The Automat is a fun place to eat, trust me.

Bess takes hold of the handle and opens the door. Inside I stop to take it all in, the aromas, the sounds, the sights. "I've missed this place," I tell her a bit wistful. There are people moving all about. This place is a New York staple and I've been dying to come back here. "Thanks for this," I say to Bess.

"Anytime," she says and I know she means it. She loves this place as much as I do. "Come on," she says pulling me by the arm toward the cashier's stand in the middle of the restaurant. At the stand we can exchange dollar bills for nickels.

Why are we exchanging dollars for nickels you might ask? That is a very good question. See, the food is behind little glass windows. Each single serving plate requires at least one nickel. You drop your coin into the coin slot, turn the handle and lift the little glass window. There you have it. There are walls and walls of options to choose from. Anything you could possibly want to eat can be had here.

Armed with a pocketful of nickels Bess and I each grab a cafeteria style tray. For a second or two we stand rooted to the floor feeling slightly overwhelmed. I turn in a slow circle trying to decide where to start. At the far end of the restaurant there is a carving station. There is a beverage station as well.

"What are you thinking?" Bess asks wide eyed.

"It's so hard to choose," I tell her. We share a smile and I say conspiratorially, "This is going to be fun."

When I say this, Bess nods. "Okay," she says, "Meet you at a table."

We split up. I peruse one wall of little glass windows. When I find something I want I stop to place a nickel into the coin slot. Turning the little knob the window pops open. Reaching inside I pull out a small plate of steaming mashed potatoes with gravy. It smells heavenly. My stomach rumbles.

I take a few more steps and repeat the action adding a small plate of meatloaf to my tray. This is fun. I do it again this time opting for a small salad. I think this is enough for now so I turn to scan the room. I find my sister already seated at a table by a window. Leave it to Bess to get the best seat in the house.

Approaching the table tray in hand I notice the large illuminated Pepsi-Cola sign vibrating with color outside in the square. Placing my tray on the table I slide into the booth across from her. "How did you get a table by the window?" I ask opening my napkin and laying it across my lap.

"It was pure luck," she says, "Along with a bit of good timing."

"Well done you," I say impressed. I'm about to say something else when I notice someone in the restaurant. It's someone that I haven't seen in a very long time. It's someone I hadn't expected to ever see again.

Bess follows my gaze. "That's George Evans over there isn't it?"

It is George. I'm surprised to see him in New York. He left the City and moved back to Newport after college. Nodding slowly I say, "Yes, that's him." Curious, I wonder what he's doing back here. Not that it's any of my business. We went our separate ways years ago.

"When was the last time you saw him?" It's as if my sister can read my mind.

Pausing for a second I have to think about it. "It has to be at least seven years I think, maybe longer."

As she and I try to remember how long it's been since I last saw my college boyfriend, we are totally unaware that he has spotted us and is approaching. "Hello," he says. I look up. He's right there. "Ellen, it's been a long time. How have you been?"

Rising from the table I stand to say hello. There are no hard feelings between us. We parted amicably. George was my first serious relationship. There was a time I thought we would get married. But, that was a long time ago. We were young.

"Hello," I say taking in his appearance. He's a little older now. His dark blonde hair is parted to one side. He no longer wears it parted in the middle and slicked back. I forgot how striking his green eyes are. "I'm well, thank you." I say politely, "And you?"

George and I met in the fall of our junior year at Columbia. Back then I spent a lot of time in the library reading and studying. One Friday afternoon in October he approached the table where I was sitting. I didn't notice him at first because I was engrossed in what I was reading at the time. Funny, I can't even remember what that was now. "May I sit here?" he'd asked. Nodding, I'd said yes.

He pulled out the chair across from me and sat down. I went back to reading. A few minutes later I looked up to find him watching me. He was just sitting there, watching. Closing the book I'd said, "Yes?" I thought maybe he was looking for a tutor. I made extra money tutoring classmates.

"Hi," he said and smiled.
"Hi," I said smiling back at him. He was cute.

"I'm George," he said, "George Evans."

"Ellen Cunningham," I gave him my name.

"It's very nice to meet you, Ellen Cunningham," he'd said.

"It's very nice to meet you, too George Evans," I'd said.

George Evans turned out to be very charming. He asked me to have a drink with him and that drink turned into dinner. Like a gentleman he made sure I got home safe and he asked if he could see me again. We dated for two years.

"I'm doing well," he says cheerily.

"You remember my sister Bess," I say. She is standing beside me. I hadn't realized that she got up from the table.

"It's good to see you again, Bess," George says and it sounds sincere. Then turning his attention back to me he says, "Wow, Ellen I can't believe I ran into you like this."

Not exactly sure how to respond to that I give him a small smile, "Me neither. I thought you were in Newport," I say lamely.

"I was," he says, "For a few years after college. Then, I joined the Navy during the war." He pauses. I had no idea. "When I got out I realized that New York is where I wanted to be," he explains, "So, I moved back."

"You were in the Navy," I say. "I was in the Navy. I just got home a few weeks ago." He doesn't say anything in reply. He looks at me and then gives a slight nod. That's it but something passes silently between us. There is a shared understanding, unspoken but it's there nonetheless.

Bess clears her throat, "I'll be right back." She walks away from the table. I can see she is heading toward the beverage station. She might be thirsty, but I wouldn't put money on it.

George looks down at his shoes. I follow his gaze. They are very nice shoes, shiny leather exquisite stitching detail. "Would it be okay if I called on you?" he says raising his gaze to me.

Oh George, I think. You are seven years too late. I give him a small smile but I think it must come out a little sad because his face falls. "I'm sorry, George. There is someone else."

His gaze flies to my left hand. He looks me in the eye. "You're not wearing a ring," he says.

"It's just a matter of time," I say quietly.

He's been holding his hat in his hands this whole time. Now he fidgets with the brim. "I'm happy for you Ellen, truly. Give my best to your sister, will you?"

Nodding slowly I say, "I will. Take care of yourself, George."

"You too," he says and turns to go. He stops himself. Looking over his shoulder at me he says, "Whoever he is, he's a lucky guy." Placing his hat on his head he walks out the door.

When he is gone, Bess returns to the table carrying two glasses of iced tea. "Here you go," she says placing one on the table for me. We slide back into our seats. The entire exchange with George couldn't have lasted more than six or seven minutes but it has left me rattled. "He's still handsome," Bess says cutting into the piece of roasted chicken on her tray.

"I hadn't noticed," I say digging my fork into the salad.

Wordlessly, Bess balls a paper napkin and throws it at me hitting me with it. "Liar," she says with a smirk.

I shrug. "He's not Ben."

We tuck into our food. We people watch. It is amazing how many different walks of life there are in this city and every one of them come to the Automat. We eat every last bite. "Are you getting dessert?" I ask.

"What do you think?" my sister says answering to my dumb question with a question.

Laughing, we rise from the table and carry

our trays to the window wall of confections. There are all manner of desserts to be had. There are numerous kinds of cakes, puddings, cookies and pies all waiting for us behind little glass windows. They beckon us forward. We are unable to resist.

As I slide a nickel into the coin slot and turn the knob to lift the window I replay the interaction with George. Running into him today was the last thing I expected. He was in the Navy. I'm glad he made it home.

Grabbing a fork from the counter I place it on my tray beside the slice of blueberry pie I selected. Picking up the tray and carrying it I head toward the coffee bar. Bess is right behind me. Over my shoulder I look to see what she picked, apple pie a la mode.

"The advertisements for the Horn & Hardart claim they serve some of the best coffee in New York," I say positioning a ceramic cup under the dolphin shaped spout of the coffee urn. Sliding a nickel into the coin slot I turn the lever. First, a measure of cream is dispensed into the bottom of the cup. Like a child I delight in the process.

Next the precise amount of black coffee

comes flowing out of the spout. Somehow the machine knows when to stop. I wait as Bess takes her turn. Dining at the Automat is an experience. One I am thoroughly enjoying.

We carry our dessert and coffee back to the table. After the first sip I say, "The ads weren't lying. This is good coffee, seriously." I am pleasantly surprised. Coffee is a luxury I missed during the wartime rationing.

Nodding Bess says, "That's because every twenty minutes they brew fresh coffee and pour out the old stuff."

"How do you know that?" I challenge my little miss know it all sister whom I adore.

"Everyone knows that," she says.

"I didn't know that," I say.

"Well now you do," she smiles indulgently at me. Lowering her cup to its saucer and fixing her eyes on me she says. "I've missed you. I hate that you're going to leave me again."

"If it helps," I say, "I wouldn't leave you for anyone in the whole wide world other than Ben. Bess, he's such a good guy. I can't wait for you to meet him. I'm so in love with him. I've never felt this way before. He's the one, you know?"

Tilting her head she eyes me. "I know," she

says. She does. She has Eduardo. "You know I'm happy for you. I just wish you didn't have to go so far away."

"I'll come visit every chance I get, I promise," I say meaning it, "And you'll come to Peoria."

CHAPTER THIRTY -BEN

I still can't believe my father is gone. The doctor said his heart stopped working, just stopped. I'm trying to keep it together as much for my sake as for my mother and sister's. They've been depending on me to take care of the things my father used to. Not to mention the deep sadness that has fallen over the house.

We lost him four and a half months ago yet I still find myself thinking that I need to tell him what happened at work on any given day or I want to get his opinion about something or other. Then I remember that I can't. I'll never again get to ask his opinion or get his advice. "Hey dad, what would you do if you were in my shoes?" I could really use his advice right about now.

Since that night I went running down the stairs to find him lifeless it feels as if someone or something has snatched the rug right out from under me. There is so much that must be done. I'm learning as I go. My mother, Gabby and I met with the attorney. Thankfully, my father had the forethought to make provisions for his family. Financially, my mother and sister will be fine. Emotionally, it's been a tough road. My dad was the anchor for our family.

Needless to say, I did not move into my own place. My plan to buy a house for Ellen is on hold. In fact, everything, all of my plans have been on hold and I don't know for how long that will continue. Ellen is supportive, as much as she can be from New York. She wanted to come out here when I told her about what happened. I wanted her to come. I wanted her to be here with me so badly but I told her no, to stay there. I could hear the hurt in her voice. I was grateful when she didn't argue though.

I couldn't tell her then why it wasn't a good idea for her to come to Peoria. How do you tell the person you love that your mother doesn't want to meet her? Under the circumstances I felt it would best if Ellen remained in New York for the time being. My mother is grieving. Respectfully, I need to give her time before I can bring Ellen here.

Ellen and I talk on the telephone once a week. I don't care what it costs. It's worth it.

On Wednesdays Gabby takes our mother out for dinner. Gabby thinks it's good for her to get out of the house. She uses the time to encourage our mother to do things that will make her feel better. Sadly, our mother has not been herself.

When they are out I call to talk to Ellen. I look forward to those phone calls. At times Ellen's voice is the only thing that keeps me sane. "I'll be there as soon as I can," I'd told her that first phone call.

"I know, I'll be here waiting," she'd said, "I'm not going anywhere until you get here."

"You're amazing, do you know that?" I'd said.

She is amazing. The problem is for how much longer will she be willing to wait? Last night when we talked I didn't mention my coming to New York. She writes. There's a letter in the post from Ellen at least once a week. I've enlisted Gabby's help in getting the mail before our mother can.

My mom is still very much decidedly against the idea of my marrying Ellen so I keep her letters in a drawer at work. The last thing I need is for my mom to find more letters from Ellen. She's still grieving. I'm holding out hope that eventually she'll come around. Stranger things have happened.

Quietly closing the door behind me, I pull a sweatshirt on over my white cotton undershirt then bend down to lace up my Converse sneakers. The air is cool and crisp this morning. I descend the front steps heading toward the street. On the asphalt I set off starting out at an easy jog.

I feel the wind on my face. At the end of the street I turn right and keep going. It is still dark outside. The street lamps glow, lighting the way. There is no one else around. I am alone. Picking up the pace I press on. Clearing my mind I run and run and run.

Ignoring the burn in my lungs I push myself hoping the physical exertion will distract me from the heavy thoughts that weigh me down most days. Following a curve in the road I pump my legs and arms concentrating on my breathing, in and out, in and out. My lungs expand and contract. I run for miles, concentrating only on my breathing and where I am going.

Eventually, the street lamps shut off and the sun makes an appearance. Only then do I slow my speed. Hunching over I brace my hands on my knees gulping in air. I've pushed myself hard. The ache in my side is a sharp knife. Standing I clasp my hands behind my head, regulating my breaths taking a few steps.

As my heart rate slows and begins to return to normal I run my hands through my sweat dampened hair. There is activity in the neighborhood. A dog barks. A newspaper boy rides by on his bicycle. A screen door slams. It is time to turn around and head back toward home.

The momentary peace I felt earlier is gone. As I backtrack toward the house I can no longer keep the heavy thoughts at bay. I'm all torn up inside. I miss my dad. I feel sorry for my mom. I miss Ellen. If things were different Ellen would in all likelihood already be here. We'd be married, working on starting our family. Instead, we remain thousands of miles apart.

If only I could forget the responsibilities I have here and just leave. I could go to New York. I could marry Ellen. I would go to her in a heartbeat if I could. I can't though. What would she think of me if I walked out on my mom and my sister and my responsibilities when they need me most? I don't have it in me to do that and I think Ellen would be disappointed in me if I did.

Does it make me selfish for wanting to? I think it makes me human. I've never walked away from my responsibilities before and I won't this time either. Gabby shouldn't have to be solely responsible for caring for our mother. What I didn't say earlier is that getting our mother out of the house on Wednesday evenings is an ordeal. She fights Gabby on this. My mother sits at home all the time. The thing is she wants us to sit at home with her.

Gabby tries to cheer her up, to make her see that she needs to keep living. "Dad wouldn't want you to be like this," she often tells our mother. Gabby usually says this when she's trying to get her to eat something or to change out of her house coat and into something else. She lets the phone ring not bothering to answer it not caring to know who is calling the house. She spends a lot of time in my father's chair staring out the window.

Gabby and I have talked about what we can do to help. We spend a lot of time at home. Gabby has pulled away from her friends to be with our mom more often. I'm home after work. I've declined numerous invitations to go to the bar for drinks after work on an odd Friday with coworkers. They don't ask anymore. The offer is always open they say, when I'm able to join them that is.

"Why do you need your own house?" my mother asks whenever I bring up contacting the realtor. "This is your home. You live here with us."

"Mom, we've talked about it," I usually say something along these lines, "When I get married I won't be living here."

"You're right, Ben you should start dating again. You need to meet a nice Jewish girl, that would make me happy," she always says. She is so stubborn.

As soon as I say, "Mom, I'm going to marry Ellen," she shuts down and the conversation is over as far as she is concerned.

As I run I can see my street getting closer with each step. The idea of going back inside that house holds no appeal. But, I need to shower and dress before work. So I pick up the pace. On the porch I pull my sweatshirt over my head and toe off my Converse. Carrying them inside I'm greeted by Winston.

Patting him on his back I say, "Good boy." He follows me down the hall toward the kitchen. There I open the back door letting him into the yard. After filling his food bowl I rinse out the other and fill it with fresh water. Then I open the door and call him back inside. As he eats, I head upstairs to shower and get ready for work.

The future looked so promising only a few months ago. Now, things look bleak. Speaking of bleak, for the past few weeks there has been something I've been trying to work out in my head. This morning on my run I've made a decision as to what to do.

Throughout the day my mind has not been on my work as it should. If it wasn't for Ann I would have missed my afternoon meeting. She had to remind me that I needed to be in the conference room at three o'clock. Grabbing my suit jacket off the back of my chair I pulled it on straightening it on my way down the hall toward the meeting room.

Eying the clock on the wall I rub my jaw. Everyone has left for the night. I told Ann that I was going to stay a while and for her to head home. I would see her in the morning. The office is quiet now except for the sound of a broom brushing against the linoleum floor as the night janitor sweeps outside my office.

Inhaling a deep cleansing breath I close the door to my office. I want privacy for what I'm about to do. Sinking into my chair I reach for the phone on my desk. I've thought about this so many times. I've tried to come up with a solution, one that would work for all parties involved.

I dial the New York number I know by heart then wait for an answer. Today is Monday. I didn't want to wait until Wednesday for this. Ellen is not expecting a call from me tonight so I don't know if she'll be home. It's seven o'clock where she is. She might be home.

My throat goes tight and for a moment I can't breathe. It's going on the third ring. Maybe no one is at home. As I am about to hang up, someone answers the phone, "Cunningham residence." It's Ellen.

I freeze, unsure about what I'm doing.
"Hello?" she says "Who is this?"
Finally, I find my voice. "Ellen," as I say her name, the backs of my eyes sting with unshed tears. "It's me."

"Ben," I track the concern in her voice, "Is everything alright? You don't sound like yourself. What is it? What can I do?"
Leave it to Ellen to want to help. There is nothing she can do to help me though. It is up to me to do the right thing for her now.

Before my courage falters I say, "I'm so sorry, Ellen. I'm not coming to New York." This is the hardest phone call I've ever had to make.

"I know, Ben. It's okay. I can wait until you're ready," she says.

"That's just it," I say, "You have waited long enough already. I won't do this to you anymore," I say. Then stealing myself, "I won't be coming to New York at all."

I can't keep Ellen waiting on me for forever. It's not fair to her. I can't leave my mother or my sister. I can't have Ellen come here. I would never ask her to leave her family and everything that is familiar to her in order to come to Peoria only to be mistreated by my mother. She deserves more than to be caught in the middle of my family's problems.

Over time Ellen would resent me for taking her away from New York and putting her in the middle of an unpleasant situation. She deserves more than what little time I could give her. She deserves to be welcomed in and made a part of the family.

I get it all out. I say everything I need to say explaining everything the best way I know how wondering if she will hate me after she knows the whole truth. "I'm so sorry. I can't give you what you deserve. I can't leave my mother or my sister and you shouldn't leave yours. It's not fair for you to keep waiting on me."

She tries to stop me. "Listen to me, Ellen," I say. "It has to be this way."

"It doesn't have to be this way," she tries to reason with me. "We can figure something out."

"It's better this way, for you," I say.

"No, it's not," she says. "Ben, please."

I take a deep shuddering breath and selfishly ask, "Please don't hate me."

"I could never," she says sadness clouding her voice.

"Forget me," I say. "Be happy, Ellen. I'll be okay if I know you're happy." I choke on the words wanting desperately for things to be different. I grasp the hard edge of the desk like it's a life preserver. I am drowning. "Good bye."

The moment I get the receiver in its cradle I bend at the waist. Covering my face with my hands I let myself cry. I am wrecked over what I've just done.

CHAPTER THIRTY-ONE – ELLEN

Have you ever been so heart sick it literally is a physical ache? Right here in the center of my chest it hurts. "Ellen," my mother sticks her head into my room, "Eduardo and Bess are out front. Are you ready yet?"

"Yes, coming," I say stepping into a pair of sandals. Earlier this week, Bess suggested we spend the last Saturday in August at the beach. Bill and Gladys loved the idea stating the children would love it, too. So, it's the last Saturday of the month and we are going to the beach. My brother and his family will meet us there.

Following my mother out of the apartment we walk down the stairs and out the door. Bess is already in the back seat so that mother may sit up front. I open the door and slide in beside my sister. I offer her a small smile to let her know that I'm doing okay this morning. I don't know what I would do without Bess. I joke that I'm her pro bono patient. In all seriousness, being able to talk to her about my break up with Ben and how I'm feeling has been helpful.

Eduardo puts the car in drive and we pull away from the curb. I look out the window at the passing apartment buildings and store fronts. As my sister and mother discuss a recipe they both tried this week I continue to stare out the window. It still stings, the idea that Ben thinks I can forget him. What must he have been thinking to say something so ridiculous? As if I could ever forget him. It's an impossible request.

Putting the pieces of my shattered heart back together is a work in progress. Bess says that with time the hurt will lessen. I wish I could be angry with Ben. Maybe, if I were angry with him I would feel better. But, I can't be angry with him not really. I know he has to be hurting, too. I know he loved me. I know he did because I loved him. I do love him.

I am angry. I'm angry at the situation. I'm angry and I'm sad. I'm sad for Ben. There is so much pressure on him to fill his father's shoes, to carry the burdens of his family. I'm sad for me. I'm sad for the dreams that won't come true. I'm devastated knowing he's out there but that we aren't together. I miss him so much it hurts.

I've been in a fog for months. I cried myself to sleep for weeks after Ben called to tell me he wasn't coming to New York, that he was ending things between us. Sometimes when I think no one is around I cry over what is lost. I would have kept waiting. I would have. Why wouldn't he let me?

I'd probably be more of a mess than I already am if it wasn't for my family. I'm trying to move on with my life as best as I can. Since I won't be moving to Peoria anytime at all, I knew I needed to find work. I was fortunate to be rehired at my old school. Classes begin after Labor Day. Hence this little excursion to the beach.

I'll be teaching High School English again. I'm looking forward to the work. Working will keep me very busy and my mind will be too occupied with school stuff to think about Ben. At least I hope that will be the case. I'm a little nervous about being back in the classroom. It's been a few years and I know there is a lot I have probably forgotten. I can only hope it will all come back to me like remembering how to ride a bicycle.

In the meantime, reading helps. While I'm immersed in a book I can escape my life for a little while. In fact one of my favorite places to spend an afternoon is in the New York Public Library. I absolutely love that place. I was there countless times this summer. There is comfort in books and in being surrounded by them.

One of the things that I love about where I live is that there are many wondrous places throughout the city to see and explore. The library building on Fifth Avenue is a prime example of one of those landmarks. This summer on my trips to the library whenever I wasn't with my nose buried in a book I walked through its marble halls. The building itself is a marvel. The artwork and architectural details throughout are fantastic. I'm sure Peoria's library is not as grand.

The wind whips inside the car through the open windows. I hold my hair back with my hand keeping it out of my face. It is sunny and hot outside already. It promises to be hot all day. I look out the window and up at the sky. From where I'm sitting I see nothing but blue skies above.

I drag my attention from the window as Eduardo begins to say something about research being done at an excavation site on the north coast of Peru. I like listening to him talk about work. I find archeology interesting. He fills the car with interesting tidbits about preceramic cultures of Peru and the importance of textiles in cultural expression. It's fascinating really and thanks to my brother-in-law and his love of ancient history the drive out to Jones Beach has passed pleasantly.

As we pull into the parking lot I see Bill, Gladys and the children. They are in the process of retrieving bags and beach items from the trunk of their car. When the twins spot us they begin waving wildly. Gladys, bless her, tries to calm them enough that they will take the items she is trying to put in their hands to carry down to the sand.

Eduardo pulls into an empty space a few over from where Bill is parked. Pushing open the door I step out of the car inhaling the salt air. There is nothing like the feeling of being near the ocean. The distant sounds of the Atlantic slapping against the shore line makes me want to hurry up and get on the beach.

"This was a good idea," I say to Bess as she comes around the back of the car. "I needed this," I tell her. Wordlessly, she smiles and gently squeezes my arm. She knew a day at the beach was exactly what I needed. Somehow, she always knows the right thing to say and do.

"Here you go," my mother hands me a large canvas bag from the open trunk. I loop the straps over my left shoulder and adjust the weight of the bag. I pull on my sunglasses shielding my eyes from the bright sun. Then as I'm waiting on the others I raise my face to the sky feeling the sun on my face. I am determined to have a good time today. I refuse to be blue on such a day as this.

As soon as everyone is ready we make our way out of the parking lot and toward the sand. Bill and Eduardo lead the way. Bill has two folding chairs and an umbrella. Eduardo carries the cooler. The twins are in charge of carrying their toys. Each has a bucket and shovel. They follow close behind their father and uncle. Behind them Gladys carries the baby leaving mother, Bess and I to bring up the rear with the beach bags, towels, snacks and blanket.

I trudge through the sand. Up ahead Bill and Eduardo drop their burdens. We spread out setting up our gear. Bill sets up the umbrella and folding chairs for mother, Gladys and the baby. Bess and I spread a large blanket on the sand and weigh down the corners with our shoes and the large beach bags.

The twins are antsy to go down to the water. Opening the umbrella and tilting it just so to block the strongest of the sun's rays my brother says, "Just a minute you two."

"Patience is a virtue," Gladys adds, much to the boys' chagrin. Gladys then looks to me and Bess and whispers, "The boys are still learning patience."

Bill finishes his task then takes off his shirt kicking off his shoes at the same time. The boys know this is their cue to do the same. They whip their t-shirts over their heads. "Okay, boys let's go in the water," Bill says. My nephews take off toward the water. Bill and Eduardo follow them down to the surf.

My mother and Gladys sit under the umbrella out of the sun while Bess and I settle our bodies onto the big beach blanket. I'm on my stomach. She's on her back facing up. "How are you doing?" she asks when it's just the two of us lying here.

"I'm getting there," I say. "I'm looking forward to going back to work. I'm not used to having so much free time on my hands. The summer has been challenging because of it. I think that working and keeping busy will be good

SHOW YOU THE STARS

for me."

"I think you're right about that," Bess says covering her eyes with her hands.

"Here," I say picking up her brimmed straw hat from the blanket and handing it to her. "Cover your face or you'll freckle."

She takes the hat and places it over her face so I can't see her. "Thanks," she says voice muffled from under the hat.

With our fair Irish complexions we either burn or freckle in the sun. I brought my straw hat, too. I'm already wearing it though. After Jane's sunburn, I never take chances. "Did I ever tell you about the time when one of my roommates in D.C. got really sun burned?" I ask.

"I don't think I heard that story," Bess says adjusting the hat that's covering her face. "Tell me about it."

"It was Jane," I say to clarify which roommate I mean. "We would go up on the roof of our building to sunbathe in the summer months. There was one time she was in the sun too long and she was starting to really burn. She wouldn't listen to anyone," I say remembering. "We all tried telling her to get out of the sun or at least turn over."

I proceed to tell Bess what happened next. It occurs to me that I should write to Jane and Phyllis to let them know how I'm doing and ask after them. I haven't written to them in a while. I think I'll do that tonight when I get home. I look forward to getting letters from all the girls. Phyllis especially though is usually up to something interesting. Her letters are the most fun to read.

"That sounds like a painful lesson," Bess says when I finish the story.

"It was," I agree. "We had a lot of great times together," I say of the girls and me.

"You must miss them," Bess guesses accurately.

"I do," I say running my fingers through the sand at the edge of the blanket. "Work at the Bureau was often tense and stressful but Bess, I made such good friends there and we had so many good times together."

Removing the straw hat she looks at me when she says, "I'm glad for your sake that you had such good friends there. When you left home you had no idea what you were walking into. I thought you were so brave."

"I'm really proud of my contribution to the war effort. If I had to, I'd do it all again," I say.

"I know you would," she says turning on her side to face me. "That's who you are." She places the hat on top of her head and rolls onto her stomach. We lay here for a while side by side on a blanket in the sun, quiet. I look out at the water. My nephews shriek as a wave crashes into them. Their laughter makes me smile.

A little while later Bill and Eduardo with the boys in tow come striding up the beach. All four of them are drenched, dripping with sea water. They grab towels from one of the beach bags and wrap the boys up in them. "The water feels great," Bill tells us. "You should get in the ocean," he says. Then turning to Gladys who is holding a sleeping baby he says, "The boys want to stay up here and play with the buckets and shovels for now."

As the boys collect their beach toys and stake a claim in the sand not too far from their mother they begin filling their buckets with sand. As they play Bill reaches into another of the bags and produces a football. "Up for this?" he says to Eduardo holding up the football.

"Of course," Eduardo says and the two take

the football down to the water's edge to toss back and forth between them.

"Let's go in the water," I say to Bess eager to cool off.

"Yes, let's," she says sitting up, "How about you Gladys?"

"I'd love that," Gladys says quietly so as not to wake baby Susan. Gladys carefully hands the sleeping baby to our mother. She is only too happy to hold her granddaughter for a while.

We three make our way down the beach to the water. The sand is hot but not burning hot where we have to run. Tentatively I wade into the sea. The chill of the water feels refreshing over my sun warmed skin. As the tide pulls out, the wet sand beneath my toes gets pulled with it and my feet sink further down.

We go out a little further stopping when the water is waist deep. I finally relax as the water covers the lower half of my body. We move a little further into the water. The waves behind us build. Turning sideways in anticipation I prepare to jump. "Here it comes," I say. At the last second the three of us turn facing the shore and jump as the wave crests.

Gladys doesn't get the timing quite right

and the wave crashes over her. She comes up spluttering and laughing. Pushing wet hair off of her face she exuberantly says, "That was fun!"
We have mere seconds to brace ourselves for the next incoming wave.

We do this a few more times before moving closer to the shore stopping when the water hits just above my knees. Shielding my eyes from the glaring sun with my hand I scan the beach. The boys are still playing in the sand with buckets and little shovels. Changing the direction of my gaze I see my brother and brother-in-law tossing the ball.

Bill catches sight of us and waves us over there. "Who's that with them?" Gladys asks as we make our way out of the water.
Bringing her hand up to shield her eyes Bess says, "I can't tell from here."
"I can't either," I say stepping onto dry sand. We start to walk toward the guys and as we get closer I recognize who it is they're with.

"Hey, Ellen," Bill says as we get closer. Clutching the football in both hands he smiles at me. "Look who I ran into." My brother looks like he's just reconnected with a long lost friend. I suppose he has. George and Bill were close at one time.

"Hi," George says.

"Hi," I say back.

Placing his sun glasses on the top of his head he says, "I saw Bill just now and had to come say hi. I'm here with some of my friends." He gestures to somewhere behind him. He looks at Bess and says, "It's nice to see you again." Then to Gladys he says, "We haven't met, I'm George Evans."

"George, this is my wife Gladys," Bill makes the introduction. "That's right, I don't think you ever met her," Bill doesn't say anymore on that topic. When he and Gladys met is right around the time that George told me he'd be going home to Newport after graduation. "Those two up there are our sons, twins and over there with my mother is our daughter."

"Congratulations," George says to my brother, "I'm happy for you, Bill. Well," he says, "I didn't mean to intrude. I just wanted to come by to say hello."

"Not at all," Eduardo says assuring George that it was nice to meet him.

When George indicated where his friends were gathered on the beach of course my eyes traveled in that direction. Who is he here with

I wonder. There is a mixed group of men and women. Did one of them in particular come with him today?

"Old chums from my college days I've kept in touch with over the years," he says in answer to a question that I clearly missed while I was ruminating. "Since I moved back here we get together when we can."

"You moved back to New York?" Bill asks curiosity now piqued. He slides a look at me and raises an eyebrow.

"I've been back for about five months so far," he tells my brother. Bess and I already know this much. George catches my gaze before he adds, "I'm here for good this time."

"That's great news," Bill says gregariously. "We have to get together and catch up," he says. I'm not sure how I feel about Bill and George rekindling their friendship. "Go get some of your buddies. We can play a game of touch football."

Thumping a hand on my brother's shoulder, George says, "Be right back."

"How about that," Bill says turning to look directly at me as soon as George is out of ear shot.

"Please don't get any ideas, Bill. That ship sailed years ago."

Bill shrugs and says, "You never know."

I say nothing. Turning, I head back up the beach to dry off and lay on the blanket with a book.

I am several chapters in when Bess and Gladys make their way back. While Gladys is busy tending to her hungry and thirsty children Bess plops down onto the blanket next to me. Bracing her weight on her hands she focuses her attention on the game that's going on down by the water. And now that's where my attention is as well. Lowering the book to my lap I close it. Noticing, Bess lowers her sunglasses and peers at me from over the rim, "I was wondering how long you were going to pretend to be reading."

Mimicking her earlier move I lower my sunglasses. Eyeing her I say, "I'm not the only one." Then I nod toward a group of girls to our right. They clearly are watching with rapt attention the touch football game that is being played down by the water.

Bill has the ball. I watch as he pulls his arm back and throws. The ball spirals through the air straight toward George. He effortlessly catches it. Bringing it close to his chest he starts running. He's being chased and I can't look away.

"It's okay, you know," Bess says quietly

bumping my shoulder with hers.

"What is?" I ask though I have a feeling I know what she's going to say.

"It's okay for you to like someone else," she says gently. A lump in my throat prevents a response.

"Ben told you to move on," she says and the words sting. "He told you he wants you to be happy." I simply nod unwilling to discuss this with her right now. "I think you should give George another chance," Bess says carefully. "You know if he calls."

"I don't think he'll call," I say.

"He'll call," Bess says with some confidence. The thing is she's usually right about stuff like this.

CHAPTER THIRTY- TWO – ELLEN

As usual Bess was right. George did call. He invited me to have dinner with him. He called here on Wednesday asking if I would dine with him on Friday evening. Ever the gentlemen he left a respectable window of time between the call and the date. Looking at the clock on my night stand I surmise that he should be here very soon to pick me up.

"You look beautiful," Bess says handing a pair of white cotton gloves to me. She waits while I pull them on before handing me my clutch. Opening the little handbag I check to make sure my lipstick is in there as well as my compact mirror, tissues, house key and enough money for a cab ride home should it be necessary.

I must be making a face at that last thought because my sister admonishes me. "Stop worrying," she says coming to stand behind me. I find her face in the full length mirror. "You really look lovely, El." She smiles kindly her eyes meeting mine in the mirror. "Just relax and have fun tonight. You know George. You know he's a good guy." I merely shrug in response. I know he is a decent man.

Tonight my hair falls over my shoulders in soft waves. My dress is navy blue with white polka dots. The skirt is micro pleated and belted at the waist. Bess thinks it brings out the blue of my eyes. Even I can admit that the cut and shape is flattering to my figure. My makeup looks good, especially my lipstick. I lean toward the mirror, turning my head this way and that for a closer inspection. Some traditions are worth keeping. I still wear Elizabeth Arden's Victory Red. It suits me I think.

I touch my gloved fingers to the strand of pearls at my neck. "Do I look worried?" my voice cracks on the last word.

"I want for you to be happy," she says resting her chin on my shoulder.

"I am happy," I say turning from the mirror. "See?" I widen my smile.

She shakes her head and collects my white cashmere cardigan from the closet. She checks her watch, a dainty piece of gold jewelry on her slim wrist. "It's almost seven," she says, "George should be here any minute. Do you have everything?"

Nodding, I follow her out of my bedroom and down the hall to the living room where my mother and Eduardo are. "Oh Ellen, don't you look lovely," my mother gushes the moment she sees me. Standing she comes over to get a better look at me. "Beautiful," she says smiling.

"That's what I told her," Bess tells our mother.

"Thank you," I say. I'm not the best at taking compliments. I would rather give them than receive them.

Eduardo lowers the Saturday Evening Post and Bess makes to sit on the arm of his chair. "I'm confident the two of you will have a great time tonight," Bess says of George and me. "From what I recall of him George Evens is very nice. He's easy to talk to, he's funny. He's outgoing and kind plus he's gorgeous."

Eduardo clears his throat with exaggerated

effort. "Darling," he says, "You do realize that I'm sitting right here?"

Bess clears her throat, "As I was saying El, George is a good catch, but he's no Eduardo." I have to laugh.

"I love you, too," Eduardo says to Bess with a hint of a smile.

Just then the doorbell buzzes. Eduardo closes the Post and stands. "I'll get that," he says crossing the living room to open the door. "Hello, it's good to see you again. Come in," I hear him say.

Invited, George steps inside. He's got his hat in one hand and a bouquet of white roses in the other. I watch as he looks around the room. He stops searching when he clocks me standing with Bess and my mother. He smiles then. Was he nervous about tonight? Did he think I'd change my mind? "Hello," he says stepping fully into the room. "These are for you."

Reaching for the flowers I say, "Thank you, how very thoughtful of you."

He ducks his gaze, just for a second. "You're welcome," he says.

The flowers truly are gorgeous. They are obviously from a hothouse and they look expensive. It does not escape me that he remembered I like white roses. For a moment I'm twenty-two again.

"Why don't I put these in water for you?" Bess says reaching for the rose bouquet in my hand.

I let her take them. "Thank you Bess."

Bess takes the roses to the kitchen. The faint sound of a cabinet door being opened is followed by the sound of running water. I turn to my mother, "Mother, you remember George Evens," I say by way of introduction.

"It's a pleasure to see you again Ma'am," George says politely.

"You look well, George," my mother says amiably. "My daughters tell me that you are in New York for work."

"Actually, I live here now. I moved to Manhattan after the war," he tells her. "Did Ellen tell you I was in the Navy? I had no idea she also was in the Navy. That is, not until I ran into her at the Automat a few months ago," he stops talking and looks at me. As he resumes speaking to my mother he doesn't take his eyes off of me saying. "While I was serving my country I realized that New York is where I was the most happy and I told myself that if I made it home alive I would do what was necessary to get back here."

My cheeks flush and I have to look away. Thankfully, Bess is back from the kitchen. She places the cut glass vase full of lush white hothouse roses on the credenza. As I pull on my cardigan sweater my mother asks, "What time should I expect you back, Ellen?" It strikes me as odd to be asked at my age what time I'll be home from a date by my mother. I had so much freedom when I lived in Washington with the girls. It catches me off guard. Shrugging I look to George.

"I'll have her home by midnight," he says. Then he adds, "We should probably get going. The cab is waiting downstairs." The entire exchange has taken place over a matter of less than five minutes yet it feels longer.

We exit the apartment building. The sun has just set and the glow from the street lamps illuminates the block. The cab is by the curb waiting for us. George holds the door as I get into it. After he is seated beside me he tells the driver where we're going, "Le Pavillon, Five East Fifty-Fifth Street on Fifth Avenue, please."

"Le Pavillon?" I say to him. I know of it, of course I've heard of it. It is one of the nicest restaurants in the city. I've just never eaten there before.

Swiveling his head to see me better he says, "I thought you'd like to go there. Was I wrong?"

"No, you weren't wrong," I say shaking my head. "You were right. I'd love to have dinner there."

He smiles satisfied that he chose well for our date. "Thank you for agreeing to have dinner with me."

I nod falling quiet beside him in the back of the yellow taxi cab as it weaves in and out of traffic. It's strange being with George again, going to dinner with him.

"Honestly, I didn't think you would," he says keeping his tone light.

"Should I have turned you down?" I ask matching my inflection to his.

"Probably," he says ruefully, "I wouldn't have blamed you if you did."

"It's water under the bridge," I say perfectly content to not dredge up the past.

"I was selfish," he says.

"You were young," I say.

"I was old enough to know better," he says.

"I won't argue with you about that," I say.

"I'm sorry," he says looking straight ahead now and the lights of the city filter into the cab casting shadows on his profile, "For being a selfish ass and only thinking about me and what I wanted. You didn't deserve that."

"It's okay, George. I forgave you a long time ago," I say.

Relaxing into the seat he rests the back of his head upon the head rest. It's as if my forgiveness has melted away the tension he'd been feeling, maybe even some guilt he might have been carrying. Rolling his head to the side he meets my gaze. "Thank you," he says softly.

This close I see the little lines by his eyes that weren't there when we were in our early twenties. I decide they make him look distinguished. He's still handsome. His patrician nose and strong jaw line are flawless. He stays relaxed allowing my gaze to travel over his features. His green eyes search my own. I wonder what he sees when he looks at me. Does he see an older version of the girl he once knew? Does he see the woman I am now? I am not the same person I was when he knew me, when he left me.

We come to a stop. George alights from the cab offering his hand to assist me out. Stepping onto the sidewalk I turn noticing the St. Regis hotel building across the street. It is a grand structure. Months ago, I had thought to suggest to Ben that when he came for me he and I should stay there on our wedding night.

"Right this way," George says offering me his arm.

I shake out the thoughts of Ben. Taking one last look at the St. Regis I tell myself, I will never stay there with Ben. He is not coming for me. He told me to forget him. With some fortitude I turn my face to George. Smiling, I take his arm and let him lead me forward. We step under Le Pavillon's long awning.

Le Pavillon is nothing short of opulent elegance. As we are shown to our table I take in the décor around us. A large mural of the French countryside fills one wall, the other walls are mirrored. Crystal chandeliers hang from the ceiling and there are candelabra on top the linen covered tables. Also, bowls of fresh flowers adorn each table we pass.

The host stops at a table set in a little nook. The seating is a plush rounded booth. I slip into it on one side as George enters from the other end. The table is set with china plates, silver flatware and crystal glasses.

Once seated, I remove my gloves and place them inside my clutch. I use the time to breathe and settle my nerves. After all these months, thoughts of Ben still have the power to rattle me.

"Would you like wine?" George asks opening the wine list. "Do you have a preference, white or red?"

I tell him I prefer red over white. He suggests a Pinot Noir. I tell him that sounds good. Then I straighten the white linen napkin over my lap.

He orders a bottle for us. It is brought to the table, corked, and after George tastes it the waiter pours two glasses. By the time the main course is set before me I am relaxed. George is making an effort to keep the conversation between us light and easy which I appreciate.

Dinner is delicious. In fact it is the best meal I have ever consumed. The beef is cooked to the perfect temperature, the potatoes are creamy and flavorful and the greens have just the right amount of crunch. Slowly, I savor each mouthwatering forkful.

When the plates are removed coffee is brought to us. George suggests I try the crème brulee. "If you insist," I say intrigued.

Using the little silver pitcher I pour cream

into my coffee, add a little sugar and stir. "May I ask you something?" George says. We've been talking all evening so I'm not sure what would prompt him to ask me if he could ask me something.

Curiosity piqued I say, "Go ahead," placing the teaspoon on the saucer beside the coffee cup.

"When you were in the Navy, where were you stationed?" That is not what I was expecting him to ask. I expected him to ask me something about Ben. I'm relieved he did not though.

"After training I was sent to Washington, D.C," I say. Then to give more explanation I tell him, "I worked in the Naval Bureau Building. I was part of Naval Intelligence. Most specifically I worked in Classification."

"That's really impressive, Ellen" he tells me. "You always were so smart," he says leaning his forearms on the table. "I didn't mean to make you blush. I'd forgotten that you don't like getting compliments."

It's not that I don't like getting compliments. It's just that I don't know how to accept them without blushing. "What about you? Where were you stationed?" I ask because I am curious about where he was during the war and also because I want to move on from how I don't take compliments well.

"I was in the Pacific," he says, "On a cruiser."

I picture George on a ship in the middle of the ocean. From my time in the Navy I know that cruisers are combat ships. Among other functions, they carried out gunnery raids on enemy held shores. It was the cruisers that provided fire support for other ships during operations in the Pacific. In other words, being on a cruiser was dangerous and often deadly.

"There were times I didn't think I'd make it home," he says quietly like he was reading my thoughts. I'm touched by his candor.

"Many didn't," I say softly. I realize that he probably knows that better than I.

"We lost a lot of good men out there," he says confirming my thoughts.

Reaching across the table to cover one of his hands in a gesture of comfort I say, "I know. I'm sorry you went through that." My words seem inadequate.

"I was planning to look you up," he says catching me off guard.

"What?" I say confused by the rapid change of topic.

"One night after a particularly fierce battle I found a quiet corner on the cruiser and I sank to my knees. I thanked God I was still alive, that the ship was still afloat and that we'd won that battle. We'd taken on heavy enemy fire and we suffered heavy casualties and I was still alive. I started thinking that if I got to come home I was going to make sure that I deserved to. I was going to be a better person. You know?"

I nod silently encouraging him to go on wondering where I fit into all of this.

"When the war was over and we finally got to come back to the States I planned to move back to New York. Never in a million years did I think that you would ever want to see me again. All the same though, I was going to look you up so that I could properly apologize for what I'd done to you. But then I ran into you and your sister at the Automat. I took it as a sign. But then you told me there was someone else in your life."

Sliding my hand across the table I place it in my lap. I don't want to discuss Ben with George. "George, I'm not ready to discuss him," I say of Ben.

"That's okay," he says, "I'm just saying that

I feel like we're being given another chance. What are the odds that we'd run into each other again, this time at the beach? I'm not going to rush you into anything you're not ready for. I just want you to know that I've grown up. I'd like to think that I'm a better person in my thirties than I was in my twenties."

I'd like to think that we all grow and change for the better, that we learn from our mistakes and try to do a little better next time around. He looks earnest and I appreciate his honesty. Is he right about us getting another chance? It does seem like fate that we ran into each other twice now. Had I never met Ben I'd be glad for another chance with George.

CHAPTER THIRTY- THREE – BEN

"Ben, over here," I hear his voice before I actually see my friend. It takes a second for my eyes to adjust to the dim lighting in this bar. I start off in the direction of where I heard my name being called. Soon I see my old friends and a feeling I don't quite understand comes over me. Joe, Dan and Tim are seated around a high top table in the middle of the bar. Looks like I'm the last one to arrive.

They get to their feet as I approach. It is so good to see these guys again. I'd learned from Joe that Dan had made it home in one piece after the war. I go to him first. "So good to see you again, buddy," I say throwing my arms around him.

"You, too," he says.

The emotions come at me all at once. I thought I'd done a decent job of transitioning from my soldiering days. But, every now and then I go back to that time when life was uncertain and unpredictable and dangerous. Seeing my buddies whole and hale in this bar with the war behind us has me feeling grateful.

Turning to Tim I shake his hand and ask how he's been. Then finally I pump Joe's hand thanking him for arranging this weekend. "I'm just glad it worked out for all of us," he says smiling. "What are you drinking?" he asks.

Looking around the table I note the guys all have pint glasses in front of them. "Whatever it is you're drinking," I say and watch as Joe raises a hand to get the attention of a passing server. When he gets to the table Joe tells him to bring us another round of beers.

"Coming right up," the guy says to us.

We climb up onto high top stools. Settling into the seat I ask, "When did you get in?"

"Late last night, drove straight through," Dan answers.

"Left right after work," Tim adds.

Next I ask, "Where are you stationed

now?" Dan and Tim both remained in the Navy at the war's end with the intention of making a career out of the military.

Tim answers this question, "Still in D.C., still at the Bureau."

"Both?" I ask looking for clarification

"Yup, both of us," Dan says nodding.

Just then the server comes back around with a full tray. He stops at our table to drop off four pints. He sets them down in front of us. I pick one up and as I do foam tips over the rim of the overflowing glass and slides down the outside. Taking my first sip the cold crisp flavor goes down easy.

Turning my attention to Joe I ask, "How do you like living in Columbus?" After the war he separated from the Navy like I did. Now he is a language professor teaching at Ohio State.

"I like it here," he says and it sounds like he means it. I'm happy he's found a place to settle, a place he likes.

"What about you Ben, how is it being back in Peoria?" Tim asks.

Gripping the back of my neck I let out a long breath. I run my hand over the back of my head. My hair is still short but I don't keep it as short as I did when I was in the Army. "You know about my dad," I begin and my friends nod sympathetically.

"Yeah, man we were sorry to hear about your dad," Dan says.

"Real sorry," Tim adds.

Dropping my hand from the back of my head to the table I stare at my beer focusing on the puddle of condensation it left on the wood. "It's been rough without him," I tell them.

Leaning forward to rest his forearms on the table Tim says, "Do you want to talk about it?"

"Actually," I say, "I think I'd much rather talk about what you all have been up to."

"I got a promotion," Dan offers. "You are in the company of one Lieutenant Commander Cavanaugh now," he tells us.

One of the things I like about Dan is that he's not an in your face kind of person. He's actually a pretty humble guy. His announcement about the promotion is not at all an attempt to brag or such like that. It was actually done with a little humility and humor.

"Congratulations," I say happy for him. I'm reminded of the good things Ellen and her friends used to say about Dan and how he was when they worked together. From what they said he was well respected and well-liked by everybody.

We catch up on each other's lives and what we've all been up to this past year. Intentionally, I let the others do most of the talking. As we polish off the beer a quick glance at my watch tells me that I've been here for almost a full hour already. It feels like minutes instead.

"We ran into Phyllis and Jane last week," Dan is saying snapping my attention back to the conversation. "They were in the commissary getting lunch when we saw them. We stayed and ate with them. Did you know Phyllis and Jane stayed in the Navy?" he asks me and Joe.

"Yes," we both answer at the same time.
"We had a great time catching up with them," Dan says.
"What Dan is not telling you," Tim interjects, "Is that he's got a thing for Phyllis."
"No I don't," Dan says.
"Yes you do," Tim says back.

"How are they?" Joe asks interrupting them.
"They're good," Tim says directing his attention away from Dan toward Joe. "They still live in that little apartment on Florida Avenue. When we asked they told us how the others are."

"Tell us," Joe insists.

Dan pipes up to say, "Jean moved back to Philadelphia. She lives with her parents. Jane says that's been a tough adjustment for Jean after living in D.C. with Vera and Lorraine. They also said she's working in an office but she's looking for something else."

"Vera went back home to Connecticut after she got out of the Navy. Phyllis is convinced she'll be engaged sooner rather than later. There was a certain gentleman she was keen to see when she got home. Phyllis promises to keep us informed on that score," Tim says.

Not to be left out Joe says, "Lorraine said she was going to move back home when the war was over. Did she?"

Dan nods, "According to Jane and Phyllis, Lorraine moved home. I thought you knew that though."

"I didn't know for sure, no," Joe says.

"I thought that was why you picked Ohio State to teach at," Dan says to Joe as if Tim and I were not sitting right here at this table.

Joe nods, "It is."

"You haven't seen her then?" Dan asks.

"No," Joe says.

"Why not," Dan asks. "What are you

waiting for?"

Joe doesn't answer that question. Instead he looks down at the table.

"What am I missing?" I ask.

"Lorraine lives in Columbus," Tim says.

"Oh," is all I can get out.

"Ellen as you know moved back to New York. She's teaching high school kids," Tim says then freezes. "Ben, I'm sorry, I didn't think before I said that."

Shaking my head, I say, "Don't worry about it."

"Look at the time." Joe clears his throat. "We should be heading over to the stadium." He looks over his shoulder for the server. "We'll tab out now," he says when the server approaches.

About a month ago, Joe suggested we come out here so the four of us could get together and attend a home football game. The second weekend in November was decided upon. He got us tickets for today's game which is scheduled to start in about an hour. Unlike Dan and Tim who drove in last night I decided to make the drive first thing this morning. I needed the sleep.

We all place money on top of the table to

cover the tab and leave a tip. Grabbing my jacket from the back of the bar stool I stand and pull it on. Then we head toward the exit, Joe leading the way. "The bar is close to the campus," he tells us as we file outside into the cold November air.

A wave of nostalgia washes over me as we're walking across the campus. I'm reminded of the years I spent as an Army instructor at Virginia Tech. "Hey Joe, how are your classes here compared to Virginia Tech?" I ask curious to know what he will say.

He goes quiet obviously thinking of how to answer. "Different," he finally says.

I simply nod because I think I understand. Everything is different now.

At the stadium we present our tickets. Joe clearly knows where he's going so we follow him. We file into the row and find our seat numbers. I'm sandwiched between Dan and Tim. Joe is to Dan's left. We're about half way up the bleachers in front of the fifty yard line. Leaning over Dan I say to Joe, "These are great seats." Joe and Tim echo the sentiment.

"You're welcome," Joe says.

The feeling in the air is one of excitement and expectation. The stadium is filled with people of all ages. Not just college co-eds. There is a roar from the crowd as the teams run out onto the field. A coin is flipped, the teams get into formation and when the whistle blows the game begins.

We follow the plays getting to our feet whenever the home team scores a touchdown. While I'm not exactly an Ohio State fan I'm enjoying watching a live game with good friends. By half time the score is thirteen to six. The Buckeyes are up over Pittsburgh.

During half time Tim and Joe leave to hit the concession stand. While they're gone Dan says, "I have to ask, what happened with Ellen?"

And there it is. The question I've been dreading. "It's complicated," I say lamely.

My lame answer it seems is not good enough for Dan. I had forgotten for a moment that he's known Ellen for a long time. Slowly shaking his head he says, "Ben, you're going to have to give more than that."

"My family expects certain things of me," I begin, "Since Ellen isn't Jewish," I pause to consider my next words.

Dan puts up a hand to stop me, "Wait, then why did you lead her on all that time?"

"No," I say shaking my head, "I never lead

her on."

"But you just said so yourself, you can't marry her because she's not Jewish," Dan says.

"I said my family expects certain things but my intentions toward Ellen were always honorable. You don't think I would marry her right now if I could?"

"Then why did you break up with her?" he asks confounded.

"You wouldn't understand," I say.

"Try me," he says.

Hanging my head I say, "When my father died my mother broke down. I mean she broke. Since then she depends on me for a lot. I thought that after enough time had passed she would come around but every time I mentioned Ellen's name she shut down." I sit back up and look my friend in the eye. "My mom want's nothing to do with Ellen. It kills me when she says that. I hate telling you this." Running my hands over my face I gather myself together.

"I didn't know what else to do but let her go. I couldn't abandon my mother at her lowest point and I didn't think it was right to ask Ellen to move far away from her family only to bring her to Peoria to be mistreated by my mother." The whole situation is miserable and it sounds even worse when I say it out loud.

"I'm sorry you've been going through all that. But," Dan stops and waits for me to look at him. When I finally do he asks, "Do you still love her?"

Nodding I tell him, "Yes."

Planting a hand on my shoulder he says, "Then don't let anything stand in the way of you two being together."

"It's too late," I say.

"You don't know that," Dan says. "She waited for you throughout the war. That girl loves you."

Something inside my chest constricts. I miss her but I let her go and now I have to live with that decision.

"I'm sorry about your dad Ben and I'm sorry that you've had a rough few years. First you got drafted. Then you were sent to the front to fight. Then when you finally made it home you found out that your dad was sick and you lost him not long after that. If all that isn't bad enough you pushed Ellen away because you thought it would be best for her. Let me ask you something; did you ask her what she wanted or what she was willing to sacrifice to be with you?"

His words have the desired effect. They make me think. The last many years have been the hardest of my life and through it all Ellen was there for me. She was waiting for me. She was my motivation to make it home alive. Why then did I let her go when she is the best thing that ever happened to me?

"Do whatever it takes, Ben. If you don't you'll regret it for the rest of your life," Dan says quietly. "Get her back."

Joe and Tim return from the concession stand their arms loaded. The second half is about to start. Tucking Dan's advice aside for now I focus my attention on the field. No matter how much I try to concentrate on the game though, Ellen is never far from my thoughts.

It's dark outside when the game ends. "Good game," Tim says as we file out of the stadium. Ohio won twenty to thirteen. There are plenty of excited football fans around high fiving and hooting and hollering. Among the chaos we head back toward the same bar where we were earlier.

"First round is on the professor," Dan says of his cousin laughing.

It's colder out now that the sun has gone down. As we walk on I tuck my hands inside my pockets. The cold wind seeps through the material of my jacket and through the thick flannel shirt I'm wearing underneath.

"The second round is Ben's," Joe says.

"Absolutely," I agree absently.

"I need to eat," Dan says.

"Me too," Tim says. "Do they serve food where we're going?" Tim asks Joe.

"They do," I hear Joe answer.

As they go on talking about beer and food and football I can't help noticing tonight's sky. It's pierced with thousands of stars. A memory flickers and suddenly I'm in D.C. on a roof top with the most beautiful woman I've ever known. "Show me the stars," she said and I wonder if she ever thinks of me.

CHAPTER THIRTY-FOUR
– ELLEN

All the lights are on. It's the first thing I notice when I get home. As I remove my coat I hear what can only be described as a squabble going on in the other room. Hanging my coat on the coat tree by the door I begin tugging the gloves from my fingers. As I do this I make my way toward the dining room because that is the general direction from where the ruckus is coming.

Rounding the corner I find a game of Monopoly in progress. From the look on my brother-in-law's face I can only assume he is winning. Sweeping into the room I bend to kiss my mother's cheek. Noting her paltry pile of colorful money neatly arranged by denomination I casually say, "One of these days, you and Bess should team up against Eduardo. I'm afraid it might be the only way to beat him."

Eduardo's head comes up swiftly. "Don't give them any ideas," he says.

Bess picks up the pair of dice and prepares to roll. "Actually Ellen, that's not a bad idea," she says letting go of the dice. We watch them roll around the board until they land. She moves the thimble five squares. Then she groans.

"That property belongs to me," Eduardo announces. "You owe me fifty-four dollars," he says to Bess.

"Fifty-four dollars?" she says in disbelief. "That is highway robbery."

"Yes, there is a hotel on that property." He fails to keep the glee from his statement. Holding up the card he shows her. "See, right here, with one hotel the rent is fifty-four dollars."

"I don't like this game," she says passing the bills across the table. "Can we be done playing now that Ellen's home?"

"You want to stop now?" Eduardo asks incredulous at the idea they stop while he is clearly winning.

"Yes, dear, let's put the game away. We've

been playing for hours," Bess says sweetly.

"We can't stop the game mid play," he says.

Ignoring her husband, Bess turns her attention to me asking, "How was the movie?"

Taking an empty seat at the table next to her I say, "It was good."

"What did you see?" she asks.

"We watched the *The Best Years of Our Lives*," I tell her.

"The one with Myrna Loy?" she asks.

"Yes, that's the one," I say.

With her elbow on the table she rests her chin in her open palm. "Who else is in it?" she wants to know.

I tell her, "Frederic March and Dana Andrews."

Bess says to Eduardo, "We should go to a matinee, maybe next Saturday?"

"If you'd like," he says then rolls the dice completely nonplussed that my sister no longer wants to play Monopoly tonight.

"And how is George?" Bess asks me while keeping one eye on the top hat as Eduardo moves the piece down the board. He lands on one of his own properties.

"George is good," I say.

It's my mother's turn to roll. She moves her piece, the little dog three spaces. "I like George," she says. "I always have."

"I like him, too," Eduardo says counting the pile of play money he's amassed. "He's a decent fellow."

My sister nods her agreement.

"George is marriage material," my mother says straightening her meager pile of real estate cards on the table in front of her.

At this Bess turns my way. When I look at her she mouths, "I told you so."

She did tell me so. Bess told me that she thinks George would make a fine husband. Bill and even Gladys said something similar. Now my mother is giving him her blessing and he doesn't even know it. Abruptly I stand knocking into the table in the process. "Sorry," I say before heading into the kitchen. I need a minute.

I'm pouring myself a glass of water when Bess follows me into the kitchen not a minute later. Leaning against the counter she fixes her gaze on me. "Are you okay?"

"Yes, fine," I tell her.

"Did something happen tonight?" she asks concern in her voice.

"No, nothing like that," I say.

She visibly relaxes. On an exhale she asks, "Then, is it too soon to tease you about George being marriage material?"

Nodding I say, "A little, yes."

"I'm sorry," she says softly.

"No harm done," I say opening the refrigerator to put away the pitcher.

She tilts her head to study me. I sip the water. "Talk to me," she says encouragingly.

Where do I begin? I think to myself. I give a little shrug. "What do you want to know?" I ask.

Bess comes over to where I'm standing by the fridge. She's close but not touching. "Anything you want to tell me," she says.

"Our mother is right, George is marriage material. I know that. Maybe I'm the one who isn't," I finally say what I've been thinking of late.

"El," my sister says drawing out the single syllable.

"George is being patient with me for now," I blurt out. "I told him that I want to take things slowly." I stare down at the water glass cradled in my hands. "He knows about Ben."

"What did you tell him?" Bess asks.

Eyes still downcast focused on the water glass I say, "I told him that when I was in D.C. I met a soldier. We fell in love. I told him that I waited for Ben for the war to end," I raise my eyes to the ceiling, "That I thought we were going to get married when the war was over but when that didn't happen," I take a moment to collect myself. I inhale a breath, hold it then release it slowly. "When it didn't happen something inside me broke."

Gently, Bess says, "Your poor heart was broken. It won't be forever, El."

Sadness washes over me. Ben and I would be married by now. I'd be his wife. He would be my husband. A knife twists in my gut. "I told George that I need time but that I'll understand if he'd rather date someone else."

"Oh," Bess says probably because she doesn't know what else to say to that. "What did he say? Is that why you're home early?"

A little laugh bubbles up to the surface and I feel a small smile emerge. Shaking my head I say, "Can you believe he said he doesn't want to date anyone else? He's content to wait."

"Huh," Bess says folding her arms across her middle. "He said that?" she asks needing to clarify she heard me correctly.

"He said that," I confirm for her.

"He really is marriage material," she says.

I bump her shoulder and we share a laugh, "Yeah."

"What do you want?" she asks.

My eyes tear up because what I really want I can't have. I give her what must be the saddest smile. Her pretty face frowns. Wrapping her arm around my shoulder she brings me in close. "Oh honey," she whispers. "I wish I could do something to make the hurt go away."

"There's nothing you can do," I say quietly. "I thought by now I would be over him, you know?"

Bess rubs my arm up and down with soothing strokes. "Sometimes it's just not that easy," she says. "Will you see George again?" She can't help herself. I know she's rooting for George.

She makes me laugh, even as I want to cry. "Yes," I tell her, "I've agreed to be his date to a Christmas party on the twentieth."

"Hmm, will it be a casual or formal affair?"

She asks trying to lighten the mood.

"You know George," I say, "It's going to be formal."

"Yes," she muses. Curiosity wins out and she asks for more. "Where will it be?"

"You know you're incorrigible, right?" I say.

"You are not wrong about that," she agrees. "Again, where will it be?"

Raising my head from her shoulder I look at my sister. "The ballroom at the Waldorf Astoria," I tell her. Her eyes go wide and her excitement does much to cheer me up. She has that effect on me and she knows it. I love her for it.

She sucks in a breath to contain her excitement. She squeezes me. "Can I help you find a dress for it?" she asks hopeful.

"Yes," I tell her and she hugs me tighter.

"Thank you," she says.

"You're a nut," I say.

"Quite possibly," she says. "But I'm your nut and I love you and I think you're strong and brave."

"Why is that?" I ask hugging her back.

"Because every day you wake up and put

one foot in front of the other and you're not giving up on finding happiness again. I think you're amazing."

Her words are what I need to hear. Resting my head on her shoulder again I say, "I think you're pretty amazing, too."

"Where did you go?" Eduardo calls from the dining room. "Bess, darling it's your turn. We're waiting for you," he adds.

"Save me," Bess says.
Steering her toward the doorway I lead her back toward the dining room table and the unfinished game of Monopoly.

The game is finally called at eleven thirty. No surprise, Eduardo having the most money and properties is pronounced the winner. I help Bess and Eduardo put away the pieces as mother washes up the few glasses and dishes left out. She prefers to tidy up the kitchen before she goes to bed rather than to wake up to dishes in the sink.

"Don't forget," my sister says placing the cover on the game box, "Tomorrow after church we're going to the tree lot."

"I remember," I say, "I've been looking

forward to it. Also, mother says that Bill and Gladys are coming over tomorrow so the children can help with the tree trimming. Then they'll stay for dinner."

"They are," Bess confirms carrying the box to the living room. I follow. Opening a drawer in the credenza she puts the box inside then closes the drawer again. "Those children are growing like weeds. Before we know it the twins will be taller than us."

"I don't believe that will be long now," I say gesturing to her obviously short stature.

She raises one eyebrow. I'm shorter than her. As many times as I've tried to mimic the eyebrow raise I can't quite do it like she can. She laughs at my attempt. I must look ridiculous.

I'm saved from trying again when our mother appears. Quietly she approaches us. Raising a hand she softly brushes the back of it against Bess' cheek then does the same to mine. "My girls," she says, "My beautiful daughters. How I love you."

"We love you, too" I tell her.

"Very much," Bess says.

"I'm off to bed now. I'll see you in the morning. Good night Eduardo," she says before leaving the room.

Shortly after that Bess and Eduardo head out and I make sure to bolt and lock the door. Since I am the last one to go to bed I make my way through the apartment turning off the lights.

In my room, I leave the lamp on by my bed. I want to read for a little while before I go to sleep. At the low book shelf I peruse the titles I own. My hand lightly skims the books lined up like soldiers at attention.

On its own my hand comes to rest on one volume in particular. I run my finger lightly over the letters of its well-worn spine but I do not pull it. I don't want reminders, not tonight. My search continues. Eventually my hand stops and this time I do pull the book from the shelf. Though I've read it three times already I carry my copy of *Little Women* with me to the bed.

The window rattles from a cold gust momentarily startling me. I make sure the latch is snug in its place and close the curtains tighter. Then I hurry up and change into my warmest flannel night gown. When at last I slip into bed I pull the covers up to my chin. Opening the book to the beginning I prop it against my up drawn knees.

By the time I reach the end of the first chapter my eyelids have grown too heavy to stay open. Closing the book I place it on the table beside me and turn off the lamp. Resting my head on the pillow as I begin to drift in my mind's eye I see Ben, his handsome smile and those warm brown eyes. Stop it, I tell myself. Don't think about him. If only that were possible, I've tried not to think about him for months with no success. It's George that I should be thinking about.

Lying on my back I stare up at the ceiling hands resting at my sides. "Tomorrow," I whisper into the dark, "I will start new." Tomorrow, I will not think of Ben. Tomorrow I will do what I must to move on because I know that no matter how hard I wish that things were different, being with Ben is not an option for me.

Flipping onto my side I face the wall. Earlier tonight in the cab on the way to the movie George reached for my hand. Interlocking our fingers his thumb gently stroked the back of my hand. It was nice. He said, "I'm going home for a few days over Christmas. I'd like you to come with me."

I'd wondered where George stood as far as our relationship goes. Now I know. I've never been to his family's home in Newport. I met his mother and father at his graduation from Columbia when they came for the ceremony. It wasn't long after that he said he was leaving New York.

"George," I said not able to look him in the eye. My free hand fidgeted with the handle of the small purse resting in my lap. "I'm not ready for something serious. I don't know when I will be." It was the right thing to do to tell him this. He's been persistent. He's asked me out every week for three months. In that time he's taken me to dinners at wonderful restaurants, to the theater, to museums, movies, parties, and clubs.

In the enclosed space of the cab I told him, "I think you're wonderful."

Shifting on the seat beside me he said, "Then what is it?"

That's when I told him about how I met Ben, how I waited for him throughout the war with the hope we'd be married when it was all over, how I was still trying to reconcile it didn't work out that way. "I'll understand if you'd rather date someone else," I finished.

"Ellen," George said softly, "Look at me." When I didn't look up he said, "Please look at me."

When I did I saw that his green eyes were full of something I hesitate to put a name to. They were serious. "I'm a patient man," he said in a low voice. "I know what it feels like to miss you. I walked away from you once. I won't do it again. I'll wait as long as you need me to. To me, you're worth waiting a lifetime for. Let me prove it to you."

What could I say to that?

CHAPTER THIRTY-FIVE – BEN

My sister called to ask if I would pick her up. Normally she walks home from her shift at the public library where she works part time. Tonight, though I'm glad she called because the weather has taken a turn in the last few hours. As I leave my office I keep my head down on the way to the car. The wind is blowing so fiercely it is howling.

The parking lot is treacherous. Taking my time I make sure to step carefully over scattered patches of black ice. Inside the car I turn on the engine and crank the heat as high as it will go. I blow on my freezing fingers to warm them. When this doesn't work I shove them in my pockets until the inside of the car is sufficiently warm.

I put the car in drive then slowly ease out of the parking lot making my way along the roads between work and the library. Snow begins to fall and I turn on the wipers. They swish across the windshield squeaking with each swipe of the rubber blades across the glass. Even over the sounds of the engine and the car's heater I can hear it.

The windshield keeps fogging. I tug off my scarf to use it to wipe the glass. I clear the area in my direct line of vision so I can see out the windshield. I have to do this every few minutes in order to see the road in front of me. Traffic is moving slowly. Drivers are using an abundance of caution in these wintery conditions.

Usually, it takes me ten minutes to get from my office to the library. Today it takes me thirty. Up ahead I see the building. I put on my blinker and pull up to the curb. Before I get out of the car, I wrap my scarf around my neck and button my wool coat. When I go to open the door, the wind almost immediately closes it on me. Pushing it back open I lumber out of the car.

I hurry into the building. Inside I scan the main area for Gabby. When I don't see her I make my way toward the information desk. Behind it is a gray haired woman wearing black rimmed eye glasses. She is rifling through a stack of reference cards.

"Excuse me," I say sidling up to the desk.

She looks up from her task. "How may I help you?" she asks pleasantly.

"I'm looking for my sister, Gabby." I tell her. "I'm here to pick her up."

"You must be Ben," the woman says. "Gabby's told us a lot about you."

"Please," I say holding up my hands, "Don't believe a word of anything my sister says about me." I am only half joking about this.

This makes the otherwise serious librarian crack a smile. "I assure you, Gabby has nothing but nice things to say about her brother. She was worried about you while you were overseas. Thank you, for your service," she says kindly, reverently.

"It was my honor," I say meaning it but very glad to be back in the States all the same.

"Gabby," she says, "is upstairs. You'll find her up there restacking books."

"Thank you," I say before turning toward the stairs.

Sure enough I find my sister upstairs. She is in the non-fiction section. Keeping my voice low I call to her. She looks my way when she hears my voice. She waves me over. "Almost finished," she says placing a book onto a shelf.

"Good, it's getting worse out there," I tell her.

She looks toward a window to see for herself. "Thanks for coming to get me," she says pushing a wheeled book cart deeper into a row of tall book shelves.

"All you ever have to do is ask," I tell her, "And I'll come when you need me."

She smiles over her shoulder at me, "Thanks, that means a lot."

"Can I help?" I ask eyeing the cart of books.

"Sure," she says handing over four books. "Take these down there. They go on the third shelf from the top. Shelve them in alphabetical order according to author's last name."

"I can do that," I say walking to the end of the row. Scanning the third shelf I search for the proper placement for the books in my arms. "How are your classes going?" I ask Gabby making conversation in the quiet library. We are the only ones up here. She's working toward her degree in library science. She is getting close to finishing.

"They're going well. I'll be done at the end of next semester," she says with a wide smile.

"Time flies," I say. "Do you like working here?" I ask.

"I love working in the library," she says pushing a book into position on a shelf in front of her. "I can't wait to be a librarian. Being surrounded by books is like a dream. It's what makes me happy." She looks over at me and I can see what she means. She does look happy. I'm happy for her.

"What about outside of work and school?" I ask. I've noticed that Gabby is getting out more. "Are you seeing anyone?" I ask fully aware I'm being nosy.

"Who wants to know?" she says picking another book up from the cart and scanning the cover.

Grabbing another book from the cart myself I say, "Your big brother wants to know."

She laughs, she's actually laughing at me. "Seriously, Ben," she shakes her head, "You don't have to be over protective or worry about me. I've been going out more with friends but I am not seeing anyone special at the moment, just so you know. For now I am completely focused on finishing school."

I don't realize I'm standing in the middle of the row holding the last book until she plucks it out of my hands. With efficiency she locates where it belongs and places it on the shelf between two other books. Placing her hands on her hips she says, "There, that's all done. Let me put this away and I'll meet you downstairs." She doesn't wait for an answer and begins wheeling the book cart toward a far wall.

Turning, I head toward the stairs and begin my descent. My little sister is all grown up. Seems she can take care of herself and what's more she wants to do things for herself. A few minutes later, Gabby bundled in warm layers, meets me by the library's entrance. Together we head into the night. The temperature is frigid. I open the door for her then hurry around to my side of the car.

When we get home our mother is putting on her coat. "Oh good, you're both home now. I was starting to worry. The weather is awful. I've kept dinner warm for you in the oven. Help yourselves."

"Where are you going at this time of night,

in this weather?" Gabby asks incredulous.

"I'm just going next door to Carol's house. She called earlier to invite me to play Bridge with them tonight."

"You're going to play cards?" Gabby asks.

"Yes, I am," our mom says. "I'll be back in a few hours. Don't wait up. Oh, and clean up after yourselves in the kitchen." Then she pulls her scarf up to cover her nose and mouth.

We watch as she leaves the house. As soon as the door closes Gabby looks through one of the narrow windows on either side of the front door. She keeps watching out the window until she's sure our mother is safe inside the neighbor's house. "Well," she says turning around, "I'll be."

Just then Winston comes into the foyer, tail wagging. I bend down to run my hands over his soft caramel fur. "Hi, boy," I say. "Did you miss me?"

"He missed me more," Gabby says petting my dog. Winston looks up at her with big brown eyes basking in all the attention.

He follows us into the kitchen. Gabby opens the oven. Carefully using a pair of potholders she pulls the casserole dish out of the oven. I get us some plates and utensils and meet her at the kitchen table. Before sitting down to eat, I make sure that Winston has food and water.

We begin eating. After a few minutes of quietude my sister speaks, "Ben?"

I lift my head to look at her, "Yeah?"

"Mom's doing good," she says.

"Looks like," I say thinking of how she went out tonight to play Bridge with the other ladies in the neighborhood. She hasn't played with them since my father died.

Now that I think on it, there have been subtle changes I've noticed in my mother. She looks better, healthier. She is taking more responsibility around the house, running errands by herself, paying the bills, making sure the house is clean. She made dinner tonight for me and Gabby. "It seems she's more like her old self lately," I say.

It does," Gabby says agreeing with me. Gabby gets up from the table and goes to the refrigerator. She holds up a bottle of Coca Cola. "Want one?" she asks.

"That'd be great," I say.

She brings the bottles to the table and sets them down. "So," she begins pouring the contents of one of the bottles into a glass for herself then sits back down to her meal.

"So," I say.

"I'm doing very well. I finish my degree in a few months and then I'll be working full time at the library," she says.

"I know, that's great, Gabby, really great. I'm happy for you." I say earnestly.

"Thank you," she says picks up the full glass and sips from it. Putting it back down on the table she keeps her hand around it. "And mom," she adds, "She's doing much better. She's getting out now and she's finding her way without dad."

I keep quiet, waiting to hear what she's really trying to say. I don't have to wait long. She leans forward and touches my forearm. "Ben, it's your turn."

Gabby grows serious. "You don't have to stay here anymore. Mom and I will be fine on our own now. I honestly don't know what we would have done without you when dad died. You kept this family together. I don't know all of the details, but I know that you made it so we could stay in this house and that the bills got paid."

I nod confirming what she has known all along. I did what had to be done.

"Thank you," she says squeezing my arm. "Thank you so much."

"I just did what anyone would do," I say.

"No, not everyone would have done what you did for us and I'm so sorry it cost you so much," she says with feeling.

I give a little shrug, not sure what to say. It is what it is. I made a decision not to abandon my family when they needed me. Life is a series of decisions. At the time I made what I thought was the right one. I knew there would be consequences. Now I have to live with those consequences.

"Ben, go to Ellen," Gabby says like it's just that easy.

I smile sadly at my sister. "It's not that easy," I tell her. "What, do you want me to just go to New York and show up at her doorstep and say, please Ellen take me back?"

"Yes, that's exactly what I want for you to do," Gabby says.

"I can't do that to her," I say.

"You miss her," Gabby says.

"Of course I miss her," I say. "I miss her every day of my life. I think about her every minute of every day. But I can't just show up in her life again and ask her to take me back," I say. "I can't do that to her."

"Yes, you can. You have to," Gabby insists.

I stare at my sister like she's lost her mind. "What world do you live in?" I ask throwing my hands up.

"The same one you live in. I want you to be happy, Ben. You, especially deserve to be happy. Ellen made you happy. Go where your happy is. Go to New York. Go to Ellen," she says and now she's crying. She's crying for me. "Go," she says quietly. "We'll be okay here without you."

CHAPTER THIRTY-SIX – ELLEN

Earlier today I spoke with Jane and Phyllis. It was so good to hear their voices. They regaled me with tales of living in Washington, D.C. and working for the Navy. It made my heart ache with longing to be there with them. Before we hung up the phone we discussed how much I would like to visit them. I promised that I would come as soon as I could. They said they would hold me to that promise.

After the call, I grabbed my purse, put on my coat and headed out. I had an appointment at the beauty parlor where I had my makeup professionally applied then my hair was styled into an elegant chignon. When I got home, I telephoned Bess and she came over to keep me company until it's time to get dressed for tonight's Christmas party at the Waldorf Astoria hotel.

Eduardo is away working on a dig site so she and mother are spending the evening together while I am out with George. I am aware that Bess will most likely still be here when I get home tonight. She'll want to make tea and sit up late like we used to do. She'll pepper me with a million questions about the party. She'll want to hear all about the music, the food, the decorations, the dresses, George.

In the living room, Bess is mid-sentence telling me a story about a scene she witnessed outside her office the other day. The way she tells it has me hanging on her every word. So I don't notice our mother at first. "Girls," she says to get our attention the way she did when we were little. We both turn our heads toward the archway connecting the living room and dining room. There she stands pointing toward the clock on the mantel. She says, "I hate to interrupt you two, but Ellen shouldn't you be getting dressed? George will be here soon."

"Oh shoot," I say getting up from the sofa. I had lost all track of time. It is easy to do when Bess is around. She jumps up as well and we move down the hall toward my bedroom.

"Wow," Bess says spying my evening dress hanging on a hook on the outside of my closet. She was with me when I bought it, so this isn't the first time she's seeing it. But I echo her sentiment. It is a thing of beauty. The sleek satin material is the color of spun gold. It is a floor length, strappy grown. The beading on the bodice and waist are breathtaking. The first time I tried it on, inside one of the fitting rooms at Bloomingdales, I knew I had to have it.

At my dressing table, I apply a few precious drops of Chanel No. 5 behind my ears and on my wrists. Looking up I see Bess removing the gown from its hanger. I straighten and admire the shimmer of the fabric in the lamp light. Quickly, I unbutton my blouse and step out of my skirt.

"Lift your arms," she says to me and I obey. She slips the dress over my head, careful of my chignon. She gives the dress a gentle tug into place and I turn for her to zip me up. Hands out at my sides, I move in a slow circle so she can get the full effect. Softly she says, "Ellen, you look stunning." Then with wide eyes she adds, "George is just going to die when he sees you."

I wave off her comment with a flick of my wrist, emitting a waft of Chanel into the room as I do. "You're my sister, you have to say nice things like that," I tell her. She just looks at me and shakes her head. "You really have no idea how pretty you are," she says. Before I can respond the doorbell rings.

The next thing we hear is our mother's voice inviting George to come inside. Bess takes my hand in hers and gives it a squeeze. Then wordlessly, she hands me my beaded clutch. I smile at her, so grateful to have her in my life. "You're the best," I say. She smiles at me indulgently placing her hand over her heart.

In this dress I feel confident, so much so, that when I enter the front room to find George waiting there garbed in formal attire I say the first thing that pops into my head, "Mr. Evans, you are looking quite dapper this evening."

His green eyes alight when he catches sight of me. "Miss Cunningham," he says taking my outstretched hands and bringing them to his lips. He kisses one then the other. His eyes travel the length of my gown. "You are a vision." George is always so attentive and complimentary.

"This old thing?" I attempt a little levity because as much as I love the way I feel in this dress and as amazing as George is, there is still something under the surface holding me back from giving him all that he wants from me. I wish that wasn't the case because my mother is right, George is marriage material. I keep hoping that with time my feelings will change and I'll be able to give him all of me. I look into his kind, smiling, handsome face. He deserves nothing less.

Bess and my mother see us out. George helps me into the cab then climbs in beside me. "The Waldorf, please," he says to the cabbie. As the cab pulls away from the curb he links our fingers letting our entwined hands rest on the seat cushion between us. "Thank you for coming with me tonight," he says.

"Thank you for asking me to come with you," I say in reply. "I'm honored to be your date tonight." Though the interior of the cab is dark, I see him nod. I sense there is more he would like to say at this moment, but he's quiet for the remainder of the drive to Park Avenue.

When we arrive, George, being the consummate gentleman that he is, assists me as I alight from the car. He proffers his arm and escorts me inside the building. Inside, my attention is caught by a tall clock tower in the hotel's lobby. George notices how it has captured my attention. He slows our steps so I can get a better look at it. "It was brought over from England for the Chicago World's Fair, eighteen ninety-three I think it was," he tells me and I want to know more.

"It is remarkable," I say.

"It is," he agrees before gently turning us away from the ornate clock. George is nothing if not punctual. I'm sure he does not want to be late to the party. As we make our way through the hotel toward the ballroom he says, "One of the Astor's purchased the clock for the original Waldorf Astoria. It is one of the only fixtures to have survived the demolition of the old location."

"I'm glad it did," I say looking over my shoulder for one last look at the clock before it is out of sight.

"Me, too," he agrees, "Especially, because you like it." His comment makes me smile. "Ready?" he asks a few moments later. At my nod, he pulls open the doors to the ballroom. Inside is a calliope of sights and sounds. The room is full of beautiful people dressed in rich clothing.

"This way," he says. We find our table and George introduces me to the ladies and gentlemen around it. I take a seat at an empty place setting. His hand on my bare shoulder he leans in to tell me, "Be right back." I watch as he heads toward the bar. He really does look handsome in his tuxedo.

While he's gone I engage in small talk with the other women at our table. He's not gone long, though. When he returns with the other men he hands me a glass of champagne. "For you," he says. Thanking him, I take the glass. I take a sip. It is very good champagne.

Throughout the evening I accompany George as he mingles with the other party goers. A few times he leaves my side to talk to this person or the other after all he is representing his family tonight. Looking around the room I notice how everyone here seems so glamorous. Not for the first time do I wonder if I could get used to this kind of lifestyle.

"What are you thinking about?" George asks sidling up to me. He's just been speaking with a friend of his father's. "You look like you were deep in thought," he says handing me another glass of champagne. "I stopped at the bar on my way back," he adds.

"That was thoughtful," I tell him because it was thoughtful of him to think of me. He shoots me a boyish grin. I take a sip then say, "I was thinking of Jane and Phyllis." It's not a lie. I was thinking of them right before I thought about how glamorous everyone around us looks. "I've mentioned them to you before?" At his nod I continue, "I spoke with them over the phone this morning. I promised I would come to D.C. for a visit soon."

"If memory serves, Phyllis is the instigator, yeah?" he says with a flash of a grin.

I can't help it. I laugh at his summation. "I think they both are," I say, then, "I miss them, a lot."

"I'm sure they miss you, too," he says. Then he places his drink glass on a nearby table and takes my free hand. "Have I told you how absolutely stunning you look tonight?" he says.

"You have," I say. I know I am blushing at the compliment. I always blush at compliments.

"Dance with me?" he asks.

"Of course," I say placing my own glass on the table with his. Then I allow him to lead me onto the dance floor.

The grand ballroom at the Waldorf Astoria is effervescent this evening. The music is serene. George and I weave our way through several dancing couples until we find a space to accommodate us. One of his hands finds the small of my back. "Are you having a good time?" he asks.

"I am," I say placing one hand on his shoulder and slipping the other into his free hand.

The party is being given by a friend and business associate of George's father. Though George is not in the habit of calling attention to himself, it is not a secret that his family has made their fortune in the shipping industry. George is representing his family this evening since his parents are not able to be here.

"It's a lovely party," I say as we move to the music. There is a five piece band playing beautifully.

George is an exceptional dancer. As he leads us through the steps his movements are effortless and graceful. "It is all the more lovely because you are here," he says. As we dance I remember how, years ago, I'd been surprised to found out that George was leaving New York after graduation. Out of the blue he'd seemingly changed his mind. He was moving back to Newport. At the time I'd been confused and hurt. He'd given me no real reason why. Up until then he'd led me to believe he would stay in New York. That he would stay with me.

Suddenly, it hits me. Oh, it makes so much more sense now. How did I not see it before? His family's business suffered financially during the Crash like so many companies did. I look up at George, into his kind eyes. He looks down at me and smiles handsomely, almost certainly unaware of my train of thought. He left New York so he could help with his family's business during those lean years.

He should have told me then why he'd left New York, why he'd left me. I would have understood. During our time at Columbia he led me to believe he wanted to stay here after graduation. That he wanted to stay with me. Oh George, I think now. I would have understood if you would have given me the chance. Reaching up, I place my palm over his smooth cheek. It is a brief caress before slipping my hand back into his.

As we continue the dance, thoughts fit like puzzle pieces in my mind. George joined the Navy during the war and that kept him away more years. He'd been gone from my life for so long I was left to think he was a callous young man who didn't care about my feelings. I was wrong about that. He is a proud man who put his family and then his country before himself. Oh, the irony.

As the song ends George maneuvers me into a graceful dip. Slowly, he raises me. When his striking green eyes lock with mine, he lowers his voice and says, "Ellen, come home with me tonight."

I should not be surprised by his bold request. Though, I am unprepared to respond. I don't know what to say. Before I can say anything at all he quickly says, "I'm sorry." Dropping his forehead to my shoulder he buries his face in my neck. "You smell amazing," he says half groaning, half laughing. Breaking the tension I chuckle.

"I am sorry," he repeats the apology from seconds earlier. "I told you that I would be patient and I will be." He lifts his head. "Will you forgive me?"

For the second time I touch his smoothly shaven cheek. "There is nothing to forgive," I tell him. On the way back to our table I excuse myself telling him that I need a moment. I leave him at the table in the company of his friends.

Stepping through the double doors I exit the ballroom. The doors close behind me and I let out a shaky breath. George is a good man. I walk down the corridor needing to put some space between me and the party. The long skirt of my ball gown swishes with each stride. I need a walk to clear my head.

My feet lead me back toward the lobby. Back to the octagonal clock tower which lures me like a siren. Earlier, when George and I arrived at the hotel I wasn't able to inspect it as I would have liked to do. Up close it is gorgeous, a piece of art really.

I'm not sure how long I've been standing here by the clock when I hear someone say my name. "Ellen," I hear again. My hands begin to tremble. I know that voice. I'd know that voice anywhere. Slowly, I turn around.

CHAPTER THIRTY-SEVEN – BEN

I stop short, unable to believe my eyes. Across the lobby is Ellen. My heart pounds in my chest. I have to catch my breath. She's stunning, absolutely stunning. Her name slips reverently from my lips. "Ellen," I say. She is more beautiful standing before me in that gold gown than my feeble memory was able to conjure for so many lonely months.

I've caught her completely off guard, I see. I'm sure she thought she'd never see me again. I didn't tell her I was coming. I just came. The look on her pretty face is one of confusion. I'm afraid to move, afraid that she might bolt. I'm afraid that somehow my showing up here might be too little, too late.

"Ben," my name on her lips makes me want

to drop to my knees right this very moment and beg her to take me back.

"Hello," I say taking several steps forward.

"What are you doing here?" she asks looking around.

Pushing through any lingering reservations I might have about showing up here unannounced, I close the distance between us. "I came to see you," I say with my heart on my sleeve. She takes a step back, shaking whatever confidence I've been clinging to. Lifting my hands before me in a gesture to show her she is safe with me I say, "I went to your apartment but you weren't there."

Shaking her head, she says, "How did you know where to find me?"

"Your sister said you would be here. She said you were at a party at the Waldorf Astoria," I tell her searching her face, looking for a sign that she is happy to see me.

She shakes her head, disbelieving. "Bess wouldn't have told you that."

"She did," I say with a nod confirming the truth of my statement.

"Bess told you where I was?" she questions still not able to reconcile that her sister would have given up her whereabouts to me.

"At first, she wouldn't tell me anything. In fact when I showed up on your doorstep and told her who I was, she nearly slammed the door in my face." That almost earns me a smile, but not quite. "I said I wasn't leaving there until I knew where you were. In fact, I threatened to stage a sit-in. I told her I needed to see you. I said it was important, that I have to talk to you, tell you," my voice catches.

"Tell me what?" she says her voice low as if she is afraid to hear what I have to say next.

"That I love you," I say my heart beating hard in my chest. "I never stopped." I reach for her hand. She lets me hold it. "I'm sorry I pushed you away and I'm sorry I didn't ask you what you wanted. I didn't give you a chance to decide for yourself what you were willing to give. I shouldn't have done that," I say. "That was wrong of me. I was wrong to end things between us." The words tumble over themselves. "I'm sorry, Ellen. I'm so damn sorry."

She breaks eye contact, looking to the side and I wonder if I've lost her for good. Giving a light tug on the hand I am still holding, I bring her gaze back to mine. "Can you forgive me? Do you hate me?" I ask anguished at the thought. Praying

I haven't lost my chance to make things right between Ellen and me, I plead, "Say something."

"I don't hate you," she says softly. "I could never hate you, Ben."

I let go of her hand only to raise both of mine to gently cup her face. My heart has worked its way up into my throat. "I don't want to live without you in my life. It hurts too much." I know she feels it too by the way she sucks in a breath, the way her body shudders. I want to lean in. I want to press my lips to hers.

"What's going on here?" a male voice interjects from several feet away. "Ellen, you didn't come back to the ballroom. Is everything alright? Who is this?"

I turn my head to see someone purposefully striding toward us. Turning back to Ellen I screw up my face. Overwhelming sadness and grief creep into my very bones. I drop my hands from around her face and Ellen turns to the man in a tuxedo, her date I presume. "I look from him to her. "Am I too late?" I ask numbly. She looks from him to me. "Am I too late?" I ask again.

"Who is this?" Tuxedo asks. "Ellen, talk to me." He's remarkably calm, I can't help noticing.

"I'm Ben," I say. My ears are ringing in my head. Who is he to her I wonder. I'm at a disadvantage here. The guy hesitates for the briefest instant then recognition dawns on his face. So, she told him about me. He knows who I am to Ellen.

He offers his hand and begrudgingly, I shake it. "Well, this is unexpected," he says. "I'm George." He releases my hand and turning to Ellen touches her bare upper arm. I hate the sight of his hand on her. "He's the one you told me about, the soldier during the war?" he asks her and she nods slowly confirming his suspicion.

I watch in silence, still as a stone. She told him about me, but who is he to her? Have they been together long? Does she love him? My heart lurches at the thought of her with someone else. Have I come all this way for nothing? Did I blow my chance? Did I ever even have a chance? "Ellen," I say to get her attention. She swivels her gaze from Tuxedo to me.

"I think you should probably leave," George says to me. I don't look at him. That is not his call to make.

Searching Ellen's face I ask her, "Do you want me to go? I'll do whatever you want, Ellen. Just, tell me what you want." I hold my breath. I won't like it, but I'll leave if that's what she wants me to do. I know I've hurt her and I know I don't have the right to just show up here and expect her to take me back. But, I want her to, more than I want my next breath.

The silence stretches. He's still touching her. I take a step back. I take her silence for the rejection that it is. Dropping my head, I turn to go. I'm devastated. I've lost her for good. I don't know how I'm supposed to walk away now that I've seen her, touched her. My vision begins to blur. I have to get out of here.

"Wait," I hear her say and hope blooms in my hollow chest. "Don't go."

I halt my steps. Looking over my shoulder, I see George's hand drop from Ellen's arm to his side. I hear him say, "Ellen, come on." He looks confused and I almost feel for the guy.

Slowly, I turn fully around but I stay where I am even though I feel helpless as tears pool in Ellen's blue eyes. She's looking at George and I know better than to interrupt. "I'm sorry," she tells him and I watch him hang his head. That was me mere minutes ago.

He looks into her face and I can just make out his words. "Is there no changing your mind?" he asks and I see the slight shake of her head.

I hear his heavy sigh of resignation. Next thing I know he's leaning into her and pressing a kiss to her temple. He lingers a little too long for my liking, but I don't have the heart to rush them. "Be happy, Ellen," I hear him say before he pulls away from her and looks into her eyes. He gives her a sad smile. I watch Ellen watching her date walking away. "Be happy, George," I hear her whispered reply.

"He seems like a decent fellow," I say from where I'm still standing several feet from her.

As George disappears around a corner she says, "He's one of the best."

I fix my gaze on the leather laces of my shoes. He clearly meant something to Ellen. Then I focus on what is most important. She chose me. When I look up, I find Ellen walking toward me. "You're not too late," she says reaching for me.

I crush her to me and the feel of Ellen in my arms again is overwhelming. I never want to let her go. I never will, I know that for certain. Kissing her feels like coming home and I have. I really have with her. On a breath I say, "I love you. Do you know that?" Pulling back ever so slightly I search her face. "I will never take you for granted, never again."

The tension visibly melts away and Ellen smiles for the first time since I laid eyes on her tonight. Her smile is radiant. She can light up a room. Her beautiful face alights with hope and love. "Tell me you love me back," I say desperately needing to hear her say the words, "Please."

Rising up on tip toe, her hands resting on my chest, she presses her mouth to mine. "I love you," she says through what I hope are happy tears and my heart soars.

Reaching into my coat pocket I slowly drop to one knee keeping my eyes on Ellen's face so I can read the emotions that play over her features. Her expressive nature is one of the things I missed so much about her.

Taking a deep breath I reach for her left hand. I'm nervous, but for all the right reasons. "Yes," she says before I even have a chance to ask the question, which makes me laugh.

"Do you even know what I was going to ask, city girl?" I say trying and failing to keep a straight face. I want to imprint to memory the way she is looking at me at this very moment.

"I'm pretty sure," she says laughing and crying at the same time. There's that sass.

I'm still holding her left hand. Schooling my features, I take another breath, grateful that Ellen had the grace to forgive me. "I don't deserve you," I say.

"Don't say that," she admonishes. I know I don't, but I let it go. I know better than that.

"Will you marry me?" I'm getting all choked up. The backs of my eyes start to sting. I drop my gaze needing a minute to collect myself. "For the rest of my life," I say raising my head, "I will do whatever it takes to make sure that you are happy every day of yours." Getting to my feet, I use the back of my hand to gently wipe at the tears she's crying. Stepping in close and wrapping my arms around her waist, I say, "I will give you the sun," I place a kiss on her forehead, "And the moon," I kiss her cheek, "And show you the stars," I kiss the other cheek, "If you'd only say yes."

"Yes."

The End.